THE STARS, THE EARTH, THE RIVER

SHORT FICTION
BY LE MINH KHUE

Translated by
Bac Hoai Tran and Dana Sachs

Edited by Wayne Karlin

CURBSTONE PRESS

FIRST EDITION, 1997
Copyright © 1997 Le Minh Khue
Translation copyright © 1997 by Bac Haoi Tran and Dana Sachs
ALL RIGHTS RESERVED

Printed in Canada on acid-free paper by Best Book Manufacturers
Cover illustration: "The Knot" (1995), oil on canvas,
        by Minhquang Nguyen, courtesy of the artist.

Curbstone Press is a 501(c)(3) nonprofit publishing house
whose programs are supported in part by private donations
and by grants from: ADCO Foundation, Witter Bynner
Foundation for Poetry, Connecticut Commission on the Arts,
Connecticut Arts Endowment Fund, The Greater Hartford Arts
Council, Junior League of Hartford, Lawson Valentine
Foundation, LEF Foundation, Lila Wallace-Reader's Digest
Literary Publishers Marketing Development Program
administered by CLMP, The Andrew W. Mellon Foundation,
National Endowment for the Arts, Puffin Foundation, Samuel
Rubin Foundation and United Way-Windham Region

Library of Congress Cataloging-in-Publication Data

Le, Minh Khue.
    The stars, the earth, the river : short stories by Le Minh Khue /
edited by Wayne Karlin : translated by Bac Haoi Tran and Dana
Sachs.
        p.   cm.
    ISBN 1-880684-47-0
    1. Le, Minh Khue—Translations into English. I. Karlin,
Wayne. II. Title.
PL4378.9.L3615A2   1997
895.9'22334—dc21   96-45139

published by
CURBSTONE PRESS   321 Jackson Street   Willimantic, CT 06226

CONTENTS

Acknowledgements

From the Editor:

My special thanks to the following people: First and foremost, to Le Minh Khue, for her stories and her courage and for forgiving me for trying to shoot her during the war: may our friendship continue to embody the possibility of hope in the world. Thanks also to the poet George Evans and to the novelist Ho Anh Thai for finding the words and for sharing that friendship with us. Sandy Taylor and Judy Doyle and everyone at Curbstone had the vision to make this book and this series possible, and I'm grateful to Carolyn Forché and Martín Espada for introducing me to the Press. Finally I'd like to thank my hard-working and often pressured translators Bac Hoai Tran and Dana Sachs for their dedication, passion, and respect for the work.

From the Translators:

We'd like to thank many people for their help with this translation. Nguyen Thanh Lam, Nguyen Ngoc Minh, Bui Hoai Mai, Jim Carlson, Viviane Lowe, Nguyen Nguyet Cam, Peter Zinoman, Todd Berliner, and Ho Anh Thai all offered suggestions that helped us toward a deeper understanding of the stories and a more sophisticated rendition of them into English. Thu Thi Phuong not only offered insightful advice on the selection of stories and the translation of idioms but she also provided us with endless cups of hot tea, bowls of Vietnamese sweet pudding, and plates of Gummy Bears. Thanks also go to Viet Anh Phuong Tran and Viet My Phuong Tran for putting up with us in their living room and for showing a restraint and good humor quite remarkable for preschoolers.

Finally, our deepest gratitude goes to Wayne Karlin for his keen eye and unfailing encouragement and to Le Minh Khue, who trusted us with her treasure.

Introduction

Although they often concern such universal matters as love affairs, the tangles of family life, greed, ambition and the tyranny of the mundane, "to understand my stories," Le Minh Khue once wrote to me, "you need to understand the history of revolution, war and struggle that my country has gone through and out of which those stories grew." Both Khue's fiction and her life were formed by and in turn reflect the tug between tragedy and hope that have marked her generation's movement through the last half century of Vietnamese history.

Born in 1949 in Thanh Hoa province, south of Hanoi, Le Minh Khue lost her parents when she was very young to the upheavals of the Land Reforms of the early fifties, a period of forced collectivization and class warfare which, as we see in her story "A Small Tragedy," left scars across many lives. Khue was raised by an aunt and uncle who were passionate about both Vietnam's struggle for independence from foreign rule and about literature, both legacies which they passed on for her. She grew up as part of a generation of young people to whom the justice of their cause was as clear as the fact of the American bombs falling on their cities; they were fervent not only with a belief in liberation from foreign domination and national unification, but also in the faith that a socially just and humane society would grow from the roots of victory.

It was that faith which led Le Minh Khue, then sixteen, to lie about her age and enlist in the People's Army in 1965, after the American bombing campaign began. She was assigned to the Youth Volunteer brigades and sent south to the highland jungles, where she received on-the-job training as a sapper. Her duty, along with the rest of the kids in her unit and the thousands like them, was to see that the Ho Chi Minh Trail—really a network of roads built under the jungle canopy in order to keep fighters and supplies flowing south to the war—was kept open. For the next four years, Khue lived in the jungle, often thirsty, starving, filthy, plagued by jungle sores, fevers and scabies, under frequent bombardment, napalm and chemical attack and strafing by the American and South

Vietnamese aircraft whose job was to shut down the Trail. The bombs were dropped while the girls huddled in caves or bunkers, where their bodies were sometimes ripped by shrapnel—Khue remembers one girl who died next to her in the middle of a sentence, a scene she describes in "A Day on the Road." When the bombing stopped, the girls would fill in the craters with dirt, defuse the unexploded bombs, or explode them after packing dynamite around them.

Khue's aunt and uncle had taught her to love reading, and during all her time in the war, she carried books by Chekov, London and Hemingway in her knapsack. She was a reader and then she was a writer: all around her, she saw the drama of her times being played out by her generation and she felt the need to add her stories to the stories that had sustained her not only because they were about tough people surviving tough times, but also because they reassured her that the complications of the human heart still existed beyond the terrible simplicity of the war. She began to be published in the army newspapers—her first story, "The Distant Stars" was written when she was nineteen and immediately received wide attention.

In 1969, Khue's enlistment was over, but when she returned to Hanoi, like many soldiers, she found that she no longer felt comfortable amid the maneuverings and self-concern of civilian, rear area society. She'd lost any romantic notions she'd had about war, but she'd left her heart at the front, with the thousands of soldiers she'd seen day by day going down the Trail, with the remnants she saw returning. She applied for and received a position as a correspondent for *Tien Phong (Vanguard)* magazine and went back to the war, traveling with combat units, witnessing, writing about and broadcasting stories until North Vietnam's final victory in 1975. She was with a unit in the jungles near Danang during the last days of the war: they entered the city and later swept further south (where they occupied the old American helicopter base camp at Marble Mountain where I'd once been stationed). Demobilized, she continued her career as journalist and fiction writer. She married, had a daughter, became an editor at the Writers' Association Publishing House, and continued to write novels and stories—seven books since 1978—that followed her generation's path back from the jungles to the more complex struggles—physical, moral, emotional and spiritual—of postwar life.

"The war years were both the worst time and the best time for me," Khue wrote to me. "The Distant Stars," written when she was just nineteen and still on the Ho Chi Minh Trail, depicts that dichotomy in the life and work of three Young Volunteers, Nho, Thao, and Dinh, who live in a cave from which they emerge after air raids to measure and fill in bomb craters or explode time-delayed bombs. Dinh, the story's first person narrator, a somewhat pampered teenager from Hanoi, is at first shocked to learn that she would have to "haul dirt." She had imagined that she would be a soldier-hero, carrying a gun, "[her] speech would be strong and terse, just like the slogans." Yet even though "The Distant Stars" was published in 1971, during the war, Dinh, Nho and Thao are far from propaganda poster stereotypes. At times irritable, vain, tender, brave, idiosyncratic, they are above all teenage girls, engaging in flirtations, crushes, quarrels, the sharing of dreams. It is the juxtaposition of that normalcy against the deadly task in which the girls are engaged, and their matter-of-fact courage at doing it, which startle and engage the reader. The story not only vividly depicts the grim details of the war but also the deep sense of purpose, idealism and optimism, the willing self- sacrifice and comradeship among the girls and the other soldiers: "I loved everyone," Dinh says, "with a passionate love...that only someone who had stood on that hill in those moments, could understand fully...that was the love of the people in smoke and fire, the people of war."

The search to achieve that sense of love and that purity of purpose, to once again subordinate one's life to an unselfish ideal —and the way men and women and their societies fail at it—drive many of Le Minh Khue's postwar stories. "The Distant Stars" becomes, in that way, a touchstone for the other stories. In "A Day on the Road," for example, when the narrator, a female combat veteran traveling from Saigon to Hanoi in postwar Vietnam, remembers vividly the death of a girl standing next to her during an American air raid, one understands, one feels like a blow to the guts, that this could have been any of the bright, courageous kids in "Stars." But even more than such direct intertextual echoes are the descriptions of the loss of love and idealism we see in many of

Khue's other stories and feel more poignantly when we remember "The Distant Stars." Often Khue's postwar stories are set at construction projects, places where a literal rebuilding is occurring, where, it is implied, attempts at a deeper rebuilding, a reconstruction of the characters' humanity, are being made—or, conversely, they're set in decaying, shoddily maintained housing projects. We see that future, those attempts, failures and corruptions through the eyes of Ninh, Nho and Thao. During the war, the country around the girls' cave is torn and scarred: "It had been punctured by bombs...neither side of the trail had any signs of vegetation. There were only stripped and burned tree trunks, uprooted trees...twisted parts of vehicles, rusting in the earth." Khue's generation in the North, and in the Southern revolutionary movement, had sustained itself through the fighting and dying with visions of the world that would be built out of the seared jungle, that would rise like a phoenix out of the ashes. "After the war," says Ninh, "When the trail we were protecting here was evenly paved with asphalt. When electricity would flow on wires deep into the forest and timber mills would run all day and night. All...of us understood this. We understood and believed it with a fierce faith." "We defeated two great powers," I once heard the novelist Le Luu say, at a meeting between Vietnamese and American veteran-writers, "we thought we could pull the heavens down to the earth if we were of a mind." But where Ninh's statement is firm and confident, Le Luu's, spoken two decades after the war, was wistful. The skills and disciplines that led to military victory didn't transfer easily to shaping a society at peace; the ashes left by the devastation of the war were too deep to allow the phoenix to emerge. Millions of the best and most dedicated had been killed, millions more had been crippled, widowed, orphaned, and the land had been scarred by bombs and chemicals. Vietnam was still divided psychologically between North and South, victor and vanquished, and was still to go through two more wars. Postwar Vietnam endured and endures the problems of poverty and the social tensions and attitudes that attend deprivation and division: with the fighting over, the Vietnamese genius for survival moved, perhaps inevitably, from the collective to the individual. That movement forms a subtext in Khue's other stories and, as we read, the three girls huddled in a cave under the bombs, their love for each other and their fellow soldiers, their willingness to sacrifice, their faith in the future, stay in our minds, and we somehow feel their silent commentary and sometimes their heartbreak. I use "we" here deliberately, because while Khue's situations are particular to Vietnam, they are also universal: what society has lived up to its own youthful ideals? The images and emotions in "The Distant Stars" form shining points of light far over the heads of Khue's characters in her other stories as well, lights that sometimes make them, and us, ache for lost dreams, that sometimes, still, act as beacons that suggest infinite possibilities.

In "The Blue Sky," also set during the war, Ninh, a naive female war correspondent who is "infatuated with soldiers and their victories, just like a thirteen year old boy," eventually develops a shell of self-survival and cynicism. Ninh's infatuation is really with anything or anyone who demonstrates the sense of heroic purpose we saw in "The Distant Stars"—but her passion can't survive her editor's cynicism, her colleagues' cowardice, their petty quarrels and jealousies at work, their domestic squabbles. All of it erodes her faith, until she finds herself even doubting the story of a hero she once idolized—the truth, her very ability to discern it, has become cloudy to her.

The normal life that many Vietnamese felt was their due after the long war years often became symbolized for them, as elsewhere on the planet, by consumer goods. The narrator in "A Day on the Road," a woman who was in the Youth Brigades during the war, who saw hundreds of people die around her in the bombing, reacts bitterly when she hears two men speaking incessantly about motor scooters and business deals—they stand in her mind for the way in which people seem to be forgetting the losses of the war and are becoming shallow, self-centered—the way her own lover had left Hanoi to go live in Saigon so he could have such luxuries as a sponge, an imported nylon broom and an electric rice cooker. In a reversal of many American stories about returning male veterans alienated from their wives and lovers who had not had the experience of combat, it is the narrator, a woman, who is the returning veteran— her lover avoided the war and when she came back to him, she could no longer tolerate his constant harping on mundane physical comforts and "luxuries," an obsession which seems to trivialize the sacrifices of the war. And yet she knows she is beset by the same concerns: "Almost every morning some inconvenience would upset me...I hoped that my pen would improve, that my tires and inner tubes would become more durable, that the rice would have fewer stones and fewer husks, that the ceiling of our house wouldn't collapse from too many leaks, and that I wouldn't have to live with mice." Later, she discovers that the two men she'd overheard were also veterans: "In our generation, it's hard to find anyone who didn't go through the war," one says to her, recalling how he'd been in a battalion that had lost 500 men—and her feelings change; she is able to see their very banality as a sign of human resilience, another kind of victory: "The driver and the interpreter were once again discussing gadgets. Now they were talking about tape recorders and record players. They said nothing about the war and I looked at them with admiration. I knew that no one could forget what had happened during those years. But they were still young and whatever they had experienced only made them stronger."

While Khue's stories all exhibit an understanding of the complexities of human nature, not all of them exhibit the same final sense of hope as "A Day on the Road." "Scenes from an Alley" is one of the four bitter social satires in this collection (the others are "The Almighty Dollar," "Tony D," and "The Coolie's Tale"); each depicts ways in which deprivation and greed corrupt human nature and tear apart family and social relationships. Quyt and his wife, a couple who have entered the ranks of the *nouveau riche* due to his time as a guest worker in Germany, rent out a room to a Westerner, who becomes the economic base of the alley in which they and other families live—a source of rent money, of cash for liquor and prostitutes and even of reparation money when, driving home drunk one night, he runs over a mentally disabled girl. "Oh, a blue-eyed, long-nosed man was a gold mine," the alley dwellers exult.

One of the other main goals of the war was the reunification of Vietnamese society, a goal achieved politically in 1975 when the People's Army rolled into Saigon. Yet, as between North and South in the United States after our Civil War, punitive policies, inefficient administration, corruption, differences of character and temperament, and the extreme difficulties caused by the economic and physical scars left from the war, have made the goal of reunification far from perfectly realized. In "Fragile As a Sunray" a woman doctor in her forties, who served with a medical unit during the war, is haunted by her memory of an enemy soldier, a Southerner wounded and taken prisoner, who she briefly encountered and treated in a jungle clearing. The two had looked at each other and had known that under different circumstances, they would have loved each other, would have spent their lives together. But he was taken away and even though she never forgets his face: "Now twenty years had passed and many different barriers had been torn down...but her hope has never been fulfilled." What can be seen on one level as a very romantic story, as only Vietnamese stories can be romantic, becomes an expression of all the dreams of reunification still unfulfilled.

Love—the search for it, the failure to achieve it, the need to find an ideal relationship—becomes another paradigm for the utopian search that sustained Khue's generation through the war and for the ways in which reality frustrated that ideal. "Rain," is again one of the stories set at a construction site, a place where new buildings are being erected, but where the humanity of the engineer, the builder, who is the story's antagonist, is eroded and hollow behind his handsome face. He seduces Ngan, a pretty young guest house hostess who has developed a crush on him, but her romanticism is shattered by his love-making, which is selfish and brutal, and which ultimately leaves her feeling soiled and exploited. She loses not only her virginity, but a certain openness to the world, a certain readiness to believe in hopeful possibilities...

Love saves Trang in "The Almighty Dollar;" she is a gentle woman who doesn't seem to fit in with her coarse and contentious family, and who is considered unattractive because she is too tall. However, she is just the right height for a visiting foreigner, who marries her and takes her abroad. Yet the dollars she sends home so that her brothers and sisters-in-law will continue to care for her retarded younger brother Ngheo become the source of the destruction of her family as the two couples fight over the right to care for the boy. One of Khue's bleakest social satires, and less a broad farce than the other three, the characters and some of the scenes in "The Almighty Dollar" could have come from the pen and the South of Flannery O'Connor; its depictions of Ngheo will put images in the reader's mind that will continue to disturb, and possibly even nauseate, long after the story has been put down.

"The Last Rain of the Monsoon" centers around an extramarital love affair between two engineers sent to work together at a construction project. The narrator, Duc, a male friend of both Mi and Binh, the two lovers, sees both become increasingly involved—and increasingly desperate as the project ends and their affair has to either be finished, or they have to decide to leave their families and commit to each other. Mi, the woman, sees her love for Binh as something that has given meaning back to a life trivialized by routine pettiness and sordidness. After Binh and Mi have met, the narrator suddenly notices how beautiful she is—"her features were bright, as if unexpectedly suffused with happiness," and then notices, as if in contrast a woman selling lemonade who had "...crude hands and unclean fingers. I fixed my eyes on her long, dirty nails, then glanced at the fat flies perched at the mouth of the sugar jar." Yet Duc doesn't have faith in love as a form of rescue or renovation: if Binh and Mi run away with each other, he warns Mi, they will eventually find their lives no different than they are with their present spouses. "The pettiness of daily life will break up even stones." At first Mi can't accept it: "Then I would die. If things are like this forever and ever, then there's nothing left for me at all. I'll erode a little more every day. I'll become stupid, lethargic, house bound. I'll be mean, wicked. I'll shout at my son, fight with the neighbors, become a penny pincher..." But Duc tells her: "To be alive in this world is the best you can hope for. On top of that, you are whole, you sleep soundly at night, you're not hungry, and you have no worries."

"You say that because you lived through the war," Mi replies, that's what Duc, the country, the story implies, has learned from the war: to settle for peace and survival—who has the time or the energy to search for anything more meaningful, and where do such searches lead except back to their starting points? In the end, Mi accepts Duc's reasoning, and, in a seemingly light moment, begins to tell him stories about the squalidness of life in the housing project where she lives, including one about a visitor who fell into an open latrine and nearly drowned in human waste, a scene so funny "it made [her] laugh until [she] cried." There's no way, finally, she feels she can escape the tyranny of the ordinary, the shit she's fallen into...

The terrible living conditions of that housing project and some of its more colorful inhabitants seem to surface again in "Tony D". The story of two petty criminals in Hanoi, Old Man Thien and his son Than, who find and attempt to sell the bones of an American G.I., "Tony D" again depicts how deprivation and greed corrupt traditionally strong Vietnamese family ties—father and son are two predators who prey on each other as readily as on any outsider, who will do anything for money. Yet "Tony D" is also a Hogarth's tour: it depicts the use of the icons of the revolution to gain privilege, corrupt building practices, the migration of peasants to the city, even, perhaps, a sly comment on the state of contemporary poetry, as Old Man Thien and two cronies sit around and make up poems "like kids farting. One after the other." Along with, and underlining all of these revelations, is the image of the war as a haunting, mocking presence, a skull-faced American ghost squatting in the rafters and laughing: the thing that will not go away until it is dug up, and confronted, and prayed to and finally brought to peace.

"A Very Late Afternoon" is a look at a time in Vietnam when association with a Westerner was illegal and would bring a Vietnamese to the attention of the security services. What's also interesting about the story, though, is the way the character, a woman named Hang who as a teenager was arrested and traumatized for having a few innocent conversations with a French boy studying in Hanoi, essentially arranges her own therapy by seeking out an act of love, shedding the virginity, the self-isolation, she's been locked into since her arrest, before she leaves the city forever.

"That wench Canh is coming home," a group of university professors tell each other: "The Coolie's Tale" again tells of someone who has gone abroad and came back wealthy, though this time the work Canh engaged in—or at least what she referred to as her second job—involved experiencing "the Western smell, which was both fatty and redolent with milk." Canh, a guest worker, had discovered a lucrative second career as a prostitute. The story satirizes an academia where (working) class background becomes both prerequisite for admission and the basis of a kind of reverse elitism, and the vestiges of class snobbery: The ever-hungry Professor Tri, who came from three generations of mandarins and who is now married to a cadre who lectures him about the class struggle as if she is shouting into a loudspeaker, can't help resenting the way "the toads and frogs always rise to the top," even as he accepts gifts of food from Canh.

In "An Evening Away from the City" Tan and Vien could have been any of the girls in "The Distant Stars—their friendship forged deeply in the war when they had both operated a communication station in the jungle. "Whenever one went off on a mission, the other couldn't sleep...Life and death were very close together. Who could know? When they finally parted, they always hugged, which made the soldiers roll their eyes." After the war, the two went to the university. But it is now years later and each has moved into her life: Vien married a poor doctor, who took her to a rural area where he kept her pregnant and abused her: the dreams of her youth have disappeared into the endless tasks of child rearing and housework. Tan, on the other hand, fell in with a group of "notables" at the university and married an older, well-to-do man, became a fashionable woman of Hanoi, living at an elegant address, wearing the latest fashions: "Who could have known that she had ever worn a uniform, that her whole body...had once been covered with scabies and tortured by bouts of malaria?" On a trip to the country, Tan decides to finally look up her old friend, but finds she is repelled by the squalor of Vien's life, horrified when Vien tells her she had thought of coming to the city. "This messy and dirty mother and children were so different from her bedroom with its white curtain and the light blue plaster on the walls. Heaven forbid if they were ever to come visit." In a burst of guilt, she tells Vien she will arrange a trip to the city for her and use her husband's influence to get her friend enrolled again in the university. She means it, but somehow, when she returns, it never happens: "The problem was that she had so little time," she thinks, as she spends her time deciding what clothing to buy, what makeup to wear—and we think of Nho, Thao, and Dinh, sitting in their cave, staring in horrified disbelief at this distant future.

Bac Hoai Tran, one of the translators of these stories, called "A Small Tragedy," the title piece of Le Minh Khue's 1993 collection, one of the most important stories in contemporary Vietnamese literature. Khue's richest, most layered and resonant story, "A Small Tragedy" encompasses the large tragedies of modern

Vietnamese history, the land reform period, the war, and its aftermath, by focusing on the life of one family, the family of the influential and powerful retired cadre Tuyen, and on a marriage between an overseas Vietnamese and Tuyen's daughter. The story opens with the narrator, Thao, a young woman journalist and a niece of Tuyen, who is on her way home after she has failed to interview, to confront a murderer—a son who killed his father. The journalist, discontent with her own lonely and rather shabby life, somewhat envious of her privileged cousin Cay, receives a letter from her uncle, inviting her to come meet his daughter's fiancee. She puts aside her assignment to come to the wedding, to witness and help in the start of this new life, but learns in the course of the story that the sins of the father cannot be put aside: the murders of the past still haunt and direct the present. This translation has appeared in *Vietnam: A Traveller's Literary Companion* (Whereabouts Press). It is presented here for the first time in its unabridged version.

Although "The River" is not Khue's most recently published story, I've placed it last because, true to its title, it seems to flow through and connect the other stories and yet also suggest a direction to go from here. If "The Distant Stars" is the ideal held in memory, then "The River", represents the continued existence of hope—it brings us back to the hope for the future we saw embodied in those three girls in a cave. But it is not the same kind of hope. Dinh, Nho and Thao looked towards a future they couldn't see. But the protagonist in "The River" is a veteran of the war and of the realities of peace. Working in the city, busy with his life, he often thinks that he should go home to the small village where he grew up, but never seems to have the time. It is only after the aunt who raised him dies that he decides to go home to attend the Hundredth Day Ceremony after her death. Thus, like so many of Khue's other stories, "The River" involves a journey. But where the others all end in the city, in the complications of modern life, this story takes the narrator back into the strong roots of his past, away from a city "scarred by too much construction." As he travels, he remembers his childhood in the village, the taste of hot sweet soybean milk and the sugarcane the children chewed and which they saw made into sweet sugar candy. He remembers his aunt, a cherished teacher, and his uncle, who always sang a French song. He remembers the end of that childhood, when the American bombers began coming, and the village dug in with trenches and shelters, and he hears the story of how his aunt gave birth while the B-52's were dropping their bombs and their house was falling around them. And he remembers leaving for the war and not coming back until now, when he meets the child born that night, when he hears again—under the sound of an English song, the noise of motor scooters, under "the urban noises that had invaded the countryside"—the creaking of a shaft being turned by oxen, grinding the sugar cane, still in the old way. The river connects, as rivers do, past, present and future. This lovely story gifts us with the strength and tenderness of common human beings, their connections to their land, and to their history, and to each other; it shows us how life and hope and love can endure.

* * *

There exists among Americans two stereotypes of the Vietnamese who were on the other side of the war, each coaxed by the holder's own politics. The first sees the Vietnamese as sadistic, heartless communist robots able to win through sheer cruelty and lack of respect for human life. The second paints the Vietnamese as saintly, simple-yet-wise peasant-or poet warriors, Third World boddisatvas who speak in fortune-cookie platitudes, super competent soldiers, who in spite of their martial skills are still gentle, just, and politically correct. Le Minh Khue's stories do not allow either stereotype to remain in the American reader's mind: one can't read them and ever look at the Vietnamese again as anything more or less than human beings, their lives configured by the same passions, angers, love, hope and despair that mark all human lives.

Le Minh Khue the writer continues to perform the task of Le Minh Khue the sapper: searching out and identifying the bombs that lay buried along the Trail along which we must move, bringing them out of the earth, and sometimes identifying them, and sometimes defusing them, and sometimes exploding them, and sometimes smoothing over the scars they leave in the earth. She never lets us forget what is buried and where; in doing so, she gently suggests the directions we must continue to travel.

—Wayne Karlin

Translators' Note

In Le Minh Khue's story "The Blue Sky," the young journalist Ninh interviews a soldier who tells her an astonishing combat story. Ninh, intoxicated by the glories of battle and infatuated by the handsome young soldier, believes every word of it. She writes a passionate article about the incident, but her editor, feeling the story "stretched the truth" refuses to publish it. He tells her to "write something more believable" and she walks out of his office, overwhelmed by tears and anger.

The process of translating Le Minh Khue's fiction into English taught us to sympathize both with Ninh's love of the story and with her editor's demand for exactness. Like Ninh's editor, English is a language that calls for precision. But, like the story Ninh heard, Vietnamese offers as many possibilities as certainties, and refuses to be pinned down.

The most obvious example of the disparity between the two languages comes in the use of verb tenses. What would we do in English without the distinctions between *go, going,* and *gone*? In English, we could hardly make it to the grocery store and back, much less through a short story, poem, or novel, without a whole suitcase full of tenses. Vietnamese travel lighter. They speak and write in the basic structure that we might call "present tense," occasionally using past or future markers, but more often leaving it to readers and listeners to fill in the time frame for themselves. One aspect of our task as translators lay in filling in such blanks. For example, when Ninh returns to her office, she asks a question, the original Vietnamese of which goes something like this: "Article day I send back publish number what you know not?" Unlike English, Vietnamese demands the active participation of listeners or readers in pulling together the meaning implied by the words. Although the sentence might sound confusing in English, it follows the rules of Vietnamese grammar and to Vietnamese readers makes perfect sense. In our final version, this sentence becomes: "Do you know what issue my article was published in?" Rendering Vietnamese into English grammar and inserting tenses formed the simplest, most straightforward part of our task.

More often than not, however, the journey from one language to the next is much more arduous. Vietnamese is a fluid language, but English readers demand the specific. When the editor finishes reading Ninh's article, for example, he tells her "*Doc xong biet la bia.*" One possible grammatical translation into English might be, "When I finished reading it, I knew it stretched the truth." Another, much broader translation might be, "Anyone who finishes reading it will know it stretched the truth." In the end, we decided to let the editor speak for himself, giving him the words: "When I finished, I knew it stretched the truth." Our sentence certainly flows better than a literal translation of the Vietnamese ("Finish reading know is stretch the truth") but we mourn the loss of all the possibilities that won't fit into English.

Vietnamese not only leaves gaps that English has to fill, but it also has characteristics for which English has no equivalent. Vietnamese identify themselves in the context of their relationships to others. The language scorns the use of "I" and doesn't even have a simple word for "you." Instead, speakers pick pronouns according to who's listening to them. For example, young Ninh calls both the soldier and the editor "big brother" and, when speaking to them, she calls herself "little sister." If she were to speak to her mother, she would call herself "child." With an older woman, she'd call herself "niece" and with a younger friend, she'd be "older sister." Unfortunately, an attempt to translate all these big sisters and little sisters into English implies a tenderness that is not always felt among Vietnamese (especially between Ninh and her boss) and it also quickly grows tiresome to the English reader.

Sometimes, however, shifts in the use of pronouns reflect subtle or more overt changes in characters' relationships to one another. Vietnamese joke that if a wife stops referring to herself as "little sister" when speaking to her husband it means that she's letting him know she's mad at him. In the Vietnamese text of the story "Tony D," a father and son change their pronouns to reflect their moods. When the two are getting along well, the father tends to be very informal, referring to himself as *tao* (an informal form of "I") while calling his son *may* (an informal form of "you"). In turn, the son calls his father *bo* (which literally means "father") and refers to himself as *toi* (an egalitarian form of "I" which, although polite, denies a certain respect to his father). Later, when the son becomes angry at his father, he stops calling him *bo* and begins to use *ong*, which literally means grandfather, but in this context asserts a formal distance between two adversaries. And the father, terrified of his son's rage, chooses the endearing pronouns *bo* and *con* (which is the most intimate form used when speaking to one's child) in order to appeal for mercy. Although most of our translation sticks to the basic English "you" and "I," at several points we shift the wording to reflect these subtle changes in the Vietnamese text. When the two sympathize with each over a shared nightmare, for example, the son calls his father "Dad." Later, during their vicious fight, the father uses the word, "Son," which we hope reflects the intimacy of the Vietnamese word *con*.

Throughout her work, Le Minh Khue relies on the flexibility of the Vietnamese language to create richly nuanced stories. In "Tony D," a public housing project comes alive not only through the details of the inhabitants' oppressive life but also through the author's rendering of evocative, often vulgar street language. In "The Almighty Dollar," Khue relies on the subtle power of words when a young woman writes a letter to a friend describing her new husband. Although we never see the letter itself, a paraphrasing of it repeatedly quotes the bride's use of *"anh ay,"* which, in this case, serves as a pronoun equivalent to "he" when referring to her husband. These pointed quotes emphasize the delight of a woman who, after giving up hope of ever marrying, has finally found a man who loves her. In our translation into English, we try to reflect this sense of joy by repeatedly putting quotes around the words "he" and "him."

Le Minh Khue, out of both compassion for our task and recognition of the difficulty of communicating with her across the vast Pacific, has given us a free hand to alter her text wherever we felt that changes were necessary. We're grateful for her faith in us, but have made as few changes to her work as possible. We hope that this collection fulfills our own goals as translators, to create stories which satisfy the precise requirements of English while maintaining the breathtaking fluidity of the original Vietnamese.

Dana Sachs and Bac Hoai Tran
San Francisco, May 1996

The Distant Stars

There were three of us. Three girls. We lived in a cavern at the foot of a strategic hill. The trail led past the front of the cave and on up the hillside somewhere, very far. It had been punctured by bombs, mixing the red and white soil together. Neither side of the trail had any sign of vegetation. There were only stripped and burned tree trunks, uprooted trees, boulders, and a few empty gas cans and twisted parts of vehicles, rusting in the earth.

Our job was to sit there. Whenever a bomb exploded, we had to run up, figure out how much earth was needed to fill the hole, count the unexploded bombs, and, if necessary, detonate them. They called us the Ground Reconnaissance Team. That title inspired in us a passion to do heroic deeds and therefore our work was not that simple. The bombs often buried us. Sometimes, when we came down from the hill we were so covered in dirt that only our gleaming eyes showed through. When we laughed, our teeth glowed out of our grimy faces. At those moments, we called each other the "Black-Eyed Demons."

Our unit took good care of us. When they had something to eat, they would say, "Leave some for the Recon Team, because they're up there."

It was easy to understand that. The unit often went out at sunset and sometimes they worked all night. But, as for us, we had to be up there even in the daylight. And being out on that hill in the daytime was no fun. Death was a serious guy. He hid himself inside the bombs. But every job has its own pleasures. Where else could you experience smoking earth, trembling air, or the roar of airplanes that only gradually fades away? Where else could you experience taut nerves, an erratic heartbeat and the knowledge that all around lay unexploded bombs. Maybe they'd explode now or maybe in another moment. But definitely they would explode.

When we finished, we'd go back and take one more look at the road, breathe with relief, and dash back into the cave. Outside, it was over 30 degrees celsius, so when we crawled into the cave, we entered a different world. The chill made our bodies suddenly begin to shiver. Then we'd turn our heads up to drink some sugared spring water from our canteens. After that, we'd stretch out on the damp ground and squint our eyes while listening to the music on our tiny radio, for which we always had batteries. Maybe we'd listen closely, maybe just think about things.

It seemed like we were about to start a big offensive. Every night, a stream of vehicles drove by on the trail. At night we usually could sleep. But for the past few nights it had been impossible. Two of us carried our spades up to the strategic hill, where we had fun joking with the drivers. Too bad for the one who had to stay in the cave to answer the two-way radio.

* * *

It was noon and very quiet. I sat leaning against the stone wall, humming a song. I loved to sing. Often I would memorize a certain melody and then make up my own words. My lyrics were so confused and silly that they sometimes surprised me and made me burst out laughing all by myself.

I was a Hanoi girl. To put it modestly, I was impressive. My ponytails were thick and relatively soft. My neck was graceful and I stood as proud as a lily. And as for my eyes, the drivers would say, "You have such a distant look in your eyes."

Regardless of how distant the look was, I liked to hold the mirror and gaze into my own eyes. They were long and narrow, brown, and were often squinted as if from a glare.

It puzzled me that the drivers and artillery men often asked about me. Either they asked about me or they sent me long letters as if we were thousands of kilometers apart, although we could greet each other in person every day. I never made an effort to please them. Whenever the girls grouped together to talk to some eloquent army man, I always stood aloof, looking elsewhere, my lips tightly sealed. But I was only striking a pose. The truth is that in my thoughts, the most handsome, intelligent, courageous and noble men were these, the men who wore military uniforms with stars on their caps.

I never said that to anyone, but the men who went by on the trail still sent me their greetings in a respectful and affectionate manner.

"You sing well, you look pretty decent, and you are an expert at detonating bombs," my friends explained. Though of course, that was not accurate.

Outside, it was still quiet. Ever since ten in the morning, no planes had flown past the strategic hill. They'd only dropped bombs further inland, as we could tell from the reverberations. It was precisely this low, seemingly fragile rumble, carried here on the wind, that made the quiet more tense, as if it were heralding something fierce. The sun burned. The wind was dry. But inside the cave, it was cool.

Each of us had her own hobby. Nho was embroidering a pillow. Thao was copying a song into a small journal balanced on her thigh. The two of them were talking, but I hadn't listened to the first part. Then, I suddenly began to pay attention.

"When will it be over?" Nho asked.

"When will what be over?" Thao didn't look up, but her voice betrayed some surprise.

Nho yawned. Then they were quiet. I knew what she meant. She would have said that when the war was over she wanted a job in a big hydroelectric plant. She would work as a welder and play on the plant's volleyball team. She would try to really slam the ball and—who knew?—with luck she might be selected for the Northern team.

As for Thao, she wanted to become a doctor. Her husband would be a captain in the military who would travel to distant places and sport a beard. She had no desire to live by his side every day because love would quickly become boring.

I also often talked about my own plans. I had many wishes, but I still didn't know my priorities. Perhaps to become an architect? How interesting! A voice-over artist in a children's movie theater? A freight driver on the wharf? Or a singer in a choir at a construction site? Any of those careers would mean happiness. I would be as enthusiastic and creative as I was now, out here at our strategic hill, where wishes and desires were born.

But these things were for later. After the war. When the trail we were protecting here was evenly paved with asphalt. Electricity would flow on wires deep into the forest and timber mills would run all day and all night. All three of us understood this. We understood and believed it with a fierce faith.

The pillow in Nho's hands was dainty and white. She embroidered careless and gaudy flowers. She made the borders thick as ropes. If anyone criticized her efforts, she would ignore the criticism and her hand would move ahead with the needle as if nothing had happened. When they really let her have it, she would bite her lips, tear the thread between her two even rows of teeth and raise her voice to a falsetto, saying, "I want it to be different!"

Nho was rather peculiar—on the one hand, affectionate and cheerful and, on the other, very stubborn. Those traits were not contradictory, but, rather, complementary, and they caused Nho to have a rather rare personality. She had lived with me ever since I first arrived at this strategic hill. At that time, everything was strange to me. I was shocked when people first ordered me to go and haul dirt.

"Young volunteers have to do this? Haul dirt?" (I couldn't have imagined it. I thought that we would be carrying guns, marching in force within a forest so deep we couldn't even see the moon or the stars. Our speech would be strong and terse, just like the slogans.)

But I just hauled dirt. And then I got used to it.

Many meals we had no broth, so we girls poured drinking water over our rice. We did this in public and we looked so miserable that some of the men cried out in pity. The first time we heard the sound of the bombs, some of us were so scared we lay down and hugged the earth.

But now we'd gotten used to it.

I joined the unit after Nho. That day, I looked lost as I set my knapsack down on a log behind the barracks. Nho walked up from the stream. Her hair was wet. Drops of water remained on her forehead and her nose. The water in the stream must have been abundant. Maybe people could swim in it, I thought. Nho paused for only a second, then approached me without saying a word, her hands busily wringing her wet washcloth. She tossed her head once, then swept her haughty eyes from the tip of my head to the mud-covered shoes that I was rubbing hard against each other.

"What unit sent you here? Where are you from? What's your name?"

I stopped rubbing my shoes together and stood ready. In my military training classes at school, I had studied martial arts. I set my arms akimbo, taking a guarded position and deliberated over whether I should punch her. Where should I punch her first? I would just hit lightly at one of her vital points. On her hand.

But at that moment, Nho turned around and stuck her hands into her trouser pockets.

"Go to headquarters," she motioned with her chin, taking off in front of me.

Of course, we'd paid a lot of attention to each other since then. Gradually, we got to know each other and at some point we became friends. Both of us had just turned seventeen. That a veteran bullied a newcomer a bit wasn't something worth resenting. It turned out that I liked her. She had a remarkable character. The boys had great respect for her, although they sometimes still managed to tease her.

Like me, Nho liked independence. We would say to each other, "From now until we're old, we'll have romance but we'll never marry. Marriage would mean too much work. Diapers. Blankets. Mosquito nets. Sawdust. Fish sauce. There would be no time left for fun. In love, he'll take you to the movies. He'll be sweet to you when you sulk. You'll have plenty of time to read books."

Nho had a guy who worked as an engineer in a machine shop. He diligently wrote to her and his letters were often so long that reading them wore your eyes out. He justified himself, saying, "In Hanoi, people have more time than at the front." He kept a photo of Nho when she was two years old. She was wearing baby's pants, with their open rear end, and a wide-brimmed bonnet, and she was holding a bunch of wildflowers at the foot of some tall mustard greens. I had read many of the letters he sent to Nho. Once, he wrote, "I'm very well. I've been enjoying playing soccer and have two muscular forearms. I look at the picture of you at two years old and it's impossible for me to imagine you as you are now. I can only think: Here you are, so small, holding flowers in your hands. Do you want me to pick you up? Take you out? Buy you some candy? Where else should we go? I'll carry you there."

His ideas were pretty funny, but we didn't laugh when we read the letter. Gravely, we turned in the direction of the north, where Hanoi lay. We had been away for so long. We missed our green city. We treasured its tranquillity as a memory. This was the place where we were growing up, but we were always thinking of Hanoi.

In Hanoi, I had a small room on the second floor. My house was ancient and deep within an alleyway where many green trees grew. Those trees were so old that creeping mistletoe now covered them. At night, I would perch on the edge of the windowsill looking out over the uneven lines of the black roofs, and I would sing. I sang with passion, loudly. Next door lived a doctor who had trouble sleeping. He would switch on his light and politely tap three times against the wall. Twenty nights out of every month would be like that. I sat waiting for sleep to come back to the doctor, justifying myself by thinking, "Only I can know the vastness and freshness of the city night. How can the doctor experience anything like this in his disruptible dreams?" It was also because of my passionate singing that once I almost fell off the windowsill. Frantically grabbing the shutter, I dizzily glanced down into the bottomless abyss. Somewhere down there was a hose which ran all night to fill a cistern. The gushing of the water gave me the feeling that it was about to rise to the windowsill. I pulled myself up and carefully drew my legs inside. I resumed singing, but I sang more softly and listened for the sound of the tapping on the wall.

In the corner of the room sat a desk that my mother had made for me over the course of two afternoons. Every time I did anything that required paper and ink, I would pull all my books and notebooks out of my drawers and my satchel and spread them out across the desk and bed, although all of those things weren't necessary for what I was about to do. For a long time, I searched endlessly among those papers, unable to do anything and also unable to put them in order. So impatient that I could cry, I shouted for my mother. She left her sewing machine and ran in, and, while lightly grumbling, arranged all the papers.

She scolded me, but without determination. "What kind of girl are you?" she asked. "Your husband will beat you. Beat you!"

Therefore, even when I was still at home, I swore to myself that I'd never marry.

Nho said, "Hey. Hurry up."

"What?" She startled me. For the past few minutes, I'd been singing. Singing and thinking aimlessly.

Nho rolled up her pillow and quickly put it into her bag. Thao looked toward the entrance to the cave. It was a reconnaissance plane, alright. Life here had taught us the meaning of silence. It was abnormal that, ever since morning, the day had been so quiet. And now, the reason for that was on the way. The reconnaissance plane was buzzing overhead and the jets were roaring up behind it. Those two kinds of sounds mixed together in one's ears to create a feeling of unsettling tension.

"They're almost here!" Nho turned her back on us, putting her steel helmet on her head. Thao fished a biscuit out of her pocket and munched on it in a leisurely manner. Whenever she knew that something dangerous was about to happen, she would look so calm it was annoying. But whenever she saw blood or even a jungle leech, she would force her eyes shut and her face would turn white. All of her undershirts were embroidered with colored threads. She also plucked her eyebrows until they were as thin as toothpicks. But as far as work was concerned, everyone respected her. She showed determination and daring.

These things happened every day: airplanes screamed; bombs exploded. This time, they exploded on the strategic hill about 300 meters from our cave. The ground beneath our feet shook. Even the washcloths we'd hung out to dry shook. Everything became feverish. Smoke rose up and filled the entrance to the cave. We couldn't see the clouds or the sky any longer.

Thao took the yardstick from my hand and, with gusto, swallowed the last morsel of her biscuit..

"Dinh, you stay inside," she told me. "This time, they only dropped a few. Two of us can do it."

Pulling on the sleeve of Nho's shirt, she flung the shovel over her shoulder and walked out of the cave.

I didn't argue with her. She had the authority to give assignments. Time became tense. My mind was tense as well. Neither the things that had happened nor those about to happen mattered any more. If my friends didn't come back, would they make any difference? The two-way radio rang. The company commander wanted to know the situation.

I shouted into the machine. "The reconnaissance team hasn't come back yet!"

I didn't know why I was shouting. There was one more wave of bombs. The smoke filled the cave. I choked coughing and my chest burned. The hill was now deserted. There was only Nho and Thao. And the bomb. And here I was, sitting in the cave. And our anti-aircraft guns were on the other side of the hill. They now responded and the sound of these guns rising up from the ground was reassuring. There is nothing more lonely and terrifying than when bombs explode around you and nothing comes up from below. Even the sound of a single rifle can give you a feeling of some protection, an impression of solid self-defense.

Feeling restless, I ran outside for a moment. I couldn't see anything except the smoke from the bombs. I was worried. Suddenly, the strategic hill next to ours echoed with the sound of the 12.7s. Great! It was the battalion of military construction workers. They had been sent as reinforcement for the men on the anti-aircraft guns, and for us. Suddenly, I wanted to shout for joy. Now, that normally deserted hill was overrun with people. The anti-aircraft gunners, the liaison people, and the engineers were all very fond of us. It was only necessary to fire off a single rifle requesting help and they would get the message and immediately appear.

Half an hour later, Thao crawled into the cave. Calm, exhausted, and bad-tempered, she refused to look at me.

"We'll need more than a thousand cubic meters of dirt!" she said.

She sat down and drank some water from the canteen. Water fell continuously from her chin to her shirt, like raindrops. I radioed the headquarters to tell them.

The company commander said, "Is that so? Thank you all."

The commander often used polite phrases like, "thank you," "excuse me," and "good luck." He was young and thin, suffered from rheumatism, and often wrote popular rhymes for the newspapers posted on the walls. His house was somewhere near the end of Lo Duc Street.

Nho had just bathed in the stream and was walking back up. That section of the stream often had time-delayed bombs detonate in it. In her wet clothes, Nho sat down and asked for some candy. I dug into my pocket. Luckily, I still had two lemon candies, although they were covered with grains of sand and melting.

Nho said, "There were only four of those time-delayed bombs. Not so many."

She put her arms behind her and leaned all the way back. Her neck was round and her shirt had delicate buttons on it. I wanted to lift her in my arms. She looked as light and fresh as an ice cream bar. The company commander had asked if we needed any help. I said no. As always, we would do everything ourselves.

"Wonderful! Thank you, all!" The company commander thanked us again. "The whole unit is opening a road for the missile regiment to go through the forest. They haven't rested since morning. I also have to go now. Just do your best."

That night, too, we would have to work outside. As usual.

I began working on a bomb up on the hill. Nho did two that sat on the road. Thao had one by the old bunker.

It was so quiet it was scary. The remaining trees were twisted and broken. The earth was hot. The black smoke floated in clumps through the air, blocking our view of things in the distance. Could the anti-aircraft gunners see us? Perhaps they could. They had binoculars that could shrink the whole earth into their sights. I approached the time-delayed bomb. Feeling the soldiers' eyes upon me, I was no longer afraid. I would not bend down. They wouldn't like it. They liked the gait of someone standing straight and calmly stepping forward.

The bomb lay within a dry bush, its head stuck in the ground and its back end painted with two concentric yellow circles.

I used a small shovel to dig the dirt from under the bomb. The earth was hard. Pebbles flew out from under both sides of my hand. Sometimes, the edge of the shovel scraped the side of the bomb. It made a sound so sharp it cut into my skin. I shivered and suddenly realized I was working too slowly. Hurry up a little! The casing of the bomb was hot. That was a bad sign.

It might be the heat from inside the bomb. Or maybe it had retained the heat from the sun.

Thao whistled. That meant that twenty minutes had passed already. I carefully packed the sticks of dynamite into the hole that I had dug. The fuse was long, coiled, and resilient. I poured the dirt into the hole, lit the fuse, and then ran for shelter.

Thao whistled again. I pressed myself against the wall of earth, looking at my watch. There was no wind. I couldn't hear my heart beat. The only calm thing, ignoring all the happenings around it, was the hand on my watch. It kept ticking, lively and softly, running past the eternal numbers, while over there, the fire burned along the fuse and entered the bomb.

I was used to it. We exploded bombs up to five times a day. Sometimes it was fewer: three times. I did think of death. But it was a vague death, not a concrete one. The chief thing was whether or not the bomb or the mine would explode at all. If not, then how would you light the fuse the second time? I considered that, and something else as well. If a bomb fragment hit my arm, that would be rather troublesome.

Salty sweat dripped down my lips and sand grated against my teeth.

The bomb did explode. It had a weird sound and it jarred me. I felt a pain in my chest. My eyes watered and it was a while before I could open them again. The smell of the explosives made me nauseated. Three explosions followed. Dirt rained down and silently disappeared into the bushes. Fragments of the bombs tore through the air with a whine, invisible over my head.

I brushed off my shirt. Straining my eyes to see through the smoke, I ran after Thao. Normally, wanting to meet Nho and me so that we could go back to the cave together, Thao would come by my place. This time, she was smiling, her white teeth shining and her scar looking glossy. She held a piece of parachute around her shoulders and ran ahead of me. The wind tried to snatch the parachute, but couldn't do it.

Thao tripped and fell and I tried to help her up but she pushed me away. Her eyes were open wide and I could see now that they were glazed over, as if there were no more life in them. I didn't understand. She grabbed my hand and pulled me down next to a mound of earth. It was a small mound, rather long, and covered with the gray explosives of a bomb.

"Nho! Where are you hurt?" Thao sobbed, but she had no tears.

I scraped at the earth, pulled out Nho, and lay her across my lap. Blood gushed out of her arm and was absorbed into the earth. She didn't look as light and fresh as an ice cream bar any longer. Her skin was pale, her eyes shut tight, and her clothes were covered with dirt. The bomb had leaped up and exploded in the air. Her underground shelter had collapsed, that was all.

I cleaned Nho with water I'd boiled over the coal stove. Using cotton wool bandages, I wrapped the wound, which wasn't deep enough to tear the muscle. But because the bomb had exploded so close to her, Nho was in shock. I gave her an injection. Her eyes fluttered and she looked comfortable; perhaps she wasn't in pain. Thao was pacing back and forth outside. She was restless because she didn't know what to do, and still she tried to do something. She was afraid of blood.

"Let me call headquarters, okay?" she asked.

Thao only approached once Nho was lying clean and tidy on the wooden plank bed.

"She won't die," I replied. "The unit is busy opening a road. We don't need to make so many people worry. Why are you in such a panic?"

"It's only normal. Those who aren't wounded often feel more pain than those who are." Thao turned her face to the entrance to the cave and drank some water from the canteen.

Nho put one arm over her eyes. She knew that she shouldn't drink any water so I mixed some milk for her in the steel mug.

Thao said, "Put a lot of sugar in and mix it so it's strong."

After she finished drinking the milk, Nho slept. The reconnaissance planes were still scraping away the silence of the mountains and forests. Thao leaned against the wall with her hands clasped behind her neck. She wouldn't look at me.

"Sing, Phuong Dinh. Sing your favorite song," she said.

I liked a lot of songs. I liked the marching songs the soldiers sometimes sang at the front. I liked the gentle folk duets. I liked the "Katyusha" of the Soviet Red Army and to hold my knees up to my chest and sing, "Return to Sorrento." Because it was a romantic Italian folk song, you had to start very low. I liked it a lot. But I didn't want to sing just then. I was mad at Thao, although I understood the feelings whirling inside her. She kept glancing at Nho, raising a hand to adjust her collar and then her lapel and her hair. She hadn't cried and she didn't even like tears. Anyone who shed a tear while we needed strength from each other would be seen as guilty of self-debasement.

Nobody said it, but we could read it in each other's eyes.

Thao sang, "Here is Thang Long. Here is Dong Do. Here is Hanoi." Her voice was both squeaky and out of tune, so she couldn't sing anything smoothly, but she had three thick notebooks that she'd filled with the lyrics of songs. Whenever she had a free moment, she would sit down and copy out a song. She'd even passionately copied out the words of songs that I'd made up.

A cloud floated by outside the cave. Then another. They were going by faster and faster. In front of the entrance to the cave, the open sky grew dark. A storm was coming in. Sand filled the air. The wind lifted up then tossed down the dry branches of the trees. Leaves flew in all directions. It was as sudden as a change in the human heart. In this season, unexpected rain often came down on the forest. But now it was hailing. At first, I didn't notice, but then I heard a tapping against the overhang of the cave. I stepped outside. Something sharp was pulverizing the air, tearing it into tiny fragments. The wind. I felt a pain and at the same time, my cheeks became wet.

"It's hailing. It's hailing!"

I ran inside, and put a few small hailstones into Nho's open palm. Then, I ran back outside, extremely thrilled.

The year I finished the tenth grade, we had also had hail. During the night, the hail had hit the walls with that same tapping sound.

I had flung open the door, run into the hallway, and pounded on the doors, shouting at the top of my lungs as if I had gone crazy,

"Heavens! Get up quick! It's hailing!"

Then, I complained to myself, "Only fools would stay in bed at a time like this."

The doctor was not a fool at all, but he proclaimed gravely, "If you continue with this noise, we will be forced to take the necessary measures."

And the woman teacher next door sighed inconsolably, "Why won't you let us sleep?"

Only the driver who lived downstairs stayed up with me throughout that miraculous night. After that, he joined the army and became a hero at destroying enemy vehicles. He wrote to me and often mentioned those hailstones of long ago as one of his "memories of the past."

Here, on this bomb-covered hill, we also got hail and my childish joy had bloomed again. Here there was no one to reproach me. Thao was busy scooping up something from the ground. Maybe it was hailstones. As for Nho, she sat up, her lips parting.

"Hey, give me some more of those hailstones," she said.

But it had stopped already, over as quickly as it had begun. Why so fast? I suddenly became dazed, filled with an unspeakable regret. Clearly, it wasn't regret for the hailstones. The storm had come and gone. But I missed something. Maybe it was my mother. Or the window. Or the big stars over the city. Right. Maybe it was those things. Or maybe it was the trees. Or the dome of the opera house. Or the woman pushing her cart filled with ice cream, surrounded by expectant children. The asphalt road at night after a summer rain seemed wider, longer, reflecting the lights, looking like a river of black water. The electric lights over the square glowed like the stars in the stories about fairylands. The flowers in the park. The soccer balls carelessly kicked by children from street corners. The hawking of the woman who sold sticky rice in the morning, carrying a bamboo basket on her head.

Maybe it was all those things. They were so far away and then, because of a hailstorm, they came in waves to flood my mind.

People asked if Hanoi women could bear three days away from home. But here we were, living on this hill for three years already. The drivers and artillery men called each of us in our unit by name, without ever making a mistake. As for us, we knew who, among those men, was in love, who had a first-born daughter, who was courageous, and who was irritable. During the night, while we were repairing the road, those men would toss us Ngoc Lan toothpaste, perfume-scented writing paper, and lemon candies. Often, we didn't even know who was throwing it because the trucks would go by so quickly. But we spread the news among ourselves.

"Those trucks were from Hanoi!" we'd say.

Because only Hanoi had those things.

In Hanoi, we'd never even paid attention to such things. But here we felt so happy to hold one thin sheet of fragrant paper, put it into an envelope, and send it to someone further toward the front.

"Get down!" Thao shouted.

As if I had just received a punch in the stomach, I doubled over and then threw myself on the ground. Bombs! It sounded like they thudded as they fell and then exploded. The surface of the earth was like a shaking giant.

It seemed like thousands of airplanes were turning somersaults over head. I dragged myself back into the cave and Thao dragged herself in behind me.

"Damn it. They don't give us a chance to breathe," she mumbled. Slender, well-proportioned, with hair down to her shoulders, her scar invisible in the dark, she stood with one hand clinging to the line where we hung our washcloths. If she had a good voice, she would have been better off in the theater. On the stage, she would have looked presentable. But her squeaky voice hurt people's ears. She herself admitted it.

"Bring the radio over here," Nho motioned.

I carried it over to Nho and then I picked up the yardstick and went back outside with Thao.

We had to run a lot and so the wound in my thigh began to hurt. I could still run, provided that the wound didn't make me limp. Thao was very determined. Of course, she wouldn't worry about going up the hill by herself.

There were so many bomb craters. We measured them and, doing some mental addition, shouted to each other the results. Thao recorded them in the logbook. There were no time-delayed bombs, but we would need a lot of dirt. The total came to two thousand cubic meters. Suddenly, as if something had shoved her in the back, Thao flew forward, grasped me against her chest, and together we fell to the ground. In a flash, an avalanche of earth came down on us. Big chunks of wet dirt mixed with the dry dirt from deeper underground. It was hot. Something pulled my head down. Thrusting my legs down for momentum, I pushed myself up, up, and up. Grains of dirt filled my nostrils. Shaking my head, I felt clods of earth fall off. All around me was the steely, ponderous gray of billowing smoke.

I couldn't see Thao anywhere. "Thao," I tried to scream but I choked. Dirt filled my mouth. Damn! I spat out a clump of earth. Groping around, my hand touched Thao's hair. I turned around and, pushing myself forward, used both hands to claw at the dirt. I found her, but I couldn't sense her breathing. Then, suddenly, she flung an arm around my neck and shakily stood up.

Back in the cave, Nho grimaced like a child. "That bad?" she asked.

Thao smiled strangely and slowly regained her composure. "A piece of bad luck," she said. "But it was really nothing."

It couldn't just be bad luck. Her body carried nine wounds, both big and small, already. Nho had five. I had the fewest, only four. I had one scar on my stomach that had been severe enough to consign me to a military hospital for three months. Being buried by an avalanche was normal.

I looked at my friends. Thao was very pale. She was exhausted. Nho brought her a mug of water and, using her pinkie, flicked the grains of dirt from her hair.

Suddenly, she philosophized, "That's life on a strategic hill!"

Thao burst into laughter, motioning with her head in my direction. "Log in the numbers before you forget," she said. As I cranked the two-way radio, Thao hurried over to my side. "Tell them everything, but let them know that we've stood our ground."

It wasn't the company commander but the liaison officer who answered the radio. He was a polite and hospitable guy who didn't smoke or flirt with the girls.

"Where did the commander go?"

"He's out giving orders where they're opening the road, because the trucks are coming through with the missiles soon. But it's late afternoon already. Nobody can sleep. What about you guys?"

"We're pretty exhausted. More than two thousand cubic meters of earth already and it's not even near dark yet. We're still standing our ground."

"If things get worse, fire off some shots immediately, you hear? The unit is always concerned about you up there. The assault troopers can get up there quickly."

That afternoon, Thao and I had to run up the strategic hill three more times. We detonated eight more bombs. And the amount of earth rose to three thousand two hundred cubic meters. Every time, I tried to find excuses to keep Thao at home. But she was smart and it was hard to trick her. As she ran, her breathing grew more and more labored. Small blue veins stood out on her temples and across the backs of her hands. I was afraid she would collapse. And every time we came back, Nho would step out of the cave again and scowl, repeating, "Thao! Thao!"

The last time, we nearly crawled back to the cave. Thao helped me lie down. I tried to open my eyes. They felt as if they were glued together. I didn't even know what I wanted now.

"I'm sleepy." I heard my voice floating by and then the coolness of the cave flowed in as I quickly fell asleep.

A squad of assault troopers came up from where they were building the road through the forest. They probably hadn't even eaten before they ran up our hill. I heard their voices as if they were coming from a distance. They asked about something and Thao answered them. They teased Nho. She got angry and then started laughing. Someone was singing softly.

Someone's hair brushed against my cheek, then the sound of breathing came down from above. It was warm and enveloped me. I felt as if I were lying in my mother's arms.

"She's a Hanoi girl!"

I recognized the voice of the liaison officer and woke up immediately. He was a Hanoi guy. His father was an electrical worker and his mother was a clothing worker. At home, he had often played hooky and gotten bad grades. One time he rolled five bombs over a precipice, forcing them to explode down there so that they wouldn't damage the road. He was polite, hospitable, didn't smoke, and didn't flirt with us girls. As for us, we wouldn't leave him alone.

"If you go out with your sweetheart, for sure you'll force her to cut her hair, wear a suit and black boots, won't you?"

He would look uncomfortable, scratch his head, and blush deeply. "In everything, there are always exceptions, dear ladies! Anyway, I've never been in love."

I opened my eyes. The cave had grown dark already. The small light had already been lit on top of the ammunition trunk. A picture of Uncle Ho was glued onto the middle of a piece of large white paper. Just beneath it, an empty explosives canister held a bunch of fresh flowers. We always had flowers there, but in the lamplight I couldn't tell their colors. Maybe someone had just brought us these. We were a priority. The liaison officer was boiling some water, his back turned to us, solid as a bedboard. But when he stood up, I saw that his waist was as slender and attractive as a ping-pong player's.

Murmurs carried in from outside. The happiest moments were coming. I told myself I had to go outside, so I put my feet against the wall and, with my hands behind me, gave one hard push. As I jumped up, pain shot through my thigh. My head and my joints ached, but I managed to stand up anyway.

The liaison officer helped me. "Are you crazy?" he asked me. "If you're tired, then you should sleep."

"I'm going out now."

"Going out!" He smiled. His lips were thin, his teeth even, and his eyebrows thick. "You're not going anywhere. First of all, you've got to sleep."

"That's silly. No way," I mumbled and went toward the entrance to the cave, groping my way like a blind person. I wasn't the only one who was crazy because Nho had already disappeared. Thao was even crazier. I could hear her laughing up on the hill.

I saw Nho among a group of military construction workers. She told me that it was nearly midnight and the trucks were about to leave. While I was sleeping, many more bombs had exploded on the hill. But everything was alright because of the assault troops.

The top of the hill reverberated with the sounds of bulldozers, hoes, and talking and laughing. Occasionally, a mine would explode. Those explosions were even bigger than the sounds of the bombs. The stars seemed to move overhead. They were very far away, but as clear as drops of blue water, and they were scattered all across the sky. How vast was the sky! Suddenly, I remembered a poem written by a forward observer who tossed it to us when his group went by. He called us "the stars above the strategic hill." They were bright stars but for some reason he thought of them as "distant." We debated with each other and guessed that maybe he just wanted it to sound literary, because it was obvious that if they were stars they would be distant. I wanted so much to meet that artillery soldier. But his group was long gone.

The trucks got on their way at midnight. The engines roared. The road became alive with noise. The driver in the cabin of the fifth truck saw us. "Hey, Hanoi girls!" he cried. "You must really miss your mothers!"

"I think that's Thang from the Quang Trung group," Nho said quietly.

The bandage on her arm glowed white. She was quiet, with a round face and straight nose. She leaned against me, looking light and fresh as a white ice cream bar.

"They said that I should go to a hospital in the rear," she said. "That's ridiculous. Shots every day. Pills. Also, meat porridge. And, please eat a lot. Yuck! Like a spoiled brat lying in bed. It's naive of them to think that they can force me to go.

How annoying!" She hissed, as if I were preparing to drag her onto the medical truck myself.

She had turned around to discuss the phenomenon of shooting stars with one of the construction workers when she saw at the edge of the forest a star fall, disappearing midway through its course.

I folded my arms across my chest and walked some distance away, not looking at that soldier but at one of the trucks approaching us. I had struck a pose and that was all. How could I help it? There was no way that I could, right at this moment, run up and hold the hand of every soldier on this hill, bursting into tears because of the youthful joy that was rising inside of me. I loved everyone, with a passionate love, a love beyond words, that only someone who had stood on that hill in those moments, as I did, could understand fully.

The trucks followed each other without lights, forming a single mass on the road. The leaves that were used as camouflage made every truck seem double its size. To me, those convoys always looked limitless and countless. Long. Numerous. Gigantic.

"Probably the Hanoi men will come tonight!" Nho said, still quietly. She was in the same state of mind as me: loving everyone. That was the love of the people in smoke and fire, the people of war. It was a selfless, passionate, and carefree love, only found in the hearts of soldiers. I put my arm around Nho and squeezed her small, soft shoulder. We said nothing to each other. She was here, brave, gentle, from the same city as me and standing with me on this night on a hill covered by bomb craters near the front. We understood each other and felt completely happy.

1971

The Blue Sky

One extremely hot day, a battalion liaison officer ran toward a bunker where several reporters were waiting.

"Ladies and gentlemen," he announced, "it's almost time for the press conference."

There was a shuffling of pens and papers and cameras. The journalists had been waiting since morning. The heroes of the last few battles were being brought about to report their achievements and even though the reporters had covered most of the fighting themselves, they didn't want to miss this press conference.

The reporters turned down a footpath leading to a makeshift shed by a stream. All of them were middle-aged, except for one young woman. She was wearing the same fatigues and floppy hat as any other female soldier in the region. The only difference was her complexion, which, at this moment, was so pale with emotion that it made people think she was only a visitor to the front. She scribbled notes, then looked outside, then scribbled notes again, her lips trembling and her pen trembling as well. The photographer, who sported a pencil-thin mustache, pulled at the shirtsleeves of a short colleague.

"Check out that girl over there," he said. "She's about to do something crazy. She's going to fall in love with one of the heroes. I guarantee it."

The short guy seemed annoyed. "Stop it. You have a way of assuming that everything will turn out bad. Anyway, why not? She's young. When she gets married, that's the end of it anyway, as far as love is concerned."

The photographer snickered. The young woman, who was full of anticipation, heard the laughter behind her, turned around, and her eyes immediately flashed with anger. But the soldiers had come: six young heroes. The face of the young woman went even paler with agitation and she forgot the laughter of the photographer.

After the short press conference, she approached one of the soldiers, a scout. The two of them went outside and sat down on a rock by the stream.

The scout swung his gaze onto the young woman. He seemed intelligent and refined. "The journalist should introduce herself first," he said.

"You can call me Ninh—in my articles I go by the name Nguyen Thi Ninh."

He shook his head. "I very rarely read the paper; I don't recognize any reporter's name."

His honesty unsettled her. She opened her notepad but couldn't take any notes. Just like any other young person during the American War, especially among those close to the front, she felt such a deep affection for soldiers that she could have opened up to him about anything in her life. She felt awkward, ugly, and shy under his gaze. Oh Lord, those eyes, that face. It seemed at that moment that she had lived her whole life waiting for a person like him.

The photographer sat watching from inside the shed. The reporters were busy getting their material, so he could sit back and relax. His pencil-thin mustache jerked spitefully. He gazed at the pair of young people talking next to the stream, gazed at their innocence and, once again, felt an urge to ridicule it.

"Tell me," Ninh said to the soldier, "Tell me about your most memorable experience."

The scout smiled. He was also young and so his heart fluttered easily. He fixed his gaze on a tiny flower growing up between a crack in the stone.

"My name is Dong," he said. "I'm twenty years old. From Hanoi."

He spoke slowly, pausing between his sentences. Ninh knew that he had become an extremely famous soldier over the past few days.

One week earlier, Dong's reconnaissance team had gone on a mission. The trail they had to cross was in the midst of fierce fighting. About a kilometer away, soldiers were fighting enemy armored and infantry divisions, while a squadron of enemy helicopters and jets occupied different positions within the airspace. Suddenly, an M113 tank* appeared out of nowhere, raced toward where they were hiding, and came to a halt right in front of them. The driver of the tank jumped to the ground and, leaving it behind, made for the trail.

"Halt!" Dong shouted. The Southern soldier looked back but kept running. His face went pale from fear. Maybe he had been planning to abandon the tank and desert his post. At that time, Thang, who was standing next to Dong, became impatient. He quickly fired a burst of machine-gun fire, but the driver disappeared into the thick jungle.

The tank stood with its engine still running, an enormous hulk in the middle of the trail. This was truly an unforeseen circumstance. The men looked at each other, both worried and delighted. They looked inside. There was no sign of any other crewmen.

Dong said, "I know how to drive. Not very well, but well enough. Let's go!"

"I'm not scared," one of the others said. "Let's do it!"

Dong jumped into the tank. He had to fiddle for twenty minutes before the thing would budge. A scout had to be a jack-of-all-trades and, in the past, Dong had learned to drive a tank, but not an enemy tank. Who would have ever thought this would happen to him? The enemy were running away like ducks trying to save themselves. Perhaps the enemy soldier had driven it away in a panic when the attack started. Or perhaps he'd planned to take it and defect.

Finally, after spinning it like a beetle, Dong managed to race the tank toward the sound of the gunfire. On the way, he spotted two of their own infantrymen running down the hillside with a B40 rocket launcher. It became clear to him, then, who was losing, since the soldiers were no longer waiting in ambush but had begun to rush forward to confront the enemy. Dong

---

* Literal translation - A M113 is an armored personnel carrier. The word "half-track" would be more accurate.

stopped the tank, pushed open the hatch and began to wave his floppy hat frantically in the air. The guys with the B40 came to a halt, understanding instantly. They crossed to the edge of the trail to get a better look, then began to run toward the tank.

Their faces were bright with admiration. "Where'd you get this thing?" one of them shouted over all the noise of the explosives. "Why don't you take it and attack the enemy on the hill over there? Those two positions still belong to them and our troops are exhausted."

He tugged at Dong's shirtsleeve, "Hey! Let me get on," he said. "I still have four rockets left. We can stop by our resupply point and pick up another B40 for my friend and ask for some more rockets, okay?"

"Done!" Dong nodded. The two soldiers quickly climbed up.

But one more time they nearly became the target of a B40 launched from their side. The guys on the tank had to stand on top, waving their hats and their hands. After that, no B40s flew toward them.

They picked up the extra rockets and B40, then continued. On several hills in front of them, soldiers were attacking the enemy stronghold. Clouds of smoke swelled and dispersed, making the scene seem to float in a thick mist. The parachute flares the enemy were shooting into the air fluttered aloft, held suspended in the air by the pressure from so many explosions. The soldiers could see the silhouettes of their own comrades running through the smoke. A helicopter was lying belly-up in the middle of the enemy stronghold, next to sandbag-lined trenches. A truck blocked the way up the hill. Dong stepped on the gas and pushed the truck down into a bomb crater. The enemy hesitated, then began to shoot at the stolen tank. Dong drove forward into the enemy defenses. His own soldiers were running on both sides of the tank, some of them so proud of this captured treasure that they were shouting with joy as they fired.

An enemy machine gun was crushed beneath the treads of the tank. One of the soldiers sitting on top of the tank shot at the enemy's ammunition pile. The target burst into flames like a gasoline torch. An enemy soldier dropped his M.72 and scrambled up a mound of earth. Dong drove the M.113 across the artillery-bracketed battlefield to the right of the fortified hillside. Then he began to ascend the hill itself, pulverizing everything in his path until he finally reached the central bunker and came to a halt. Here, he met comrades from his battalion. The scouts already knew this area as clearly as the palms of their hands, which is why Dong was immediately able to thrust in the right direction. They had taken over the entire battlefield and the soldiers were already hoarse from cheering. A guy Dong knew handed him a cigarette.

"So you finished enough of your scouting duties to give you time for this sort of thing?" he asked..

"Plenty of time. Tonight, we'll fight even more."

Soldiers surrounded the tank, inspecting and discussing it.

The enemy commander was led out of the bunker. He was a bald-headed, fat colonel with small eyes. He paused for a moment, looking calmly into the eyes of the victors.

Dong stopped speaking. The young woman journalist grew tense.

"And then what happened?" she asked him.

"After that, I was dragged all over the place, answering questions about what had happened. I didn't enjoy it."

"Why?"

"I don't know. For a soldier, fighting is easier than talking."

The young woman looked at the soldier's hands: two rough, sinewy hands whose apparent experience contrasted with the youthful face.

Ninh tried to restrain herself but, unable to do so, asked a question she had thought of earlier. "When you go out onto the battlefield like that, do you feel any fear?"

"No! At those moments, you're only fighting. That's all. The first hillside I drove up was so steep. You can't imagine. Sitting inside the tank, I could only see the sky. When the front of the tank slammed down onto the hill again, that was how I knew I'd finally reached the top."

Ninh scrawled a quick note on her pad, "Sitting in the tank and only able to see the sky." During the rest of his story, she hadn't been able to write down a word. But it seemed as if she could remember every pause and expression on his face.

She didn't want to think of saying good-bye. Her heart beat painfully in her chest.

Ninh didn't know when she'd started to be infatuated with soldiers and their victories, just like a thirteen-year-old boy. The quality of this emotion made it difficult for her to distinguish between love for an individual soldier and love for all of them. But she'd never felt like this before. Her delicate hand sat motionless in the hand of the scout.

Dong was surprised to see the tears welling up in the young woman's eyes. He turned his back toward everyone else as if to protect her from their stares.

His voice seemed altered.

"Good-bye!" he said. "See you around."

She shook her head, the tears streaming down her cheeks. "Where will you be that I can meet you?"

Dong was the last to leave, to cross the wooden bridge that led back across the stream. The truck waited for the soldiers. Ninh had already dried her tears and her face looked normal, but when the engine started on the other side of the stream, she could no longer contain herself. She ran into the shed, threw herself onto a chair, and burst into tears. Fortunately, there was no one in the shed.

That evening, the group of reporters stayed in the barracks of the youth volunteers, relatively far from the front.

The photographer finished off a huge can of pork sausage in a few swallows. He looked over at Ninh's untouched ration box and then at her listless face and snickered, "You miss him a lot, huh? He's number how many hundred already?"

The young woman carried her ration box to a hammock and sat down to eat her food. In general, she didn't like to talk to the photographer. She didn't have the wit to compete with a man twenty years her senior, who had lived through the French occupation of Hanoi and had four children in addition to two mistresses who traipsed in and out of the office all day. In general, he was small-minded and mean. He'd even noticed the way the hem of Ninh's black pants had barely touched her ankles when she first came to work at the office. He'd even made fun of her blue flip-flops. And when Ninh sat reviewing her French in the office, he laughed when she mispronounced a word. Within the rosy mist that always enveloped Ninh, he was the wooden stake piercing through to torment her. He had written a ditty, which he read aloud for everyone to hear, comparing her to a chicken who had dared to join the peacocks. Even now, among all these good-natured people, he still hadn't changed. His thin face only became alive when there was no sound of bombs or guns. He was not only mean but unusually afraid of dying and he always got in people's way.

How could a man like that understand me? Ninh asked herself, nibbling at her canned meat and scowling at the cowardly face of the photographer. Now wonder he has a pot belly, she thought. He eats like a tiger.

That night, sitting in her hammock with her flashlight on, Ninh finished the article about the scouts and Dong's captured tank. First thing the next morning, she handed the article to the army reporters and ventured off toward the front by herself. The photographer also headed off in that direction. Ninh knew that he must have had a compelling reason to go. She had never met anyone as afraid of death as he was. Anyway, she found it more pleasant to go alone. She was in the habit of taking a backpack, jumping onto trucks, and traveling for long days to get closer to the fighting.

This time, she had asked to go forward in hope of meeting the scout again.

At the moment they had parted, her love for Dong had been so fierce that she would have sacrificed everything simply to be allowed to go with him. Her article, full of fire for him, had been submitted. She had scrawled all her emotions, admiration, and the fluttering of her heart across the back of a discarded piece of mimeographed paper. Pretty soon, that article would fall into the scout's hands. Would he read between the lines of words describing his achievements?

In the following days, she calmed down and was able to see him as one among the thousands of soldiers with whom she had met and spoken. Sometimes, she laughed at her own emotions. But if she wasn't in love, then how could she write?

She stayed for two more weeks, visiting the artillery and infantry units. Many more faces and many more victories made her heart beat painfully when she had to say goodbye.

On the truck taking her back to the city, Ninh was impatient to read the article she'd written about Dong. In her rush, she'd forgotten to ask what street he lived on and his address. Where could she find him?

After dropping her backpack off at home, she ran straight to her office. The peacefulness of the place amazed her. The painter was slouched in her chair, discussing dress fashions with the treasurer. The photographer, already cleaned up, was standing in the courtyard with a friend, talking loudly and roaring with laughter.

Seeing Ninh, the photographer yelled, "Ah! The busy lover has returned, huh?"

Ninh tried to contain her anger.

"I just got back," she said. "Do you know what issue my article was published in?"

"It was cut," he said indifferently.

"Why?"

"Go on in and ask your boss. It never even made it to the editorial board."

Ninh rushed into the editorial office. Three heads. Three pairs of glasses perched on the tips of three noses. The sounds of chairs sliding back. Greetings.

"So you got back, Ninh. Was it a safe trip?"

"Yes, so to speak," she answered. "Why wasn't my article published, Khang?"

"Have something to drink and relax first. Have you had a chance to clean up yet?"

Ninh became impatient. "No, but I can wait until I get home later."

Knowing Ninh's character, the department head pulled out a chair and asked her to sit down. He fumbled through a drawer to find her article. She looked at his bald head and smiled sourly. Before she'd come to work here, the sound of his name had made her heart flutter. Tuan Khang! She'd imagined him to be youthful, healthy, a man who wore white sports clothes, whistled often, and took the stairs three steps at a time. The day she returned from her journalist's training, she was assigned to the public housing building where he lived. People pointed out Mr. Tuan Khang. Carrying a spittoon in his hands, he walked down the stairs one step at a time. He had let his hair grow long around his ears so that he could brush it over to cover the bald crown of his head. Every morning, he coughed loudly and spit into the toilet. People also told her about his stinginess, many of the stories so bizarre that it was hard to know if they were true or not. But people knew for sure that he was the boss of everything in his house. He allotted the matchbox to a corner of the pantry and always set aside three matches for the day. Often, his wife had to go ask a neighbor for a light because she'd already used up all three without getting the fire started. In the privacy of their home, he would beat his wife for boiling five cents worth of water greens for only one meal.

Now, looking at the few hairs brushed across his bald head and remembering those stories, Ninh felt creepy.

"Let me explain, Ninh," he began. "The article you wrote was full of zeal and was able to convey the atmosphere of the battlefield. But you went over the top. When I finished, I knew it stretched the truth."

Hot-tempered to begin with, Ninh couldn't bear to hear what the department head had to say. She was so angry that tears came to her eyes. It was a long time before she could speak.

"There's no lack of unusual stories from soldiers. You might not believe it, but you have to publish it. The soldiers will know it's true."

The bald man calmly looked at the young woman. He believed that she was rather unbalanced and, although likely to explode over anything, she'd probably lose interest eventually anyway.

He took his time. "There's no lack of other role models either," he said. "Coming back this time, you probably have plenty of material, so just go ahead and write about something more believable."

Ninh jumped up, her face flushed, her lips trembling uncontrollably. But then she quietly walked out of the room. When she reached the stairs, she burst into tears. The photographer was standing there grinning.

It wasn't the first time she'd seen him grin that way. Once, he and Ninh had gone to a timber forest in Central Vietnam. During wartime, the timber forests were calmer than other places because all the work was carried out in the woods and the trees made people feel protected. That time, the man in question was eloquent and more intelligent than ever. An engineer who had just come back from studying abroad, he was full of enthusiasm and beautiful but impractical ideas. He worked in a technical office. Seeing that the timber workers' administrative section was too big and cumbersome, he came up with an innovation: Leaving only a third of the staff inside, all the rest of the office workers would participate in clearing a route to transport the wood from the newly harvested area to the main road. He volunteered to work as a team leader and his friends followed suit.

Ninh and the photographer went there during the days that the administrators began to work on the new route. During one crystal clear afternoon in the ancient forest, Ninh met the engineer and fell in love immediately. His health, energy, and clear-mindedness completely suited Ninh's ideas. Mostly, though, she was drawn by the fact that everyone else admired him. He could have remained comfortably back in the office. What had made him jump headlong into this difficult work? She was also moved by the fact that the corps flag marking the front line was always near where the engineer worked.

In the evening, back in the guest house, a passion-filled Ninh sat writing an article about this man and his friends. She sent the article back immediately and spent another week in the timber forest. Her undeclared love for the engineer began to fade because there were so many other men around. But everything had been declared in her passionate article.

When they parted, Ninh said to the engineer, "After you read my article, if you have any response, please write to me."

But Mr. Tuan Khang hadn't published it. Why not? Her eyes had opened wide with consternation as she'd peered into the department head's face, a face like a big red pumpkin.

He had taken his time. "Calm down, calm down," he'd said.

"No. How can I calm down?" she'd asked. "A story like that, and you won't publish it? Look, at a time when everyone is complaining that the support sections are too big and hogging too many workers, a story like this is really important."

The department head had pushed his few hairs from one temple to the other. He'd pulled open a flimsy wooden cigarette box, drew out a cigarette, broke it in two, then carefully placed one half back inside. Ninh had never seen him have the courage to smoke an entire cigarette. His method of smoking unnerved her. There was something so extraordinarily greedy about it, maybe because he had struggled so long before finally giving in.

She had impatiently asked him, "So why?"

"Where would it lead? That team that's building the road, once they've finished what will they do?"

"They'll do something else! There's a lack of laborers in the timber forest. There's so much to do!"

Ninh was flustered. Clearly, she had never asked herself this question.

"Will they become permanent manual laborers, then?" he had wanted to know. "And in the article you say that most of them are technicians. Technicians are trained to deal with technology. Because of their fervency, they've dropped it all to become laborers. Now the timber forest will have to find some other technicians. How do you think that will turn out economically?"

While writing the article, Ninh had never actually considered this issue. But didn't she have the right to commend their enthusiasm?

"That won't do, Ninh," he had told her. "You might commend them, but the readers will want answers. When you put forward a new concept, you have to consider all the possibilities. You can't rush into praising everything."

Ninh had run toward the stairs in indignation and met the photographer, who had been grinning in the same way he was grinning today.

* * *

Now, the department head watched Ninh go to where her bike was parked, take it, and rush out of the compound.

The cold water he had thrown on her enthusiasm about Dong's story was too much, too brutal, and it made her feel faint. With his outlook on life, could he see any good in the world? Ninh rushed home and threw herself on the bed, sobbing to release her anger. She looked through the window at a patch of blue sky and felt pity for the loss of the blue sky that the scout had seen while he was driving the tank. Suddenly, she felt so much love for him. He was far away now at the front. For so long, he had been without a good night's sleep and even a hot meal while the people here didn't even believe him.

That room over there was the photographer's, right near the entrance to the apartment building. Whenever any young people came up to the young women's common room, he would know it. One day, he complained at a house meeting that the young women's room wasn't enforcing the rules strictly enough. A young woman had even been seen kissing her lover while her roommates were away. Such things couldn't be permitted. The communal house had to be a true communal house. If outsiders had seen this kissing, they would have thought the communal house lacked culture.

At that meeting, a man had asked him directly, "How do you know that people were kissing each other?"

The photographer shamelessly replied that the window had been open and so he had looked.

The man asked another question. "If you were in love, wouldn't you kiss?"

The photographer had exploded, saying that he would request to move, but they all knew that it was a hollow threat. With a wife and a bunch of children, where could he go? He was the peacock who believed that all the chickens were about to soil his feathers.

The room on the other side of the public fountain was the department head's. As his belly grew fatter, his head grew full of dark suspicions. Recently, in a room next to Ninh's, a woman had heard someone call through the gate at about eleven at night. She'd gone out and spoken to someone who had given her a piece of news that made her immediately begin to cry. She was from the countryside and expressed her emotions openly and noisily. As she trudged back up the stairs, sobbing, she caused a commotion throughout the whole building. Ninh had opened the door and the woman grabbed her.

"Oh Ninh, Manh is dead. Oh, little brother! You were so young and you've left me already! Only three days ago, we were eating together. Why did you rush off like that?"

Ninh had turned pale. Manh had been a soldier on the missile brigade. Three days before, when he had come to visit his sister, he and Ninh had joked around. His unit had gone down to the Fourth Zone and he'd died there.

Because Ninh's boss often had trouble sleeping, he'd heard the loud noise and came upstairs to find out what had happened.

When he heard the news, he pontificated, "Whatever happened, it's late and you ladies need to keep quiet out of respect for the rules. Tomorrow, people have to go to work and if they can't sleep, they won't be able to function."

The women had gone to their rooms and shut the doors. Everybody was quiet. They were all afraid of him and whatever plots were in his head.

But that night, Ninh couldn't sleep at all. Her nineteen-year-old heart was in excruciating pain. She had also loved Manh and now he was dead. How could death come so swiftly and unreasonably?

For a long time now, Ninh lay looking out the window and thinking. Her thoughts were scattered and her tears blurred everything.

Through her sobs, Ninh sang the words of her favorite song: "Even though winter passed, the beautiful images have faded away and the leaves are already pouring from the branches. I will remember you all my life. You'll return, you'll return."

Among the countless faces she had loved, the face of the tank-driving scout came back to her more than any other.

* * *

Two years passed. The small reporter continued to go back and forth in the dusty convoys. The war against the Americans was moving toward victory. As the days progressed, the department head grew fatter and became more and more confined within those four walls. He always acted aloof, although one day he had thrown a basin full of water at his wife because she lost the ration ticket for their remaining three kilos of meat. When she cried loudly, he dragged her into the house, thrust her head against the wall, and hissed, "Shut up right now!"

He was afraid that his reputation would be affected.

He had succeeded in passing some of his indifference and cynicism about everything onto Ninh. These days, after hearing a story, she would hesitate a bit. Writing her articles, she would stop to consider whether anyone would believe it and whether anyone would question her or not. She didn't fall in love as easily, either. Now, almost every one of her articles passed the department head's inspection. They were accurate, temperate, and no longer as full of fire as before. She understood this was necessary for a journalist.

One afternoon, while walking home, she heard someone call out loudly, "Ninh!"

An army jeep came to an abrupt halt by the side of the road. A soldier ran toward her.

"Ninh! Ninh!"

"Is that you? Oh, my!"

Ninh looked at the soldier and her "Oh, my!" was so temperate that he stopped quickly and his expectations immediately diminished. They asked about each other like two people who had come from far away to meet, like two people who had known each other a long time. While Ninh spoke to him, she wondered why, back at the front, she had thought him so handsome and unreachable. It seemed as if, at that time, he had been taller and his gaze more intelligent. That day, in the forest destroyed by American bombs, he had had the beauty of a knight. Standing next to him, all the calamities of war had seemed smaller and less disastrous. She had felt prepared to follow him to the ends of the earth. She had loved him fiercely and didn't care to know anything else about his life beyond his achievements and his looks.

"It was such a shame," she said. "The story I wrote about you was never published."

He smiled. "I was so busy; I couldn't have read it anyway."

He was on the point of saying something else to this girl whom he had once protected, shielding her tears from other people's curious eyes. He wanted to say, "I didn't dare to write, but there wasn't a moment when I didn't think of you." Now, he thought better of it. She had changed. He shouldn't think that things were the same as before.

After saying good-bye to the scout, Ninh returned to the communal house. The photographer had mistakenly put something into the pot of porridge that his wife had prepared for the children and now she was berating him. He was terrified of his wife. The more chivalrously he acted outside the home, the more cowardly he became in contact with the two iron hands of his wife. He was wearing shorts and an undershirt and his arms and legs were deathly pale. He was so afraid of his wife that he didn't even dare to glance up at Ninh as she walked by.

Ninh walked into her room, opened the window, and saw the sky. She thought how Dong had said that when he was driving the tank, he could only see the sky. Was that a lie or the truth? Maybe, she thought, it was a lie.

1986

A Day On the Road

The car dropped me off at a newly opened construction site. I picked up my two canvas bags and got out. The two men who had given me a ride also got out. One of the men was very fat and spoke in a falsetto. The other man was very thin and scowling, with the kind of face that makes people worry. I thanked them and said good-bye. But they were busy discussing who had been promoted while they were away. A moment later, the door to the car shut again. The fat man caught sight of me and extended his hand. His palm was moist.

The thin man said, "Go on in there and rest. Don't be afraid. I told them to make a portion of rice for you. There's space for you—you can sleep with the waitresses who serve the specialists, okay? I'm going to return the car and I'll be right back. Go on. Don't be afraid."

I went inside. The communal room was very spacious; it contained a few dozen single beds and was crowded with girls and women. The young women of the Central region are very healthy and talk loudly. They walk around quickly, stomping. When all of them are packed together, they sound like a noisy train station during the days before Tet. I was led to a bed at the end of the room. I sat down and looked at everyone, feeling lonely because I knew no one and no one paid any attention to me.

My two bags were very heavy. Everything inside was Duc's. When I was about to leave, he had asked me to carry some gifts back for him to Hanoi. Afraid that I would mix his things up with someone else's, he'd opened everything for me to see: A large container of Phu Quoc fish sauce, five kilos of sweet sausage, three or four kilos of dried fish and squid. I had felt like laughing as I watched Duc's slender, girlish hands open all these large and small packages in order to show me what was in them. There had been a time, during the frenzied nights that the B-52s bombed Hanoi, when we still loved each other and I brought Duc two loaves of bread and he ate them, blushing from shyness. Back then, Duc wore straightleg pants and white plastic flip-flops that slapped the floor when he walked, just like almost all the other young people in Hanoi. He often read me sad lines of poetry by Russian poets who wrote about love. And when we went to see a romantic movie, both of us would nearly swoon from emotion. All the material things, however, made us uneasy. Just like all of our friends during that era, neither of us ever had any money. Our minds were completely occupied with headier things. Whenever we could all get together, we discussed lofty issues. All the while, our stomachs cried out for something to eat. Those hands of Duc's, which I used to think so beautiful, I now remembered pulling open a bunch of dried squid.

He'd told me, "I bought all this with money my mother sent me. Please tell her when she gets everything to write and tell me explicitly so that I won't have to worry."

At that time, I hadn't given Duc's request a thought, but now I was really mad. These two big canvas bags were exuding the smell of fish sauce, fish, and sausage. Here I was, carrying them until my arms gave out, and he'd been worried that his mother might not get it all.

I'd met Duc this way: A woman from my office had said, "I know a guy, the younger brother of a friend. You should get to know him. This guy is so sweet, if any of his friends liked his girlfriend, he'd probably be willing to give her up." I had wanted to see a man like that with my own eyes, a man willing to sacrifice everything for a friend. And we'd liked each other right away, very naturally. Everything at that time was natural, cheerful. Duc had his own room in his parent's two story house right in the center of Hanoi. So much space was a rarity at that time. We often had a relaxing time after work in his room: reading books, listening to music, and chatting softly without fear of any eavesdropping, judgmental neighbors. This was no communal house. Duc's father, who, I'd heard, was a merchant before the Revolution, was now very old, fat, and slow. He often walked by the room, saw me sitting there, and nodded hello without saying a word.

Perhaps I was too worn out after traveling several hundred kilometers. When I thought about my leave-taking the day before, a bitter feeling washed over me, filling my eyes with tears. I hadn't felt this way out on the road. Only now, sitting alone among strangers did I look at myself and wonder why I had ever loved Duc so much. A very trivial thought crossed my mind: There is nothing that can burst into flames and then be extinguished without a trace so easily as love.

At that time, almost all of my friends had joined the army and gone to the front. There were also a lot of people who had stayed in Hanoi to work, like Duc. That was normal. Back then, Duc was raising a small turtle. The turtle crawled aimlessly around the room, out onto the porch, under the bed, and occasionally even crawled onto my feet, terrifying me. Duc laughed gently, his glasses flashing. He was still young but, because he was very shortsighted, he looked much older and I couldn't help but compare him to the turtle.

And then suddenly, Duc's disposition changed. I didn't understand why. That summer, after joining the army and being sent to B5 for about six months, I returned to Hanoi and immediately ran over to Duc's house. I'd been with a special services unit, all of whom were good-natured and full of enthusiasm, and the atmosphere of the front still enveloped my being. I went to Duc's house hoping to find something new in him, but I found him sitting on the porch, from which were hanging pots of orchids. The turtle was wandering around close by. Duc's face had filled out but it seemed strange, both tense and disdainful. The neighborhood was so quiet and calm it astonished me. Nothing had changed at all. Coming back from the battlefield, I assumed that there had been fierce fighting everywhere. It turned out that in this small corner of Hanoi the sound of gunfire was very far away, inaudible. Duc was happy to see me again. He used his foot to push the turtle away. The turtle withdrew its head into its shell very quickly, then immediately stuck it out again and walked into Duc's room. Like the turtle, Duc walked slowly into the house and his voice surprised me.

"Well? What's new? Are you sick of the war yet?"

He sat down on a stool made from the base of a tree and left rough so that it would look artistic. I sat down on another stool just like it but at that moment I felt that his furniture was very snobbish. He made tea in an eel skin teapot the size of two matchboxes, then poured the tea into cups the size of his thumb. His gestures were very restless. He'd been like that in the past, but I'd gotten used to it. Now, though, I'd just come back and the place I had inhabited for half a year was entirely different from this room, from Duc, even from his turtle. It seemed that, during my absence, something had changed in his life. He asked me if I'd seen my friends.

"A bunch of fanatics!" he mumbled.

I was very surprised. "Why do you think so?"

He smiled disdainfully, but didn't answer.

Without thinking about it, I picked up one of his books and noticed a quote that he had written in the margin: "We experience terrible misfortunes, the first of which is that we have to live at all."

Throughout all the exciting and memorable events that happened in the next few months of the war against the Americans, Duc continued to live in that room, to go to work, and to speak to me in a voice that was very listless. For the life of me, I couldn't explain his new disposition, but I could see that he had taken on someone else's gestures and speech patterns to such a degree that for a long time I treated him like a friend instead of a lover.

He came to see me off again on the day that I returned to the front at the end of 1974. We didn't mention love. Looking at his glasses, I found him rather pitiful. Maybe I still cherished him, cherished that person I had known in the early years of our relationship. But I had to go to the front.

We followed the soldiers from their base down to a city in

the central region. I really wanted to have Duc with me to share the joy in those first few days after liberation. Then those days were over. Coming out of the jungle, my friends and I had a lot of work to do in that city, and just like everyone else who had just emerged from the jungle, none of us thought about buying anything. We only thought about the North, which was entirely different from here. The city was ferociously hot, which made me dehydrated. I was always unsettled and homesick, missing Hanoi. In this city, all the houses had corrugated roofs and the streets were bare of trees. How could anyone live in a city with no greenery? The young men wore bellbottom pants forty centimeters wide and the women let their hair grow long and cover both sides of their faces. Stores sold plastic goods. Elegant rooms buzzed with the sound of air conditioners. Everything seemed unstable. The city seemed to float in midair, without clinging to anything solid. I thought that I could never be part of this picture. A very pure emotion made me restless. I longed for the calm, healthy life in the North. Duc would be there, the Duc I remembered from the early days of our relationship.

Only one month after the liberation of the South I returned to Hanoi. The moment I stepped down from the bus, I could already see that everything had changed. People were racing all over the place in a great commotion of selling and buying. It was as if a fever had infected the city. I immediately went to Duc's house and I saw change in his room as well. Three big suitcases and a couple of large bags were sitting in a corner of the room. Almost nothing was left of his furniture. He had packed everything.

"I've got documents allowing me to go to Saigon already," he told me.

"So you're leaving for good?"

"For good. I want to get to know somewhere else. It's too boring to stay too long in Hanoi."

I thought back over those years of war against the Americans. He had never once left Hanoi. He had called our friends who went to the front a bunch of fanatics. Many of them had died.

And Duc would be the first to go and live in that city that they had helped to liberate.

Duc introduced me to a young couple sitting in his room. "These are my new friends," he said. "Thu has just come up from Saigon to give a performance and she has to get back immediately."

I looked at Thu. She was rather pretty. Hers was the same beauty that I had seen among young women in Central Vietnam. It was hard to know if it was real or fake: her face was plastered with make-up, but her gestures seemed very mature. All four of us sat around that artistic wooden table. I didn't know whether Duc planned to take his eel skin teapot with him or not because he hadn't packed it yet. Thu drank tea as strong as a man would. Her boyfriend continually scratched his leg, complaining that there were too many mosquitoes.

Thu spoke very slowly about the things she was interested in. Normal human beings deserve a better life than this, she said. Only when she got to Saigon did she recognize that. In her aunt's house, when they washed the dishes, they used a big sponge. In Hanoi, if they even have a pair of print trousers, they had to hide inside the house. They wouldn't even dare to step outside the door. But her cousins in Saigon, when they went to sleep they wore white gauze nightgowns. At her aunt's house in Saigon, they cooked their rice in a Japanese electric rice cooker. They slept on mats made of Thai nylon. When she thought about this, she realized how long it had been since she'd lived like a human being. In Saigon, everything was so convenient and they had enough of everything. Even the baskets looked really civilized. All of them were made of plastic.

"Even their brooms are made of nylon!" I blurted out, looking at Thu. She was so carried away with what she was saying that she didn't notice the tone of my voice.

She looked at me, brightening up. "You may be right!" she exclaimed, adding, "I hate to say it, but you could even use their toilet paper to stuff your pillows!"

Duc laughed with a great deal of satisfaction. He forcefully set his cup in its saucer as if to express his determination: I've got to go.

I stayed for a few more minutes before going home and when I went into the street I began to cry. If I had come on a scooter, maybe Duc would have had a different attitude toward me. How could I have known he had such a craving for modern conveniences? Suddenly remembering, I asked myself who Duc could have given his turtle to, because I hadn't seen it wandering around the room anymore.

* * *

The thin man appeared in the doorway and wove his way through all the women in the communal room to tell me that he had managed to find me a seat in a car going to Hanoi. It was a car reserved for technical experts and so he had had to do some persuading. The car would depart at six the next morning. I was very happy because it meant that I would probably be home by late afternoon, back to my work that was waiting, back to my mother.

On the day that Duc got on the train, I didn't go to see him off. A long time, perhaps nearly a year, later, I received a letter from him. He told me that he had just gotten back from a mission to the Western region. Wherever he went, everything was "huge"—the ducks were "huge," the fish and shrimp were also "huge." And he didn't have any emotion at all except that he missed Hanoi and really missed me. If possible, he said, I should come South on a mission to stay with him for a while.

I asked my office to let me go down immediately. I wanted to see Duc in order to clarify our relationship. We hadn't declared anything to each other regarding our sentiments and this uncertainty had lasted a long time. Over the past year, he had been too busy with the glittery life, which was his passion. For my part, because I was a woman, I had to be reserved. This journey south was very important to me.

I sent a telegram to Duc immediately, telling him which

train I was taking and hoping that he would come to meet me because I had no friends in the city. Duc did not come. I had to ask to stay in the guest lounge of a branch office with which I had worked in the past. After I had made all the arrangements for my stay, I went to Duc's office in search of him. Everyone told me that he had been gone for two days. I wrote down my address for him, then went back to kill time in my room. Immediately the next morning, Duc arrived, looking for me. I got the feeling that he had wanted me to take care of my accommodations myself. Once assured that I had taken care of it, he came. Our conversation was aimless.

Duc was the same—noncommittal and slow. His face contained a new and strange tension. Maybe he had to struggle a lot with his new life, his trivial ambitions. He invited me to come visit him. He was staying in a spacious room in the large home of his father's older brother. It was apparent to me that he had attained what he wanted. He had a big sponge to wash his dishes with. He had a nylon broom. An imported nylon broom. An electric rice cooker. All the necessary appliances. Even a plastic toothpick holder. And he wore pajamas at home. They were gray, with stripes. I hated him in those pajamas.

"It would be even better if you had the turtle," I teased.

He looked at me with suspicion, afraid that I might have meant something by that. In fact, I didn't mean anything deep at all. His pajamas made him languid and didn't suit a thirty-five-year-old man. How suitable the turtle would be in this scenario.

After that, I avoided him. Yet as far as Duc was concerned, if I avoided him or met him frequently, it made no difference at all. He was like a wall. All the flutters of excitement and despair that I tried to hide hit against that brick wall and bounced back. And I remembered the first few things that people had told me about him: This guy is so sweet. If any of his friends liked his girlfriend, he'd probably be willing to give her up.

Now I understood. But I still didn't understand why Duc was so obsessed about that sponge.

Our only outing was memorable. He invited me to go eat at

a restaurant that served northern-style noodle soup. It was extremely crowded and tables and chairs had been dragged out onto the sidewalk. The young boy who made money watching over people's scooters approached Duc before we parked his Vespa. "Do you want me to watch it?" he asked.

"No," Duc said. With determination, he dragged his Vespa toward the base of a tree. "No watching. I don't want to be ripped off."

The boy scowled at Duc and said nothing.

After we ate, Duc pushed his Vespa back into the street. We couldn't go anywhere, though. Both of the tires were flat. I laughed to myself. It wasn't Duc that had been ripped off. It was his Vespa. No doubt, that pained him. He sweated profusely as he pushed the scooter to a repair shop. The inner tubes had been slashed to shreds. While the owner of the repair shop was busy working on the Vespa, I sat quietly, looking out into the street. I didn't dare look at Duc any longer.

The charge for changing the inner tubes and repairing the tires was very high, but Duc had only brought enough money for noodle soup. I had to shake the money out of my purse, all the money I had saved to last me a week in this city. That was the only time the two of us went out. I thought Duc would never come by again. But then he came, the day I was about to leave, his arms full of packages and parcels. They smelled terrible, even though they had been wrapped up in nylon bags! I don't know where he managed to find the ten herbal cough lozenges he gave me to suck on the way home.

During those days in the north, during the war against the Americans, he had been a simple young man who blushed when I brought him a loaf of bread. At that time, we treated material things lightly, or with embarrassment, or caution. But now, he was like this. Maybe he hadn't changed. Maybe he had become his true self. But it still pained me whenever I thought of this: how could a sponge attract Duc so strongly?

* * *

I went to catch the car earlier than I had planned. A night without sleep made me very uncomfortable and it gave me a throbbing headache. The drizzle that fell like dust in front of my face made it difficult for me to see the car come to a stop right in front of me. Get on! A voice that was both imperious and playful boomed at my ear. An elderly foreigner with a gray mustache, who must have come here as a technical expert, nodded at me. His interpreter gave me a hand with my bags. Finding them heavy, he asked if he could put them in the trunk. I was happy to agree. From now until my arrival in Hanoi I would not have to carry those precious things anymore and I would not have caused the people sitting next to me the unpleasantness of that combination of bad smells.

The driver, who was about thirty, sat behind the wheel looking straight ahead. Even though I was sad, from the way he was sitting I couldn't help but notice that he was handsome and strong in a way that had probably made a lot of women love him.

But I was disappointed when he abruptly turned around and said, "Hey, when you get home remember to ask if that Vespa has been sold. If it hasn't, buy it, okay?"

"So quickly?" the interpreter answered.

"And that thing that you mentioned a while ago, consider it done."

He glanced at me, obviously choosing to be vague about their discussion. I laughed to myself. Sitting in that position staring straight ahead, he had made me feel that he was meditating on something, but it turned out that he was only meditating about business. I still had the foolishness of a young girl when judging the outward appearance of a young man. My older sister had not been teasing when she advised me, "Don't fall for a guy just because he picks up a guitar to strum in front of you. Those guys are more useless than anybody."

I yawned, squeezing myself into the far corner of the car in hope of taking a nap. The driver and the interpreter continued their conversation about the scooter which had been interrupted when they stopped to pick me up. Another Vespa! I listened with bitterness, closing my eyes and remembering Duc's Vespa. I didn't understand why everywhere I went I had to listen to people talking about motorbikes. This motorbike fever was so intense. Nowadays, everything was like a fever. The two men released torrents of opinions about engines, speaking with great enthusiasm, as if they were ready to sell their souls for exhaust pipes, tires, inner tubes, and spark plugs.

The interpreter gestured with his hands excitedly. "Can you imagine?" he asked. "The day the guy who fixes motorbikes opened his shop at the corner of my street, I stood there in a trance, just watching him take apart a Honda. It took almost three hours. I kept standing there watching until my wife finally came out to look for me. She was carrying the baby and she had to whack me on the butt to wake me up."

The two of them started laughing. The old foreign expert also joined in the conversation and something that the interpreter told him made him hold his sides with laughter. I observed the clothing of the two Vietnamese. Driving cars and working for foreign experts had given them the chance to dress rather well. The interpreter was wearing a very fashionable shirt. It probably cost him what many people pay in rent. His watch, his American jeans, and his shoes, all of them must have cost thousands of dong. Some people could afford to be so happy. They grew up, went to school, found jobs, and then were able to wear their money.

I started to doze off. I tried not to think of Duc with bitterness or amazement, tried not to hear the people around me talking about things to which I could never adapt. Yet. I was obsessed also by the inconveniences I met in my daily life. My building was so overcrowded that it had had to be partitioned into many sections, many temporary rooms. At night the mice took over. They crawled over feet and wove across sleeping bodies while searching for an exit. All of this would interrupt one's sleep. Waking up in the morning, I would hear the sound of people quarreling. On my way to the lavatory, carrying my wash basin and my clothes, I would face crowds of people. Everyone was in a hurry, everyone had their needs. Some days, I could only cursorily wash my face and leave, yielding to everyone else, because the stream of water was as thin as a chopstick and if one person did everything then no one else would have a chance to do anything. Then, starting to prepare my breakfast, I'd realize that I'd forgotten to refill my kerosene stove and that the dry rice was full of stones, which I should have picked out the night before. The mice had eaten most of the cabbage, leaving me nothing to do but throw it away. I moved around the crowded room that housed my whole family, constantly running into my brothers, who were tall and wore only shorts, and who, in this summer heat, made everything even hotter. Even they were ashamed of their size. My mother was angry at my father because she had told him to carry the chicken coop up to the porch but he kept forgetting. My father said that we didn't even have enough space for all the people anyway, so we shouldn't have ever gotten those chickens. My sister-in-law scolded her children, "Go out and sit on the stairs. If you stay in here, I'll kick you."

Even so, the mornings passed. Almost everyone left and I also got ready to go to work. But when I picked up the ball-point pen I'd just bought, the ink would not come out. After I combed my hair, I tried to put on a hair clip, but it wouldn't snap. Every day I had to fiddle with it to make it snap. And my bike had a flat. People said that phony inner tubes and tires had flooded the stores, and with bad luck you could be one of the people who bought one. The boy who blew up tires would, with a certain sleight of hand, break your valve and then you'd have to buy one of his at a price that was a rip-off.

Almost every morning, some inconvenience would upset me. But why did I still cherish that life and hope every day that it would keep getting better? I hoped that my pen would improve, that my tires and inner tubes would become more durable, that the rice would have fewer stones and fewer husks, that the ceiling of our house wouldn't collapse from too many leaks, and that I wouldn't have to live with mice.

As for Duc, he went looking for a more comfortable life in a city to whose liberation he had contributed almost nothing. I had been to his room, and seen all his conveniences, but the familiar life of my own city still had a magical power that pulled me home. Duc had told me to transfer to the south where, he said, things were very good. But I had a feeling I couldn't be happy in a life that lacked the simple atmosphere I'd grown used to, despite all its inconveniences. Such simplicity, that pure rhythm of life that my generation had known and embraced, would be hard to find in the city Duc had come to love. Some things I can't explain.

The car braked very suddenly. I opened my teary eyes and saw a big river in front of us. A ferry was leaving to cross to the far shore.

"We're already at Pha Rang," the interpreter shouted.

Everybody got out of the car. I hurriedly looked around. Pha Rang! In 1968, the Americans stopped bombing north of the 20th parallel, but hit the area between the 17th and 20th parallels even harder. Thick smoke and fire covered this ferry dock day and night. One night, as many as eight people in my unit were killed. Everyone was petrified by the scream of the planes, the bombs, and the strafing. Perhaps that was the bunker where Cay and I had spent the night together. Both of us had just turned 17. Cay was a country girl who had an innocent appearance and a very pretty face that often made the soldiers turn around to look. She had never eaten ice cream. What's an iron? Will lipstick make your lips itch? All day, Cay bothered everyone with her questions. But she was very brave. I have often thought that if this ferry dock hadn't had people like her then our victory would have taken longer. On that evening, the enemy flares lit up the dock, making it possible to see every grain of sand. We were exhausted from carrying dirt, from hoeing, from leveling the earth. Only when a B-52 dropped a bomb would we take shelter. I was sitting by myself when I saw Cay run by and I called her over.

Cay giggled, put her head down on my shoulder, and said, "Tomorrow, we get to have pork."

"Liar. There's no way."

"I'll bet you. The supply truck came. I know."

"Great! We haven't eaten anything but shrimp paste in a month."

"Longer than that. It's funny how thinking about a bite of pork can really wake you up."

"That's only because we've been awake for so many nights."

"Hey, I'm going to sleep a little. When you hear the whistle, wake me up."

At that moment, Cay screamed and twisted her body in a very strange way. I hugged her, calling out her name. I shifted a bit to let the light from the flares fall into the shelter. One side of Cay's face was covered with blood. She wouldn't wake up. When I was able to call out for help, some people from the next shelter came over, but she was already dead. Shrapnel from a bomb had penetrated our shelter. One hit her side and another her temple. That was a death which obsessed me for many years.

I approached the side of the road. Maybe it was right here. This spot still had a gigantic rock that looked like a person swimming. Cay died when she was 17 years old, before she had ever tasted so many things, with so many unanswered questions in her innocent eyes.

The interpreter stood near me. His arms were folded, and he was looking across to the other side of the river. His expensive shirt and jeans fit beautifully on his healthy, well-proportioned body. Suddenly, I hated with all my heart this person who had, perhaps, been born and raised with so much comfort and happiness. He spoke French so well. He had such a good education. And Cay had been so full of questions because she'd never even eaten ice cream. What does ice cream taste like? My home is so far from town. I didn't go to school, so I've never been there. Is that sad? What does a trolley look like? Does it run on electricity? Her shiny, round eyes made her look even younger, as lovely as my youngest sister.

The interpreter turned around when he heard the sound of my wooden clogs. For a moment, I was rather surprised. The handsome, rather smug face that I had been looking at all morning now looked much older. He pursed his lips and he looked very grave.

"Do you know what time it is?" I asked in order to have something to say.

He looked at his watch and answered, "Noon exactly." Then he mumbled, "Some ferry. During the war it wasn't even as bad as this."

We waited. To alleviate my impatience, I made small talk. "I guess you often come through here, right?"

"Occasionally. But I used to be stationed here."

I glanced at him. His American jeans were extremely beautiful on his long, straight legs. His expensive watch shone like a light on his wrist. He was still looking across the river.

"Were you an army engineer here?"

"No, I worked with missiles. An artillery soldier."

Perhaps he recognized the strange look on my face, because he smiled lightly. His face was unforgettable. There are some faces that we encounter for a fleeting moment but which, even years later, when we close our eyes, we still see clearly. Once, a girlfriend and I were walking on a sidewalk in Hanoi. A small car drove slowly by. A man sitting in the back seat turned around and looked at us. My heart had been pained by the realization that that young man had just gone through my life and I'd never see him again. Many years later, I could still clearly see his face. It was straightforward and sincere, with an expression that could envelop you, warm and protective, like that of an older brother. That look could understand every thought that was crossing your mind.

Now, for a single moment, I tried to imagine Duc's face. His eyes. His nose. His mouth. His smile. But I couldn't. I had known him nearly ten years. But I couldn't remember his face, although he hadn't faded from my mind.

"Do you find that strange?" the interpreter asked. "In our generation, it's hard to find anyone who didn't go through the war, especially if you're a man."

"Even so," I said, "how did you manage to learn to speak French so well?"

"I managed. If you try, then you can do it."

Once again, he looked across the river. The ferry was slowly heading back toward us. But he wasn't thinking of the ferry.

"It's really strange," he said. "It's impossible to see anything from the past here anymore. Anyone who comes by can't possibly imagine how fierce the fighting once was here. Our battalion lost something like five hundred people here, but still I managed to survive. Some were remarkable guys. You can't possibly know. Some were so handsome."

His voice was trembling. He shook his head full of beautiful hair and then, raising his voice, called to the driver, who was washing something in the river.

"Get the car ready," he said. "Try to get in front of that Lada over there."

"Don't worry," the driver answered. "I'm coming up right now."

"That guy will never yield to anybody," the interpreter smiled, and then said, as if by way of introduction, "He was an army driver in the Truong Son range during the war against the Americans."

We started back toward the car. As we passed the big rock, I was planning to tell him that this was the place where Cay and I had sat for the last time when we were both seventeen years old. But on second thought, I said nothing.

The old foreign expert was talking to the people who had been riding in the Lada now parked behind us. A woman, whose nationality was hard to guess, made a wide gesture with her arm, talking about something. She was strangely large but very coquettish. The sun started to sizzle. The strong smell of her perfume spread across the dock, making people as nauseated as they would have felt had they inhaled condensed poison. As if through that puddle of poison, the woman cast a haughty glance toward us. Encountering our answering gaze, she blushed.

I said to the interpreter, "In the West, people treasure women, unlike here. They say that women are flowers. But how can you treasure a flower like that one over there?"

The driver had been walking behind us for some time. He spoke loudly, "Well anyway, they can have her, no problem. Don't worry about that."

The woman, who perhaps came from Northern Europe, could guess that we were talking about her and she hurried toward her car. Two bearded, blue-eyed men followed the waddling woman like two footmen. The sun had turned their skin so red that they looked like they'd been deep-fried.

The old foreign expert smiled at me. Perhaps he was surprised that I had managed to throw off the funereal expression I'd worn all morning.

The interpreter translated what he said to me. "He says you probably miss your mother and are anxious to get home."

We crossed the river. Later, we crossed several small bridges that had once been important American targets. Now, everything was peaceful and safe. In some places, where bridges had once spanned ditches between two fields, those ditches had been filled in and the bridges replaced with roads. I quietly looked out the window, feeling warmth in my heart, no longer feeling lonely from the memories that had agitated me.

The driver and the interpreter were once again discussing gadgets. Now they were talking about tape recorders and record players. They said nothing about the war and I looked at them with admiration. I knew that no one could forget what had happened during those years. But they were still young and whatever they had experienced only made them stronger. They still had a long life in front of them. They still had to struggle, to build their families, and to attend to their work in many different places.

Once again, I tried to imagine Duc's face. His eyes. His nose. His mouth. I gave up. I couldn't remember. Duc was so far away, among his sponges, his Vespa, the elevator that he liked so much, and the AKAI stereo that he kept on all day. So far away. How could he be compared to these people?

The sky had already been dark for a while by the time we reached Hanoi. I said good-bye to my new friends.

The driver teased me. "Hey, on just one trip you've managed to bring back this much?"

I laughed without saying anything.

I immediately carried the two bags to Duc's house. I had to call from the gate. I had to wait. The house was quiet and lonely. A thought crossed my mind while I stood there: If only a catastrophe would strike this house. By some miracle, through two wars, no one in this house had ever had to leave Hanoi. They had gotten married, given birth, and grown healthy and bright in this house. And the only person who ever went far away was Duc.

Handing the bags over to Duc's older sisters, I made them examine all of it and write everything down. Then, I directed them about what to do, saying that it was essential that they write to Duc and let him know that they had received it all.

Now I only had my leather briefcase, holding some fabric I'd bought for gifts and the clothes I'd brought for the trip. It felt as if the briefcase also heaved a sigh of relief. I walked down the long, dark hallway. Everything in this house was dark. The door to Duc's room was open. Someone with a hunched back was sitting at the table. I didn't recognize him. Just then, someone walked out the door. It was Duc's oldest brother, who looked exactly like their father. He was carrying a heavy chamber pot toward the stairs. He walked very slowly. Everyone in this house was slow.

I involuntarily glanced into Duc's room, searching for the turtle, but it was no longer there.

1987

Scenes from an Alley

In the past, honest people rarely dared to enter this dark and smelly alley at night. In those days, the alley had no electricity. It was a place where people dumped their trash and where squatters built huts out of stray pieces of wood and sacks of rice. Over the past two or three years, it seemed like this alleyway suddenly awoke from a stupefied sleep. It came alive, full of houses with trees and plants. The faces there were also transformed. They were human now, no longer as feral as before.

In the depths of the alley lay Quyt's two-story house. In the past, Quyt's father had received the death penalty for murdering somebody. Instead of remarrying, his mother picked trash to raise her child. By bribing someone, she arranged for Quyt to go work as a laborer in the Great Nation of Germany. Five years later, he returned and transformed their miserable hut into a two-story villa. Western currency could perform magic more powerful than a fairy's. If you wanted a multi-story house, it would instantly materialize. If you wanted a guard dog or ornamental plants, they'd be yours in the blink of an eye. And you could even have a wife who was as beautiful as a dream, a real intellectual, and fluent in English. Every day, Quyt and his wife came and went like a prince and princess. They had a son who inherited all of the traits of his father: a pouting lip, eyes like slits, a crooked nose, and stunted limbs. But he always dressed in the most fashionable clothes and he always wore foreign cologne, so he wasn't such an eyesore.

The couple and their son slept on the ground floor. The second floor was very spacious and they rented it out to a Westerner who was as big as a steamroller. The Western guy did some kind of work for a foreign company in the center of town. He was seen driving his own car and every morning he could be heard breathing laboriously through his exercises in the alleyway, showing a body that was as hairy as a gibbon's. Every night he came home late, smelling of whiskey, and every night he brought a prostitute up his private stairway. It was said that Quyt and his wife even got something on top of the rent for allowing that. Money makes money, as the saying goes.

Before Quyt went away to work as a laborer in Germany, there was never a time when his house wasn't full of the sound of quarreling. Now there was only sweet talk. As for their son, Quyt's wife complained to the neighbors that although the house was always full of such delicacies as pork sausage, fresh milk, and imported apples and pears, the boy would never touch them. She dressed like a queen, worked for a foreign company, and sometimes you could see her laughing until her eyes puckered up, saying, "Well! Well!" in English to the Westerner who rented their house.

That man was a fiendish drinker. Every time he came home at night, he revved his engine at the head of the alley and then raced on in. It would be disastrous for anyone who was too slow to get out of his way. For some time, people had been afraid, and by ten o'clock at night they'd already be in a state of suspense, not daring to show their faces in the street. When they heard the sound of his car from far away, the old people would plug their ears and crawl under their blankets. Even on nights when the car didn't make a lot of noise, when he was only slightly drunk, people still knew that there was a woman in the car. They'd learned his ways. It wasn't until the last days of the month, when he was at his drunkest, that he would be alone. That was the time that his money was running short and he could only afford alcohol and nothing else. Once he'd gotten to his room, he'd go out onto the balcony and sing at the top of his lungs. Hearing him even from far away, children would huddle closer to their mothers and dogs would race to their gates and howl. The whole neighborhood was in an uproar.

Near Quyt's house lay the home of a gentleman who'd just been promoted to a big position in one of the city's more important companies. His given name was To and when he was young he and his mother had picked trash in this neighborhood. Thanks to his hardworking mother, To was able to make it to high school. He became a soldier in April of '75, a convenient time to enter the army because that was the month the war ended and too many people had died already. He was sent to a city in Central Vietnam as part of its military government and took on the responsibility of weeding the place of capitalists. When he returned to the north, he looked like a person who had made so much money he had no need of making any more. The company where he worked found him very conscientious, so they promoted him to the top rank. Once he had established his career, he dropped his peasant's name in favor of something more refined. Now he called himself Toan. He had a secretary and whenever they rode in a car together, he would get out first and open the door for her. He entertained his customers with Western whiskey. But even though he'd attained a high position and a great deal of wealth, he was uncultured. After work he would order the chauffeur to drive straight to a club. He was crazy about massage and he liked to hold the tender thighs of the young women sitting on his lap in this dark and dreamy atmosphere. All of his colleagues liked that as well. With a woman on either leg, the men would wrap their arms around the women's waists, open their mouths, and wait to be fed like babies. This was an unusual form of enjoyment that men in our country loved.

For some months it had been known that he kept a mistress, which fulfilled the last remaining requirement of a peasant who had risen to a high rank. He had bought her a house and whenever he wanted entertainment he could go there. In order to maintain her husband's reputation, his cunning wife never picked a fight in public, but in secret she often bit and hit him. One day there was a welt as big as a guava on his forehead. He tried to explain it by saying that the stairs in his house were too slippery.

Toan's poor father was over 90 years old. Although he was both deaf and a slow walker, he still had a good appetite. All day long, the old man would pay attention whenever he saw anyone's lips moving. He loved to sit and watch, just like a baby who hadn't learned to turn over yet. Maybe it was because of him that Toan didn't dare to pick a fight with his wife. At any rate, the daughter-in-law was still willing to wash the old man's hands and feet, blow on his rice to cool it down, and cook him bowls of vegetable broth. He would have had to wait forever for his son to do that. The son was always in a meeting. After work, it would be massage and beer and women.

"Damn this man born in obscurity, with his feet buried deep in the water of the fields. Now that he has money, he looks at everything with desire and he imitates other people just like a monkey." The wife would curse at random and the deaf old father-in-law would prick up his ears like a donkey.

Sometimes, his uppity son would look at him with rage, thinking, "Why don't you just hurry up and die?"

* * *

One evening, the Westerner renting Quyt's house got completely drunk. He drove his car home earlier than usual. When the car entered the head of the alley, he ran into something and hit the brake in a panic. He sobered up immediately. The residents of the alley rushed outside and in an instant there was a crowd. Whose child is it? She's dead already. Pick her up! What a tragedy.

The car had run over her head. Her broken neck tilted to one side and her blood streamed into the street. It was Miss Ti Cam—Little Mute—the daughter of Mrs. Tit. The two of them had come here together and no one knew where they'd come from. People would only see them build a fire at night to cook some rice under the *sau* tree at the head of the lane. Miss Ti Cam, who was both mute and rather crazy, would sit idly waiting for her mother. Mrs. Tit went scavenging and she would wash out the pieces of plastic that she'd found and lay them to dry on the sidewalk. She also collected empty cans and bought scrap metal. In short, she did anything in order to raise her daughter.

Being both mute and rather crazy, one day Miss Ti Cam found her way to the train station where a gang of rough young men dragged her into a back corner. She lay quietly while they molested her. Passersby felt their hair stand on end when they heard the hoarse laughter of the beasts mixed with the grunts of Miss Ti Cam, who sounded like a bitch in heat. The noise coming from behind the station, the noise of sin, and the noises of the night enveloped the sobs of poor Miss Ti Cam. Over the past three months, her stomach had grown, bringing Mrs. Tit to the verge of tears. Pregnant, Miss Ti Cam seemed a little less crazy, and she no longer went back and forth smiling to herself. Instead, she sat listlessly at the base of the tree. Several times, a charitable organization would bring a car around to pick her and her mother up and take them to its headquarters so that the government could care for them, but after a few days they always found their way back. They were like wild grass accustomed to living in a field. How could they bear to live in a cage?

Mrs. Tit threw herself across the body of Miss Ti Cam. "Oh my child, I brought you into this miserable life and now you have to die like this!"

Toan and his wife came out to the spot to see what had happened. Toan's expression was very strange. Something like the flash of a great discovery appeared to cross his face and he brightened up for a moment.

Quyt and his wife looked terrified. They would probably lose their renter because of this. After this incident would the Western guy dare to stay? If he wanted to stay, he would have to spend a fortune on bribery.

The body of Miss Ti Cam was still warm and dozens of people were already busily thinking of profits and losses. The whole neighborhood was as noisy as a broken beehive and the Westerner was flailing his arms, shrugging his shoulders, and screeching like an ancient record player with a dull needle. His breath still smelled of alcohol..

Within a few days, people had completed their measurements to determine who was to blame. As it turned out, Miss Ti Cam had thrown herself under the Westerner's car. As for him, he had been drunk and therefore had not been able to apply the brakes in time. Otherwise, he hadn't broken any rules. Because of that, he wasn't indicted, but he still had to pay Mrs. Tit damages amounting to 10 million dong (US $1000) on top of the funeral expenses.

After burying her child, Mrs. Tit couldn't believe that she now had 10 million dong. It was said that the Westerner also gave her a gold chain that weighed three tenths of a tael. In the space of an instant, Mrs. Tit had become a millionaire. She immediately bought herself a place in the alley, built a kitchen and then remodeled it, all of which cost three million. She didn't deal in scrap metal anymore. She bought a small glass cabinet and brought it home to display sundries for sale. She was just over fifty years old and she had money, a shop, and a chain weighing three tenths of a tael of gold around her neck. It was still a peasant's neck, but now it was also a wealthy one, so a few men often parked their scooters in front of her glass cabinet in order to chat with her. Who knows, perhaps in the near future she'd be riding in a bridal car. The neighbors were already huddling together gossiping about her, the same woman they once spit on whenever she and her daughter accidentally made too much smoke while cooking something under the tree. Mrs. Tit herself had been transformed. She spoke more gently, used fewer obscenities, and one day she bought herself a flowered hat.

Toan and his wife didn't tell each other what they were thinking, but both were obsessed with the same idea whenever they looked at the old deaf man sitting in the rattan chair reserved for him. Summer had arrived. People in the neighborhood often pulled chairs outside to catch the breezes. During these days, Toan and his wife made a show of their love for the old man. One could see them carrying out the chair with him in it and setting it down by the front door. Often, the old man was already fast asleep. There were times when Toan's wife forgot him after she turned on the electric fan inside the house and fell asleep. Sometimes it was nearly midnight before she'd remember the old man in the chair outside.

During this time, Toan's business was prospering. His company was doing so well that he had hired an extra secretary to help him. She often wore miniskirts and was unlike the first secretary, who was reserved and came from a good family. If Toan was dozing off in the director's office in the afternoon, this new secretary often came up behind him, put her hand on his forehead, and pressed her breasts into his back. Her hands were so cool that his heart almost stopped beating and the sound of her whispering in his ear made him melt like water. He thought gloomily of his children and also of his wife, who often fondled him dutifully in a corner of the kitchen. He couldn't leave his wife because he needed her. He needed her as a nurse for his old deaf father, who seemed unwilling to die anytime soon. Oh, this horrible fate of his.

Every night, both the husband and wife thought about Mrs. Tit. They wished that they could be like her, finally rid of their terrible burden while at the same time suddenly finding themselves with some extra millions in their pockets. This family was rich already. But who would turn down a few million more? If luck came their way and the drunk Westerner happened to plow into their 90-year-old father, they wouldn't accept only 10 million. No, it would have to be more. Double that. Westerners were very rich. Anyway, the most important thing was to have a legal way to rid the family roster of the old man's name. To think that a beautiful house like theirs was dirtied by an old man's stinking urine! How could their fate be so horrible??

Whenever their obsession reached such a point, although neither husband nor wife said a word to the other, they both pricked up their ears. It was still summer, and only in summer could they use the pretext of the cool breezes to let a 90-year-old man fall asleep outside. But why during these days was the Westerner so rarely drunk? He no longer sped into the alley, but instead drove very slowly. Surely, though, one day he would forget the past and drive again like he used to, like he had on the night he ran over Miss Ti Cam!

The husband and wife looked at each other, breathless because they had the same idea, but neither dared to tell the other.

* * *

Deep inside the alley, Quyt's house was located behind a fence covered by creeping vines and the light in the Westerner's window still burned brightly. Quyt's wife was speaking English with the Westerner, caressing him and warning him not to drive recklessly into the alley as he had in the past. The Westerner said "okay" many times and did not forget to kiss the hand of Quyt's wife, his thick lips lingering on the ruby ring she wore on her little finger.

Quyt was more devoted than ever to the Westerner who rented his house. He brought prostitutes home for the renter. He brought whiskey home for him. There was also the night that Quyt's wife even disappeared from his bed and he just ignored it—as long as the Westerner continued to rent the house. As long as he forgot the past incident. As long as he continued to pay the bribes and insured that they had their effect. Oh, a blue-eyed, long-nosed man was a gold mine.

And every midnight, Toan and his wife came out and carried the rattan chair with the old man in it back into the house. It wouldn't look good if they let him sleep there all night.

* * *

One night, the alley was already nearly empty by nine o'clock. There had been heavy winds in the late afternoon but it hadn't rained. The cool air had sent people to bed early. Toan's father was sitting outside in the rattan chair, just like any other night. He was breathing softly, like a child. Suddenly, an uproar started among a group of gamblers squatting next to Mrs. Tit's house. Two punks grabbed each other's money and one chased the other down the alley. One of them ran like an arrow. The other followed him, screaming, "Bastard! I'll break your head open!"

He hurled the brick in his hand at his rival. It arced toward the ground, ricocheted off the base of a tree, and flew into the head of the sleeping 90-year-old man. The two punks vanished. The old man was strong and so he wasn't badly hurt. He only fainted. Toan and his wife carried him into the house and from that day on he was bedridden. He ate well but couldn't make it to the toilet.

The doctor came to examine the patient and told the daughter-in-law, "He can't walk yet, but he's still very strong. If you take good care of him, he may even live to be a hundred!"

Toan and his wife looked at each other in dismay. Suddenly both of them cursed the Westerner. Damn him! Why had he been driving so carefully? How could things have come to this?

1992

Fragile as a Sunray

For years, I didn't understand why, at certain moments of leisure, my mother seems sad. Our family is rather well-off. My parents opened a private clinic that has plenty of patients. I am studying medicine and sometimes go home to help them out in the clinic with diagnosis and treatment. My younger brother and I are devoted to our parents. My brother has even won some prizes at the math competitions for high school students.

But why is my mother still so sad?

She is just over forty and very beautiful, but her eyes are filled with sadness. She mixes with many people every day. Occasionally, she gets angry. If she is cheated out of a bit of money, she'll cry. And she also argues with the neighbors. She's no different from anyone else. But I still didn't understand what makes her so sad. I tried to find out and one day I did. And then I learned that even ordinary people have secrets. The heart is never at peace.

* * *

Late one afternoon, a military ambulance pulled off the road onto a footpath, preparing to wait until dusk in order to cross the pass. The doctor and two male nurses strung their hammocks alongside those of a unit headed South and fell asleep immediately. The woman with them, who looked like any other well-educated female soldier, enjoyed roaming a bit and so she went down to a shallow section of the stream, where one could wade through water that only came up to the ankles. On this side of the stream were a few soldiers washing up. On the other side a scene appeared to her that seemed extraordinary to a female soldier making her first visit to the front. Truly extraordinary. Blood rushed to her head. On the patch of pebble-covered shore, sat about a dozen men wearing camouflaged fatigues, each eating from a ration box.

"These are the prisoners from the battle of Route Nine," the soldier standing next to her explained.

She sat down on a rock on this side of the stream, pulled out a towel and slowly washed it. The most extraordinary thing about this moment, the first moment she had ever seen the enemy, was that the only emotion she felt was curiosity. Most of the prisoners were busy eating and there was nothing extraordinary about those faces. Except for one. He was still very young, not much older than twenty. He had a strong build, but not the kind that comes from working in the fields. He looked more like an athlete. All of his features were symmetrical and harmonious. He was holding his ration box in his hand without eating and staring sadly into space. She'd never seen a face like that in her life. That was the face she imagined when she read novels. While still at home, she would linger in bed under the mosquito net in the mornings, listening to the sounds outside and daydreaming until her mother called her. During those moments, she often imagined a face like that one. It was impossible to separate the features on that face in order to describe it, impossible to talk about it, but she had dreamed of spending her life with a man with a face like that.

Her heart pounded in her chest and her arms and legs suddenly went icy. While her hands kept washing the towel, her eyes were fixed on the scene across the narrow stream. The enemy soldier abandoned his despondent stare, looked down at the ration box, then, looking up again, suddenly noticed her. Two pairs of eyes met. During that brief moment, a terrible lightening struck her "wanderer's" soul. "Wanderer" was the word her worried mother always used to describe her.

"You won't be lucky in life," her mother used to say.

Startled and guilty, she jumped up. On the other side of the stream, the enemy soldier did the same thing, as if he, too, were shocked. The gesture caused one of the guards to abandon the conversation he and the other guards were having and to point the barrel of his gun at the prisoner's temple, forcing him to sit down. But his gaze still burned her. She walked dazed and unsteady back to the ambulance, pulled out her hammock, strung it between the trees, and climbed into it. Her heart rebelled, but fear overwhelmed her. How could she allow herself to think such thoughts? He was the enemy.

She lay in the hammock for most of the afternoon. Finally, the senior doctor got up and hurried them along, saying, "Eat and finish your washing; at dusk we'll get going."

But she continued to drift along in indescribable sadness. Like that. Like that. The sounds of conversation penetrated her sorrow. The voice of a stranger asked, "Are you a doctor, comrade?"

"Yes, I am," she heard the doctor reply.

"Can you please help us? A soldier is running a fever from a swollen wound and tonight we have to march. Can you help him so that he can walk?"

"Is he a prisoner?"

"Yes, just captured."

"Okay, I'll come right over."

She sat up immediately, her gaze fixed on the doctor. He looked at her. "Ah yes, please come with me and bring the medical kit," he said.

It was him. His eyes were clear and innocent, and his face was peaceful. It was a face that existed outside the war. Her fear of herself increased when she dared to look into the face of this enemy officer, but she did so anyway, unable to turn away. With the afternoon sunlight piercing through the branches of the trees, and the guns momentarily silenced, the war seemed more cruel, embodied in the contrast between the cold features of the guard and the hopeless face of the prisoner. She watched carefully as the doctor examined the wound in the prisoner's thigh. He frowned when he saw the infection.

She washed the wound with alcohol and cotton wool. She could hear the prisoner clinching his teeth, but he didn't cry out. When the doctor turned away to let the guard light his cigarette, she spoke softly to the prisoner.

"Try to bear it!"

"Do you know where they will take us?"

"No. I wish I did."

"I'm a doctor also," he told her.

"Really? How did you end up here?"

"War knocks on every door. I tried to avoid it but I couldn't."

"I know."

"Can you help me?"

w

The doctor and the guard turned back around.

"Are you done yet?" the doctor asked.

"Yes. I gave him an injection," she said, trying to avoid the burning gaze of the prisoner. It wasn't a gaze of fear. Absolutely not. And it wasn't a gaze of pain or begging. It was a clear gaze of amazement that in this life he had discovered a person who could have belonged to him, who could have understood him, who could have spent her life with him. And that there should be no chasm, no division between people.

With compassion, the doctor asked the prisoner, "Are you able to walk?"

As if a certain hidden strength suddenly woke and pushed against his back, the prisoner stood up, his face white with the pain and determination.

She knew that it was thanks to her presence. War could not cut the loving thread that linked the hearts of two people. But how would fate treat him, with his wounded leg and his resolution? Carrying the medical kit, she followed the old doctor back across the stream. The group of prisoners were preparing to set off and the steely voices of the guards rose around them. Surreptitiously, the prisoner raised a hand toward her. His face was full of sorrow and despair and a hope that there would be something for them in the future.

Now, twenty years have passed and many barriers have been torn down. And yet her hope has never been fulfilled. If only they could meet again, even for a minute.

* * *

During those moments when my mother isn't busy earning a living, she is sad. Everybody has a secret, a sorrow, a memory.

I believe that my mother has been able to live until now because of such a secret, such a sorrow, such a desire.

1992

Rain

In the early '80s, the construction site expanded across the river, making the whole area bustle. Vehicles from all over converged here. There were crowds of people, crowds of beautiful girls. Every day, the guest house received one wave of guests after another. Each of the women selected to work as an attendant was as beautiful as a dream, but even among them Ngan stood out.

Ngan had had serious training at the school of dance and had become a dancer for the provincial troupe. Because dancing these days didn't earn much in the way of money, she had asked an uncle to help her find work as an attendant at the construction site guest house. She didn't have to wear an *ao dai*, but merely the uniform of the guest house. The short aquamarine skirt came to just above her knees. The long-sleeved, buttoned-up white shirt was accented by a small black bowtie. This outfit wasn't much but it was enough to cause a stir among members of the opposite sex. Although it hid almost everything on that body, which was fragrant as ripe fruit, it revealed her long, slender legs, shining in her transparent skin-colored stockings. The members of the opposite sex—from dignified ministers who came to the construction site on missions, to engineers, to those who'd earned gaudy doctorates from abroad, to seventeen-year-olds who had just begun their careers—all of these people watched Ngan as she walked by.

Under the circumstances, the gazes of the men were very different from those of the women. The women compared themselves to her jealously while the men gazed with tenderness and desire and speculated on the sweetness of that ripe, unpeeled apple.

Maybe Ngan was aware of all of this. But Ngan's mother was a provincial teacher who had taught her daughter since childhood how to behave around a man. She knew how to keep a safe distance and, though always cheerful, she stopped there.

She didn't lose herself and go too far. The members of the opposite sex only advanced as far as they were allowed.

But Ngan wasn't able to keep her guard up around Quoc, who, though only an electrical engineer, had a pull stronger than electricity. Quoc was one meter seventy-eight and weighed 69 kilos. He had the just-ripe body of a thirty-year-old. His face had an arrogance which was matched by the coldness in his beautiful eyes. Although Quoc often came in for coffee, he never paid any attention to Ngan, which is the reason why she began to like him. That's the fatal flaw of women, all through the ages, and Ngan was no exception. A worthy man was the one who paid no attention. Ngan vaguely understood this tactic, but still became crazy when, even in her brilliant white shirt and beautiful new shoes, she attracted no more of Quoc's attention than a brick would. After work, Quoc often sat by himself with his glass of coffee, looking aimlessly at the mountains and hills that stretched into the distance outside the window. Ngan didn't understand that Quoc also lusted after those shiny legs. But he knew that women chased after mystery and so his eyes became even colder, even more indifferent. Night after night, Ngan cried quietly over that gaze that intentionally ignored her.

This situation lasted for so long that Ngan's acquaintances began to see clearly the signs of her physical and emotional deterioration. Ngan put on her makeup more carefully but couldn't conceal her pale complexion and her sunken, sleep-deprived eyes. Her wristwatch, which had once fit so perfectly, now became loose and threatened to slide off. Quoc, who also noticed this, held back for a few more days so that the glass of water would become even more full. Then one afternoon, he turned around and, looking toward the refreshment counter, replaced his once-lofty gaze with something new. The rainy season was approaching, causing work at the construction site to taper off, and fewer guests were coming in to drink or dine. Ngan was sitting by herself behind the money drawer when Quoc stood up from his familiar table and approached her. Feeling as if a mountain was weighing down on her fragile heart, Ngan stared down at the book of checks, unable to look up. Her cheeks flushed and she felt light-headed, as if she might faint. Quoc knew this very clearly because such things were not strange to him at all. Quoc was in no hurry to begin the affair. He tenderly picked up the delicate hand. The electric current that emitted from him had the destructive power of dynamite. The girl's heart exploded and tears streamed down her face. This was the end of several months of pain and hopeless waiting. Her nightly torments. Her questions without answers. Her inability to breathe when he was near.

"Don't worry," he said. "I'll always be beside you, my little sweetheart."

A beginning like that was so sweet. What woman wouldn't melt like water upon receiving such an offer of protection? What woman—whether her life was as rare as crystal or as common as the trees—wouldn't exchange that life for those few words "my little sweetheart"?

Quoc lived in the building set aside for engineers. It was built precariously at the edge of the stream, in keeping with the wishes of the engineers when they first came to the construction site. His room was like any other temporary room at a construction site. Quoc shared it with a civil engineer who was currently at a meeting in Europe, putting together contracts for the building of roads. The room was simply furnished with two single beds, several suitcases, and two desks covered with papers. As a matter of fact, though, Quoc was rather wealthy. He was the son of a rich farmer in the South. Although he was working in the North, he could afford to spend money like water. His VCR and piles of videotapes had a dizzying effect on Ngan. Outside, it began to rain, the first of the long August rains that soaked the trees and made Ngan feel content now that her dream had come true. She was now beside him, the man who had never courted her but still attracted her as if by some magic she couldn't resist.

"Ngan, do you agree that from now on we'll live together?" he asked.

That Southern accent was so seductive and that question was so simple. Ngan rested against his broad chest like a small ship that had put down anchor. The child-like way that she lifted her arm around his neck and pressed her cheek against his served as her answer: "I'll give my life to you!"

But Quoc was a man with an overabundance of libido, and he didn't notice the tenderness and sacrifice of her offering. He rushed his lovemaking like an athlete racing toward the finish line, never stopping to admire her smooth skin or the romantic curves of her body, not even noticing the subtle fragrance on the white breasts of this virgin. He devoured her quickly, deeply, greedily. Night after night. Ngan was astonished that what she had held precious seemed merely the prize in a contest to Quoc. Was this love or a strenuous form of exercise, a kind of mountain climbing? How could love be like that? Sometimes Ngan let her spirit fly toward something more romantic. In some rare moments while they were having sex, she wanted to ask him sweetly that question which is a woman's luxury in such circumstances: "Do you love me?" But her hands only touched the sweat on his back, her body nearly breaking from his weight and lust. Romance seemed like the greatest luxury then and she didn't even bother to ask.

At the same time, the television next to the bed would be showing a video of naked bodies. It was a very mediocre film, but it contained one extremely interesting message: "Men only need to have a place but women always need a reason."

And the eyes of the girl filled with tears when Quoc, sated, lay fast asleep beside her.

This continued for a month, a month of long rains and a roommate still absent in Europe. Night after night, the wind howled as it came down from the mountains and blew across the valley. Ngan had never felt such loss, so vulgarized and used. Now, she understood everything clearly, but she had nothing left to save. All she wished for now was to make a small family. Quoc, had never promised anything, had never even said, "I love you." However, despite all that, he treated her like a wife, didn't he? And, if she were a wife, then why should she take precautions?

Around midnight, Ngan would get up by herself, her feet feeling around for her flip-flops beneath the bed, her body covered with goose bumps from the sound of Quoc's snores. Only a pig would sleep like that. Ngan went back to her room in the guest house attendants' quarters. Every night she bathed and washed out her clothes but when she finally climbed under her blanket, she always felt that something wasn't right, that she wasn't worthy of her body. She burst into tears. She always wished that tomorrow Quoc would announce to everybody that he would marry her. She would try to envision their wedding.

After the roommate returned, Ngan and Quoc rarely saw each other. Ngan's hatred for Quoc began to equal her passion. Making love without a bed was degrading. Quoc was ready to climb on top of Ngan anywhere that he could find the space, regardless of the smell, the inconvenience, the dinginess, and even the curious eyes. He began to sense Ngan's detachment and discomfort and so he began to make promises about a family and children. Ngan believed him and became more passionate for him after he made those promises. But a short while later, Quoc received a transfer to a construction site in the South. As it happened, Quoc's father had pulled this off so that the son could be near his parents.

"I'll go first, then send for you later," he told Ngan.

Ngan's tearful farewell took place in that familiar room about which she knew every detail. It was the room in which, while her nude body was being ravaged, she had stared at the landscape Quoc's roommate had hung over the head of his bed. She looked at it as if she were pleading for help, as if she were searching for something within that small forest, bright beneath a spring rain, and she wished that others could have the same sentiments about beauty as those of a woman in love.

Quoc left the construction site on the same day that the long rains stopped. The site became busier because all the contracted engineers were reporting for work. At the vehicle unit and the construction unit, people were swamped with work. As for Ngan, she faced no consequences from her nights with Quoc; maybe, she thought, because he was so experienced about such things. She continued to work in the guest house, waiting for the time when she could go South and marry Quoc, as the two of them had discussed before they parted. Ngan continued to wear the attendant's uniform with its long-sleeved white shirt buttoned to the neck, the small black bowtie, and the aquamarine skirt that reached to her knees. But the dignified ministers who came to the construction site now nodded their greeting to her in the same way that they nodded to everyone else. The educated young men walked by her as if they were walking by a wall. Even the workers who drove the earth movers, who had the habit of making crude passes, no longer even tried to get her attention. Was she like an apple with its skin peeled off? Ngan felt abandoned. Maybe she had magnified her problems somewhat, but her heart was still tormented. What she didn't realize was that the light of happiness had drained from her face. With that light missing, her magnificent expression became as mediocre as any portrait of an anonymous girl on a third-rate calendar. Tired, Ngan walked back and forth carrying trays of glasses among the noisy customers. Night after night she pulled her blanket up to her chin and dozed off. She never recalled those sessions during which Quoc had done his exercises on her body. It was too crude, too insulting. She didn't remember and she didn't bear a grudge but she wasn't able to recover her balance either.

After a very long time, Quoc wrote Ngan a noncommittal letter. Expressions in the letter like "I miss you" and "me and you" were as dry as stones. Quoc said that if Ngan wanted to come down then she should come down. His new construction site also needed attendants of her caliber. She could beat out the rest of them because, while those girls had good legs, their faces couldn't compare to that of a Northern girl like Ngan. They exchanged a few letters and then Ngan quit her job and took her suitcases back to Hanoi. She bought a ticket for a sleeper on the North-South Express, which left at eight in the morning.

Everything was going as planned, except that the sound of the train whistle frightened her. It signaled something faraway and dangerous. Most frightening of all was the fact that she would see Quoc again. If only Quoc had never known her body. If only he had never labored on the fertile field that he had so desired. If only her body were still a secret, then she would rush to him and put down her anchor at his port. But now some strange awkwardness prevented her from stepping onto the train which would take her on the longest journey of her life.

Instead Ngan went back to her province to visit her parents. Seeing her daughter so pale and sad, Ngan's mother wouldn't allow her to return to the construction site. Instead, she told Ngan to stay home, where she had just opened a small storefront selling cosmetics. Day after day, Ngan sat behind the glass case reading a book, occasionally chatting with the young women who came to buy the products. She developed the strange habit of looking at these women with intense curiosity. Has she been peeled yet? Has she known what a man with a broad chest and a sweaty back is like yet?

The rainy season arrived, making the town mud-covered and dismal. A doctor in the local hospital often came to drink tea with Ngan's father. He often leaned against the glass case making small talk. The doctor was rather good-looking and, even though they were friends, he was much younger than Ngan's father. At the end of the year, he didn't come by any longer, perhaps because he didn't want to fall into an awkward situation. Ngan cried silently because she knew she could no longer attract anyone. But she was still young and every day she tried to forget what had happened. Every day she still thought about the landscape that had hung in Quoc's room. She remembered the forest that brightened in the rain, remembered her tears, the desire for happiness she'd felt during those days.

And Ngan sat looking out at the rainy street, waiting.

1991

The Almighty Dollar

The earth-shaking fighting between the children in Old Man Truong's family began at three o'clock in the afternoon. With great excitement, children and adults flocked toward that corner of town, but no one dared to risk their lives by getting too close. Every member of that family was violent, so anyone going near them ran the risk of getting hurt. Only after considering the possible routes for their own escape did everyone stand in small groups watching the scene from a safe distance.

It began with Qua, the wife of the Old Man Truong's eldest son. She'd been a meat seller for many years. At seven months pregnant, she was healthy as an elephant. Carrying the extra weight as if it were as light as cotton, she ran to the house where her husband's twin brother lived. Qua's husband's name was Khang and his twin was An. Khang, An*. For a long, long time Old Man Truong had wanted his family to be blessed with peace, so he gave his first born twins names those meaningful names.

Qua planted one foot on the ground and set the other on the decorative tile porch and began to "sing." When a long-time meat seller in this town begins to "sing," nothing in this life could surpass it. Among the rubberneckers, even the toughest men blushed to their ears. The women glanced at each other, feeling embarrassed in front of the men. Qua treated An's wife to all her best lines. The two women had been enemies ever since they set foot as daughters-in-law into Old Man Truong's family and, therefore, whenever the opportunity arose, they offered up their most vicious curses. But the town's population had never seen the two of them as full of energy as they were today. When it came to fighting, An's wife was no slouch either, but, naturally, she couldn't compare to a meat seller. Now, she hid in the kitchen hut near the pig sty, hurling back the barbs that Khang's wife had thrown at her family with such generosity.

* Khang means well-being. An means safe.

This was truly a colorful chorus. The town's children, who recognized this moment as a fine opportunity to enrich their vocabularies, clung to each other, whooping with delight.

Khang and An had not yet made a sortie into the fighting because they were brothers and, moreover, twins, only distinguishable from each other by one scar on one cheek. The scar was not the result of any effort on the part of Old Man Truong, but rather was produced during a fight between the two brothers while they were in prison.

At the moment, they were watching their wives from two different places, neither one willing to make a move. Khang, sitting across the road in the dog meat shop owned by the cripple Diem, was keeping an eye on his wife's stomach. An was sitting next to the ebony platform bed near the kitchen hut. Neither man missed a single word uttered by either of the women and their blood began to churn as if they were intoxicated.

The fight was reaching its climax when Can, the younger sister of Khang and An, came home from the market. She parked her crimson Honda Cub right out on the road. The townspeople had a great deal of respect for her because she was the first woman to drive a Cub in the whole town, the first person to own one of such an impressive color. She wore dark red French silk outfits and her fingernails and toenails were painted a deep scarlet. Her wardrobe was like those of the women who sold sundries in the town market. She owned the biggest aluminum goods shop in the whole town: the biggest, the brightest, and most successful shop on her street. She was the most famous woman in town, so sweet but also so sharp that even the weeds would cringe to hear her curse. At this moment though, walking with a supple grace into An's house, she looked calm. She planted herself between her two sisters-in-law and began to speak. Within this fiery atmosphere of hatred, her normally sweet voice was so cold it sent shivers down the spine.

"Stop it. Please. My family has been cursed enough already," she said. Then, she raised her voice. "Ngheo, where are you?"

Ngheo was gentle and dimwitted, suffering from a congenital deformity which gave him a limp and two arms that he could never raise up to his face. Because of this, he could never wipe off the drool that ran freely down his shirt.

Ngheo came out of the house, turning his head up to the sky, laughing. He was well-dressed, wearing Thai jeans, embroidered with gold thread along the seams. Drool soaked his shirt around a pocket embossed with an image of a naked Western woman. Can grabbed her pitiful youngest brother by the nape of his neck and thrust him first in the direction of Khang's wife, and then toward An's.

"I invite you, my sisters," she said. "Go ahead and cut him down the middle. Each of you can have half. How nice of you. Such a worthless thing suddenly takes a seat on the throne. Everyone pampers him. What can we do but cut him in half? No one can complain because if he lives or dies it doesn't make any difference. Then, the two of you won't have to wear yourselves out taking care of him."

Khang's wife protested vehemently, her swollen stomach shaking. She had the feeling that the son inside her also had a temper and that gave her even more strength. Although she was speaking to her husband's little sister, the words came out like a curse on An's wife.

"You don't have to attack me," she said to Can. "You know that dwarf-faced woman too well already. She's the daughter of a bitch, so she's greedy, too greedy. She's been hanging on to the boy for two months already. Two months, so that she can save up enough dollars to buy a dog's head to offer to her own ancestors. Today, she has to let the boy come to my house. But she still hangs on to him, even though it's been two weeks already. I kept sending her reminders, and even came over here myself, but still she wouldn't let go of him. I'll slash her face. I'll throw gasoline on her husband, that man who doesn't even know how to teach his own wife and just hides under her skirts. Why are they so greedy?"

Things had come to such a point that nobody could stand each other anymore. An raced out of the house. A sharp knife, the kind of knife that commandos used in the war, pierced the target of Qua's belly, right where the child was lying. Later, some people even claimed to have heard the sound of the baby screaming. Khang's wife gasped. Her stomach, seven months pregnant, hit the ground first, and then her face hit the edge of the porch after. Khang raced out of Cripple Diem's place carrying a steel pole that was one and a half meters long. He was in no hurry to help his wife. In a frenzy, he sprinted after his brother, but people were able to hold him back. Can stood frozen in front of the horrifying scene, an outcome she had never considered possible. The blood gushed out from under Khang's wife's belly, spreading across the stone courtyard. Can released her grasp on Ngheo's neck.

Ngheo paid no attention to the ruckus going on around him. Instead, some unintelligible sounds came out of his throat. A few moments later he walked over to the water container, drew out a gourd full of water, and drank from it laboriously. Both the water and drool streamed down to the ground, forming a puddle.

* * *

When he was younger, Old Man Truong was a cadre who had left his family to work in the city, far from home. He was only an employee in the financial department of the municipal trade union office. But in this remote town, everyone thought that he had a very important position. During those years before the town got electricity, he used to carry an Oriental radio as big as his head and wherever he went it blared out music and the children followed him around in droves. Every Saturday night he would peddle his "Favorite" brand bike home from the city, his face exuding self-satisfaction. He'd sit in his courtyard making tea for the town elders, conversing with them about the East-West situation, about icons like Mao and Stalin. No one could know what his life was like in the city where he had to sleep on his desk, where, at six o'clock every morning he had to wake up, fold his blanket and roll up his mat, then put them away in the cabinet. Every meal in the communal kitchen cost him three *hao** and whenever he got there late because he had too much work, the girl in the kitchen would throw curses in his face.

Truong concealed all these things from his wife and children and the people of his town. He even concealed from them the story of the month he had to sell all his food-ration tickets in order to pay off his debts. Consequently, he wasn't allowed to eat in the dining room at all and had to subsist by eating bread with salt. He also didn't tell them about the time he got back late to the office after the security guard had locked the door, and had to spend the night under the eaves in a driving rain. He had gotten so sick he almost died.

Before their youngest child Ngheo was born, Truong's house didn't even look like a house. For some unknown reason, the old man suddenly became depressed, and then he had an awakening. He told his tea-drinking pals that in the final analysis the once-idolized Stalin and Mao were really quite ordinary. He didn't need another icon. That was his awakening. After that, Truong's life took a different turn. When his twin sons Khang and An had just turned twenty they were drafted, but only six months later the South was liberated. The old man asked the army to discharge them but was refused. Then, he urged his sons to desert.

The North-South passenger train almost never passed through town without the old man and his sons in it. Small and agile, Khang and An could hide themselves brilliantly and none of their business trips was ever a failure. First, they traded in women's underwear. It had been so many years since women in this country could get nylon underwear that now that they could get hold of it, no matter how expensive it was they would buy it. The old man also carried dried garlic, anise, and cinnamon from the North to sell in the South. Once he had built up a pretty

* Hao is equivalent to a dime.

decent surplus of capital, he trained his sons to trade in gold. After Khang and An had mixed with the train traders for only six months, wherever they went, people kept out of their way. Even savage dogs, seeing the two brothers walk by, would whimper and run. Up to now, they each had three prison sentences on their records. Still, every time they got out of prison, their faces looked even haughtier. If they kicked someone as they walked down the street, their victim would simply look at them humbly and apologize.

Truong built a house for Khang and An and picked daughters-in-law that were worthy of them. One was a meat seller and the other owned a gambling den. Procuring this gambling den owner as a daughter-in-law was truly a blessing. The whole town was drawn to her establishment until, at the end of the year, the district police raided it and took everything. Even so, Truong's daughter-in-law behaved like a heroine. For months, without shedding a tear of self-pity and while pregnant, she carried food to her husband in prison. After she gave birth, she opened a beer bar. How many years had it been since the townspeople knew such delights? She became noticeably richer, but when her father-in-law borrowed one-twentieth of a tael of gold, she demanded not only that he pay her back, but that he include the interest, never subtracting even a *trinh*.*

Even Truong winced at his two daughters-in-law's greed for money. Once, Khang's wife borrowed some ironwood from her husband's parents in order to build a kitchen. When the kitchen was completed, she invited Truong to come see it.

"I was so lucky," she said, smiling sweetly. "You gave me such good wood that I would have had to pay a fortune for it and I still could never have gotten such good quality."

The old father-in-law had a bitter taste in his mouth but he couldn't say a word. Because Truong had worked for so many decades as a cadre, now, when his daughter-in-law tricked him, he still had too strong a sense of manners to argue with her. Still, he felt indignant when he realized that she wanted him to

---

* Trinh is equivalent to one penny.

think he had misunderstood and that she hadn't borrowed the wood but had asked for it as a gift.

After Khang and An, Truong had two daughters. Can's character was exactly like that of her twin brothers, but her outward appearance was completely different. Her build and strength were like those of a farmhand and, during the lean years, she never had a chance to eat her fill. Although she was so big that she walked with a heavy thud, she agreed to marry Lan, a very thin man who had just come back from studying abroad. Over there, Lan had been caught smuggling with some Arabs and so that country had deported him. The Vietnamese embassy let Lan go home without any questions because his grandmother had, in the old days, brought food to a secret bunker sheltering a man who was now a bigwig in the government. Before going abroad, Lan had failed the university entrance exam six times. On the seventh they finally let him scrape through and go to Europe. But after several years overseas, Lan still didn't even know enough of the language to say a few basic sentences when he went shopping. Nevertheless, he got very rich. He brought home seven containers of goods, including two thousand irons, four thousand aluminum basins, three refrigerators, fifteen hundred electric kettles, one thousand pressure cookers, and many other miscellaneous items. Everything was valuable. Lan hauled his heap of goods back to the town during the time when the poem "Ten Loves" was just becoming popular.

One, I love you because you wear an undershirt
Two, I love you because you have a good supply of dried fish
Three, I love you because you use a washcloth on your face
Four, I love you because you have enough toothpaste to use
every day
Five, I love you because you have a pipe . . .

At that time, Lan's future in-laws had even adapted Kieu and would recite:

If heaven forces us to be naked, then we have to be naked
*If heaven allows us to have an undershirt, then we can wear it**

After Lan arrived in the district, the topic of every conversation centered on him. Can was conspicuous among the young women in town who were intoxicated by all the glistening pots and pans that Lan had starved himself for so many years to amass. She was conspicuous for her sweet voice and her two hands that would do any work willingly. Lan thought that by marrying Can his heap of goods would, instead of disappearing, begin to multiply. Walking along beside Lan, Can looked like a mountain looming over a tree that had been struck by lightening, but she considered herself extremely lucky for finding such a wealthy husband. She opened a shop right in the center of the district market, where all the shoppers would have to pass. Once every two weeks, she went to the city to buy supplies. After a while, she didn't even have to do that anymore because a truck would come to deliver the goods.

Even after dozens of government inspections caused her to close the store, Can's enterprise still did well. She was so successful in building up capital that she was able to construct a two-story house. Once, acting on some order, a group of reporters from the city came to photograph her house. They took a lot of photos of her shiny tile bathtub, which was the first of its kind in town. That's what the reporters said. Her house with its tile bathtub made it into the paper with the criticism, "Living like the bourgeoisie." Can ignored all this until, when the government appropriated one of the floors of her house to use as an office, she really got mad. At that time, she saw many acts of protest go unpunished all around her. It seemed like anything was permissible and so she came up with a bold plan. One day, she took off all her clothes, smeared herself from head to foot in water buffalo dung, then lay in the courtyard in front of her house kicking and screaming. But the authorities came and

* The original lines from *The Tale of Kieu*, Vietnam's great epic poem, are: If heaven forces us to live a life of hardship, then we must live like that. If heaven allows us to live a life of ease, only then can we live like that.

handcuffed her. They escorted her to the city, where they charged her with speculation, smuggling, getting rich dishonestly, and resisting the law. She received a suspended sentence of 18 months. And ultimately, the district small handicrafts industry office still moved into the second floor of her house anyway. She loathed it, and so she built a separate staircase for the new office. As for the ground floor, because her family both lived and stored supplies there, they had little room left to maneuver. But she was able to secure a new trade license, this time under her husband's name, and continued to multiply her capital. Now she was in an even bigger hurry than before because she wanted to make up for her lost investment.

Can's younger sister's name was Trang. She had the most gentle nature of anyone in the family and was the only one who had finished high school. She was unusually tall, about 1.75 meters. In this country, it was almost a certainty that no man would marry a woman that tall. On top of that, her eyes were slanted up and her cheekbones were high and looked like they'd been carved from stone. A woman like that was considered ugly. Throughout the time she was in school, the town boys, who were as frail as withered plants, never once would walk with her. They never had any sweet words for her and never even glanced in her direction. Trang was filled with sadness over her fate. When she finished school she stayed home, working as a seamstress. After the war, the sewing profession seemed useful.

At home, she rarely laughed or spoke. Khang, An, and Can all had houses of their own. Trang lived with her parents and her crippled brother Ngheo in the old family house. Since Old Man Truong first began to trade on the North-South train line, the house had been remodeled, using brick, and now had a flat roof which made it look like the Southern houses he had seen. Although it was more spacious, the house was always filled with cursing. The older Truong got, the more reticent he became. Sometimes, he fixed his eyes on his daughter, then sneered, "Hey, thickface! You should go to the pagoda and ask the abbot for a sweeper's position. Even a bum wouldn't marry you, so don't sit around waiting for it. You're just an eyesore."

His laugh sounded callous, but upon close observation one could see tears in his eyes.

As for Old Lady Truong, every day she got sharper. Although she was very skinny, her curses rang out as loud as the sound of a copper bell. She was very alert. Whenever she felt like cursing, she searched for any excuse. She would curse over everything from a broom on the floor to the basket that Trang had forgotten to hang on the wall and left on the table. Any of these things could cause her to curse about the old days, the days when Truong traveled happily between the city and the town, while his family endured so many hardships. She cursed the days when she had to hunt for crabs and snails just to feed Khang and An, and Truong would whisper in her ear, "You have to bear it. The whole country is enduring hardship so that, one day, we'll have a global family. It's not just us who are suffering." And then Truong would pick up his big radio and disappear until the next Saturday. On Sundays, back home, he would eat like a tiger, not even giving candy to his children, and when he left the next day he'd steal two *hao* from his wife's purse. She never had anything more than two *hao*, but, even so, he'd take it. Once, he even stole a piece of fabric meant for his children's clothes, and went out and sold it. The house had so many leaks that when it rained it seemed to rain inside. When Can was born, she ate rice porridge with salt. Khang and An waded through the puddles in the house, picking up feces and eating them. During those days, Truong's income was so small that it wouldn't even satisfy what, these days, An's wife would spend on salted apricots. What a bum.

Day in and day out, that was the line she used. Every time she said that, Truong exploded. He would smash whatever he could lay his hands on.

One July, during the height of the rainy season, he smashed his wife. The continual rain had no effect on the flat roof of the house, which Truong had constructed after his great awakening, when he started to trade on the North-South train. Outside, it was gloomy. Little Ngheo crawled out to the porch to play in the rain water. The sound of Trang's sewing machine was depressingly steady. Truong's wife saw the sewing box lying under the bed and started to curse.

"A sewing box left under the bed," she yelled at her daughter. "You whore! That bum of a father of yours once took some stupid pills and I gave birth to a worthless idiot. When bombs were falling, I sent him a telegram and he wouldn't even come home. When a bomb made the house collapse, I had to carry Can in one arm and use the other to drag a container of rice out from under a pile bricks. If I hadn't done it, then who would have fed my children? Take a look at that gorgeous face of yours. You don't even deserve to lick Khang's wife's heels. She started out empty-handed and now she's built a fortune."

Truong had been drinking liquor. Holding the empty bottle, he clenched his teeth and hurled it at his wife. Old Lady Truong cried out, then fell down. Shards of glass had pierced her brain. Back home from the hospital, her fever rose and fell uncontrollably for several months before she finally succumbed.

Two months later, Old Man Truong drowned after going for a swim in the pond when he was drunk. When Trang went to look for him, she found him lying face down among the water hyacinths, his body as stiff as wood.

After their parents' burial, the Truong children struck out in different directions in search of money. The old house at the edge of town got emptier. Trang's sewing machine clicked and clacked all day long. Ngheo, cocking his head to one side, played with his drool. Sometimes he pulled off his clothes, walked naked out to the place where his father had drowned, and stuck his legs in the water.

When she was almost thirty, Trang had become even more coarse and ugly looking. Her friend Canh, who sold chili sauce next door, talked to Trang about going to find a guy to "give" her a baby. But because she had a sweet nature and rarely socialized, the thought made Trang blush to the ears. "You fool!" she said, scolding her friend.

Canh retorted, "You're the fool! Do you want to die without any children? Is what you have so precious that you need to preserve it?"

Trang, unable to answer, began to sob.

Suddenly, her dull town began to bustle as if the opera troupe were about to arrive. The small, obscure cement company at the foot of the mountain was being expanded and experts and workers from some remote country were coming to help. The road through town was widened and paved with glittering asphalt. Convoys of gigantic trucks hauling construction materials drove past Trang's house on their way into the foothills. During these days, Trang became so restless she could barely get any sewing done. Imitating all the other establishments in town, she spruced up her sewing shop. She bought a glass cabinet to display her new line of cosmetics, because she'd heard that the Western men who came here brought their wives along with them. Then she went to study English at a class taught by the English teacher from the district school. She hoped that, in the future, she'd be able to converse with her customers. Every night she sat pronouncing, "Well, Well," which made Ngheo, who found this strange, turn up his face and laugh. Trang was the most intelligent in the family, like a star that had wandered into the dark galaxy of Truong's house. She learned English rather quickly and her pronunciation was quite accurate. Her English teacher remarked on this, and for the first time a man condescended to look at her, even though she was so tall he only came up to her shoulder.

The Western men and their wives began to arrive as soon as the construction of their villas at the base of the mountain was finished. How fast! The dollars pouring in really made a difference and the buildings went up swiftly and were exceedingly beautiful. They'd even imported bricklayers all the way from Saigon. In no time at all, flowers were blooming in the raised circular beds in the villas' yards. Creeping vines already covered the iron fence surrounding the compound. From the outside, the scene entranced people. At night, the heat of the tropical climate wouldn't even make those people sweat or smell bad; they kept their air conditioners humming twenty-four hours a day. The town's children circled the compound, observing, but, complying with the age-old customs of their ancestors, they knew that local people couldn't enter and so kept their distance.

One morning, the people of the district, looking through the iron fence, saw a very hairy man in shorts playing with a ball all by himself in the fancy paved courtyard. The old gardener stood looking at him with admiration

In this area, there was no place for entertainment and the "Mr. Westerners" would sometimes go out for a walk through the town. The town was extremely tiny for people born and raised in faraway Northern Europe. But they liked it here because it was quiet, because there was a row of *xa cu* trees, and an ancient well that, though covered with duckweed, had brickwork which was still extremely beautiful. Everything else looked exactly like every other town. Sundry shops. Mechanic shops. State stores. Slogans strung up everywhere, some bright red, others pure white. They strolled at a leisurely pace, interested in everything. The children ran noisily after them, like a swarm of tropical flies seeing for the first time a piece of cheese. Whenever a piece of cheese turned to look at them, the flies would buzz away, and then, moments later, swarm right back. Sometimes, those "Mr. Westerners" looked into Trang's glass case but they very rarely bought anything. Trang now had an opportunity to use her rough English to converse with them. She found that, not only could they understand her, but she could also understand them.

One Sunday, Trang was wearing a Thai pullover shirt that came from Saigon. She had washed her hair that morning and left it down so that it would quickly dry. She had also put some lipstick on her lips. The interesting thing about cosmetics is that they make people who wear them more self-confident because they feel less ugly. She examined herself in the mirror, then went to sit down, looking outside and feeling happy.

About noon, a man from the compound went out into the town. Because it was during the heat of the day, only a few "flies" were swarming after him. He rarely went anywhere. In fact, today was the first time he'd gone out into the town. He was wearing shorts and looked uncomfortable under the tropical sun that was beating down on him. He went to Trang's shop and bought two bars of soap and a bottle of French cologne. When she stood up to get him his change, he gazed attentively at her tall body that, in this country, didn't interest men. He thought she was lovely. He looked furtively at her slim waist. Her two tanned bare arms and her long hair pleased his blue eyes, which squinted with delight. Trang said good-bye to him, and invited him to come to her shop again. He told her that he would be back and exclaimed earnestly, "You're so beautiful!"

After thirty years in this town, this was the first time anyone had told her that she was beautiful. Now, a man of a different race was praising her in English. She was absolutely positive that she had misunderstood or that she hadn't clearly heard what he said. She was shocked when, the next day, he reappeared after work. He bought a handkerchief and when he left he said again, "You're so beautiful!"

Trang hurried over to the house of her friend Canh, who sold the chili sauce. Together, they checked in the dictionary. He really had said, "very beautiful." Was he honest or making fun of her? The two of them looked at each other in wonder.

After that day, as if there was a fire burning bright inside her, Trang's coarse features and slanted eyes became transformed. She diligently used cosmetics, wore fashionable pants, and a pullover shirt, and let her hair hang down, covering much of her back. The Western man had bought nearly every item she displayed in her glass case. The neighboring stores had gotten used to his presence every afternoon. He had a name that was very hard to pronounce. Trang had said it to everyone many times but no one could repeat it. They only remembered the syllable Xen at the end, which is why they called him Mr. Xen. He often sat in a chair next to Trang's glass case. Once he drank green tea that she had made him. Whenever he stood up to leave he always asked permission to kiss her hand. The first time that he did that, she went pale from fear because the gesture was so unusual. Then, one day, he proposed to her. He told her he was 53 years old and had two sons. His oldest son was thirty. He already had grandchildren, but his wife had died. He had come to work here because he was so sad. He was a civil engineer and would stay here for only six months because he still had a job back home. When he went back to his country, he wanted Trang to accompany him.

Trang felt pity for him. Judging by their outward appearance, Westerners seemed to lack nothing. One thought that they were happy, but they could just as easily be sad. Some were even miserable, like this Mr. Xen whose wife had died, whose children had moved out, and who lived a lonely life. Oh, it was destiny. After accepting Mr. Xen's proposal, Trang couldn't sleep that night. She lay crying about the fact that her parents hadn't lived to see her become so lucky, about her crippled brother Ngheo, and even about her pretty neighbor Huong, who had had flocks of admirers but married a locksmith who now beat her every day.

As it turned out, all the formalities for marrying a foreigner were expedited very quickly. Both Westerners and locals came to Trang's house in droves. Everyone on Trang's street became very excited because such an event didn't happen every day. Khang's wife and An's wife were filled with envy. It was clearly a case of the blind cat getting the fried fish. Can pressed her finger against her younger sister's forehead. "You've got seventy generations of luck," she said.

Khang and An, more reticent than ever, were each thinking: "This is a gold mine. What can I do to exploit it?"

Their parents' property was divided among them. Trang used her portion to buy gold in case of a rainy day. As for the kitchen, they built a separate door so that Ngheo could go in and out. Every day the brothers and sisters would have to make sure that

Ngheo had something to eat. Can kept Ngheo's money so that she could increase it and use the profit to feed him.

Mr. Xen would pick up Trang and her family and take them to Hanoi for the wedding. The people on Trang's street gasped when they saw the diamond ring that she wore on her finger and the necklace with a crucifix as big as the cap on a fountain pen, which she wore around her neck. Both of these pieces of jewelry were gifts from Mr. Xen.

When the day for picking up the bride arrived, the whole town took off work and flocked into the streets as if it were a political rally. On that day, Trang wore a full length dress and white flowers in her hair, and was holding a bouquet of roses. She stood as high as the groom's shoulder. She looked so gorgeous that the district school English teacher choked with jealousy. She had been the ugliest of all his female students, so ugly that he had not allowed her into his class until she paid him extra money.

Khang and An were wearing black suits, which made them look even shorter and their faces more forbidding. Can had her arm through her husband's. She was wearing an apricot-colored *ao dai*, with a chain of white beads hanging around her neck. Skinny Lan walked with difficulty next to his wife. The bride and groom drove in their own car decorated with white flowers. Her relatives went in a bus. The car with the bride in it drove very slowly and the people on Trang's street walked along behind it. Ngheo stood alone in the kitchen courtyard. He babbled for a moment, then pulled off his clothes and went to dangle his legs in the pond. A leech stuck to his leg. Ngheo pulled off the leech then set it on his head. It was such an exciting game that he didn't see the wedding procession fading into the distance.

Two months later, the townspeople were still discussing the wedding. It wasn't unlike the story of a peasant girl who'd been offered to the king. Her marriage represented the highest honor, as well as unequaled wealth. In this life, luck is better than wisdom!

Every day on her way to the market, Can would drop off a food container for Ngheo. The boy knew how to eat half and save the other half for the evening meal. When she returned from the market, she often brought him a cake or a bit of sausage. She seldom let him go hungry. But she couldn't find the time to bathe him. Now the children on his street invented a new game. They surrounded Ngheo in order to pick the lice from his hair. They could collect the lice in handfuls and then set them on the paved courtyard, whooping as they watched the lice march around. In the winter, Ngheo got even dirtier. Once, when Can went to Saigon, Ngheo went hungry. One couldn't fault the sisters-in-law for disliking Ngheo, but even his brothers couldn't stand him. Once, Khang even threatened to stab the boy, saying that such an eyesore didn't deserve to live. Ngheo lay down to sleep wherever he found himself and sometimes he even slept in his own excrement.

Winter arrived and Trang had most likely settled comfortably into a villa that had an electric fireplace. There was no way that she could know about the situation in which her beloved younger brother was living. While Can was gone, Ngheo caught some disease that produced ulcers all over his body. Even the children didn't dare to go near him anymore because of the unbearable stink. When he was cold, he was smart enough to go into the garden to collect twigs for a fire, but the heat made him even itchier. He would take off his clothes and pull the scabs off his skin. He roasted the scabs until they burned on the coals and then he ate them. He seemed to find his scabs very delicious. A few days later, when the scabs appeared again, he would pull them off again and roast them.

One day, An's wife came by to throw Ngheo a loaf of bread and when she saw him roasting his scabs, she vomited so severely that, after that, she never dared to venture back. Khang's wife, who claimed to suffer from dizziness, said that if she looked at Ngheo she would faint. When Can returned from Saigon, she found Ngheo sprawled on a mat covered with excrement and urine, surrounded by a swarm of blue bottle flies. He was at the point of starvation. She went and bought him some noodle soup, cursing all the way back from the noodle shop. In her curses, she named no names, but everyone knew that she was referring to her two cruel brothers and her two wicked sisters-in-law.

The first letter from Trang set a fire burning in every house. In this small, dull town, even though people at one end of the street knew everything that people on the other end of the street ate for dinner, a fabulous story like this one was hard to come by. In her letter, Trang said she'd had a safe journey. She felt well-protected with "him"* because "he" was very thoughtful and took care of her every need. He had a two-room house in a small city near the sea. She really liked the garden behind the house where she often went to sit and knit. She had knitted for "him" a series of sweaters, poor thing, and he really appreciated that she could cook for him. "He" sometimes took her to restaurants and also for outings outside of town. Here, everyone drove a car just like everyone rode a bicycle back home. She had met "his" sons, both of whom worked and had families of their own already. Both of "his" sons treated her quite respectfully. One day, when she went shopping with "him," the owner of a small grocery store in a shopping center asked if she wanted a sales job because her previous employee had just left for America with her husband. She accepted immediately and "he" was also pleased to let her work a shift because when "he" went to work, she might get sad at home all by herself. So now she had a job, but it wasn't hard work. Ever since she'd begun to work as a saleswoman, the owner said that the shop was full of customers because everyone thought she was so pretty. How strange!

She said that from that month on she could send money home for her family to use to raise Ngheo. Every month she would send one hundred dollars. Each family would take care of him for a month and would receive a hundred dollars and after that month someone else would take him. One hundred dollars! Khang and An nearly came to blows at the next family

* See translators' note on page xxi.

meeting. An's wife succeeded in securing Ngheo first because, in dividing the money over the sale of the house, Khang's family had gotten an extra three-fortieths of a tael of gold. That reason gave Khang's wife a bitter taste in her mouth because she was the one who had kept the extra gold and now she couldn't do anything about it.

When An and his wife went to Ngheo's house, they no longer felt disgusted. After all, Ngheo was An's flesh and blood! Therefore, he was An's wife's flesh and blood as well! An's wife rolled up her sleeves and washed Ngheo, applied ointment to his ulcers, cut his hair to get rid of the lice, and then the two of them led him back to their house. The very next day, Ngheo was wearing blue jeans. In this town, people were crazy about Thai blue jeans, Thai pullovers, and Thai soap. Ngheo was so spruced up that everyone in town looked at him like a forgotten oil lamp that was suddenly burning brightly. Sometimes, An's wife even spoon-fed Ngheo, making sure someone witnessed this, so it could never be refuted.

At the end of that month, Khang carried a knife to An's house when he went to pick up Ngheo. But An also carried a knife out. Who, he asked, had had to clean up that disgusting mess that Ngheo had been in for months? Who had cured him of scabies and lice? Whoever had put up with those things deserved to be compensated. He wanted one more month. Then Khang's family could have him for two months in a row. Now go home!

If the two of them weren't brothers, Khang thought to himself, he would go after An and his wife right then and there.

Ultimately, Can had to intervene. She was sick of the whole thing, but she didn't dare to say so. Instead, she told both of them to give in a bit, or otherwise the whole town would shit on them. Khang went home but his wife stayed, cursing until nightfall without interruption. People up and down the street could hear it. After that, Khang's wife continued to bear a grudge and every time An's wife went by her butcher stall she would pick up two knives and made a terrifying show of sharpening them against each other. She had been waiting until today. What had to happen had happened.

* * *

People carried Khang's wife to the emergency room of the district hospital, but neither she nor her seven-month-old fetus survived. The police had to handcuff Khang to keep him from killing his brother. The whole town held its breath, waiting for something to happen.

That very night, the police arrested An and took him to the city. He received the death sentence because in the course of a single moment he had killed two people. An's wife appealed for leniency, begging the court to consider the fact that An had two small children, and his sentence was commuted to life in prison. As for Khang, he went crazy. People wondered why, after causing blood to flow so many times and remaining cold and haughty, the sight of his wife and child dying made him crazy. Or did he go crazy for some other reason that no one ever knew? For a while, he mostly sat with his hands over his head, sometimes screaming out loud but never cursing anyone. Then they sent him to the city mental hospital. Can was forced to raise his two daughters. Business at her shop these days was very bad. Competition had gotten worse but the main reason for the decline was that she often had headaches and couldn't keep as big an inventory as she had before. Only Ngheo remained happy. An's wife took even better care of him than before. She had received two hundred dollars. She held up the money for everyone to see, then rolled it up and put it away. Every few nights she went to the pagoda and very piously made offerings.

The townspeople had the opportunity to discuss the event extensively. Only Trang's friend Canh said nothing, because she also received Trang's letters. In these letters, Trang sometimes admitted that she was sad. "On rainy nights, when the wind is blowing in from the sea," she wrote, "I'm very homesick. I remember the days we used to fry corn and eat it together. I crave the chili sauce that your family makes. They don't have it here. When will I see our homeland again?"

These days, wherever Canh went, people asked her many questions. You see, it was unusual to have a friend overseas. She tried to look modest, however, saying little about Trang, maintaining her reserve for a friend who had attained such an impressive position. When the district school English teacher saw this expression on Canh's face, he felt very annoyed. He often went to Diem's dogmeat shop and the two of them got along extremely well after a few drinks. The English teacher was full of bitterness, but he didn't know what he was so bitter about. Every time he felt that way, his stomach churned and he became nauseous. This weird sensation had begun when Trang put on that long dress and glided past him. Trang had never even seen him in the crowd. She was too busy gazing at the gray beard of her fiancee. Right at that moment, the teacher had first felt his stomach churn. Damn it! He mumbled the curse as Trang got into the car decorated with flowers. Perhaps he was cursing himself.

At this moment, sitting with Diem and thinking of Trang, the teacher got really upset. When Diem brought up the story of how Khang and An had fought and committed murder over dollars, the English teacher sat silently, staring at the dish of dogmeat.

Diem gulped down his drink and slammed his glass on the table. "Fuck!" he said. "It's worth it if you kill each other over dollars."

The English teacher nodded. When he spoke, his words were strong but his voice lacked emotion. "Still, it was so vile," he said. "Extremely vile. Don't you agree?"

1990

The Last Rain of the Monsoon

In late August, our group of three engineers was assigned to go to a work site in order to supervise and expedite a new phase of building based on the blueprint we had designed the year before. It was already the beginning of autumn, but the weather was still hot. The asphalt on the road shimmered. The trees were motionless and bleached white by the sun. On such days, people lose control of themselves. They often become bad tempered, restless, and unreasonably depressed. Tuan was nodding off and Mi, my close friend, was looking out the window of the car. The heat was wreaking havoc on her fair complexion, but she didn't seem to notice. She appeared so listless and bored that anything could have happened and she wouldn't have cared.

I spoke out loud. "Hey! What's the matter?"

"Nothing. Nothing's the matter."

She made no effort to continue the conversation. She was preoccupied, but not because of the heat. Mi was a good engineer who made a good deal of money from her construction designs. She also loved her son, whom she often talked about, and was a dedicated wife. But ever since she achieved this position in life, she seemed to be sinking. Her personality and beauty began to deteriorate. She was always busy, always a mess. I felt angry at her, but what could I do?

Yet the farther the car moved away from the city, the more I could see Mi change. Her gloom disappeared, to be replaced by a tense restlessness. I couldn't pay much attention; it was too hot. At some point, I drifted off to sleep.

When we reached the work site, the director shook our hands and greeted us warmly. I asked about any difficulties we might have, as I had heard that there were some problems at the site.

The director laughed and patted me on the back. "Don't worry, Mr. Engineer!"

When I turned around, my friends had already disappeared. I went to the room that had been assigned to the two of us men. Tuan had just finished bathing.

He grinned. "Bathe first. Why wear ourselves out by rushing off to work?"

"You're right. But his reasoning was so flawed I had to tell him what I thought."

I went to bathe. The water was very cool, pumped directly from the river without any filtering, and so it smelled of diesel fuel and algae. When I'd finished, I went out onto the balcony. A breeze was blowing up from the river. The atmosphere was pleasant here because there were still quite a few trees around. On another balcony, a group of young people came out to enjoy the breeze. They had arrived in a van a few minutes after us.

A hand was raised and a voice called out, "Is that you Duc? It's me, Binh!"

"Binh! Oh my God! Where did you come from?"

We both ran down to the courtyard, extended our hands, and laughed. The strength of Binh's grip expressed his feeling.

"How strange. I didn't imagine we'd run into each other here."

"I never would have expected it."

Two years before, we both spent two months at Work Site B, working, drinking beer, discussing matters, and even going out dancing. Since that time, we had never written, but we still remembered each other very clearly.

"Is there anything to drink here?" Binh asked, looking around.

A man walking by pointed to a row of trees by the river. "There's a place over there," he said. "It's as good as Hanoi."

"Thanks! Let's go."

Binh had the typical good looks of Southern men. He was one hundred percent Saigonese and girls hung on all his gestures. They enveloped him with their glances, their smiles, their voices. But he never appeared affected, or showed any signs of weakness in his soul. You could see that clearly in his warm eyes, in his robust and resilient body.

I asked, "What did your team come here for?"

"For the electrical wiring, just like last time."

The two of us went to the refreshment shop, a solid brick structure. The two rows of tables were stained from spilled drinks and marked by the burns of cigarettes. The shop was crowded with people. A board listed beer, lemonade, and ice coffee for sale. While the two of us were looking around for a place to sit, the clear voice of a woman called out.

"Duc! Come over here."

We elbowed our way over. It turned out to be Mi's voice. How strange. Mi was sitting at a table with some men we knew from working here, all of them tipsy. The glasses of beer were foaming in front of them. As on every beer drinking occasion, only one person remained sober—Mi. She liked to sit amidst the bedlam, aloof, watching the men getting drunk. Many times she had told me how much she enjoyed the solid feeling of watching others lose themselves.

She stood when we approached and gave us a fresh smile. "I saw the two of you from far away. These days it's very strange to see men who look as dignified as you two. It's as if you're not from this miserable world, but came down from another planet." She laughed.

I pulled her arm. "Let's go over there. It's so noisy. How can you sit here?"

We found a table outside the shop. When I was arranging the chairs, I noticed Binh looking at Mi. It was a strange look, as if nothing in life had ever surprised him like that. She sat down and seemed comfortable on her wobbly chair.

"Duc, I never knew you had a friend like this . . ."

I introduced them to each other. Something swift and powerful passed between them. They looked at each other quickly. Someone called for Mi from inside, from among the group drinking beer. She had left her purse inside. She ran in to get it.

Binh sat transfixed. "She's so beautiful!"

I was surprised. "Beautiful? How so?"

"Just beautiful! You don't see it?"

While listening to Binh talk, I looked in the direction of the men drinking beer. Two of the men were blabbering. One held Mi's purse and wouldn't give it to her, wanting her to sit back down with them.

"Just look at her hair, at her long neck, her shoulders . . . . Is there anyone else like that? She looks so pure."

Binh's southern accent became more tender. Mi was heading back toward us, her purse swinging from her hand. Her shirt had two white stripes running diagonally across her left breast, which made her body look like a tree reaching up toward the sun. Her features were bright, as if unexpectedly suffused with happiness. Suddenly I understood. Binh had caused all these swift changes in a woman whose beauty I had failed to notice. She gave her hand to Binh so that he could help her sit down on one of the three chairs. He sat down next to her, without looking at me.

I asked, "What do you two want to drink?"

It was as if the two of them answered together: "Whatever. It's up to you."

I went to the counter and ordered three glasses of lemonade. The girl who made the lemonade had crude hands and unclean fingers. I fixed my eyes on her long, dirty nails, then glanced at the fat flies perched on the mouth of the sugar jar and at the chunks of ice covered with rice husks to keep them from melting. She took a while. I watched them talking. When I returned, Mi stood up to take the glasses from me. She was no longer agitated and looked as lovely as a young girl. We drank the lemonade and talked about the upcoming soccer matches, about the work site, and about Mi. I told a few funny stories about what a mess Mi had been when she was raising her small boy. Binh seemed unable to believe it. He spoke to Mi with his eyes when I averted my gaze. The garden stretched down to the riverbank. At this moment, the weather was cool. The work site itself was on the other side of the river, covered with piles of steel, lime, mortar, and several cranes. On this side was the workers' housing, which lacked amenities but still offered some of the atmosphere of

Hanoi. All the professional workers came from the capital, as did the people under contract, like us. It was pleasant enough.

We sat for a long time, a very long time. Most of the people in the shop left. While Binh spoke, he couldn't take his eyes off Mi. And Mi was looking at me with a tense, begging stare. I understood her look. I hurried to finish my drink and stood up. Binh also stood up.

"Where are you going, Duc?" he asked.

"Don't get up. I have to go meet with the general manager to talk about our work for tomorrow."

"You don't have to hurry," Mi said weakly, her face reddening. She was never a very sincere liar. That was what I liked best in her.

I said, "I do have to hurry. You stay here and tell him about Hanoi."

Binh looked straight at me. For a second, both of us stood looking into each other's eyes. A fleeting sadness crossed his face. He was sunburned and handsome, but not in the ordinary kind of way. He had the kind of face that would make any woman feel secure. Mi was intelligent enough to see that and she wanted, temporarily at least, to drop her anchor here.

I walked along the river's edge. I felt the two of them looking at me, but only to have something to look at. Both of them were breathless. For a moment, I thought about Mi's husband, but then I scolded myself: To hell with it. What good will it do to worry about everyone else's problems?

I worked with the general manager for more than an hour. As it happened, he'd been a colonel in the army. We talked about the war years.

He shook his head, complaining about his twenty-year-old son. "He's melancholy. Twenty years old. Why should he be so sad?"

When we said good-bye, he gave me a pack of 555 cigarettes and said he hoped that my group wouldn't fall into meaningless liaisons that we hadn't planned on when we signed our contracts.

After that, I wandered around. When I got to the dining

hall, everyone had gone already. On the table reserved for our group, all that was left were the portions for myself and Mi. There was a plate of stir-fried beans, a bowl of mustard greens with broth, and a saucepan full of rice. The buxom cleaning woman was flipping the chairs upside down onto the tables so that she could wash the floor. While she worked, she told me to go ahead and wait for whoever was coming. Whenever we finished eating, we should put our plates in the wooden cabinets to keep the mice from getting to them and she'd come in and clear them out tomorrow morning.

I sat and waited, then I pulled out the newspapers and magazines that I had borrowed from the general manager's office to read. All the papers had photos of the approaching World Cup tournament in Italy. I looked at the photo of Maradona. I didn't know why, but I felt worried when I looked at this man who was standing at the pinnacle, whom everyone on the planet was watching. There's nothing to be happy about when one has to keep one's balance at the top, especially when everyone else is forcing you to stand exactly how they want you to stand. If that was me, I would disappear, escape, or cease to make a sound when I had reached the top. No one could rise forever or be great forever, either.

After I'd read all the papers, I looked at my watch and saw that it was ten o'clock. I had said good-bye to Binh and Mi at four. I was examining a photo in a local magazine of a woman with a flat and haggard face when Mi came up from behind me. I wanted to give her a very stern look. But as soon as I saw her I knew that I couldn't do it. Her face was fresh from the cool breeze, the mist, and the moonlight. Happiness made her breathing uneven. She sat down softly. She was like a being infused with a current, growing bright, then brighter until she would amaze anyone who saw her. After working with her and being her good friend for four years, only now did I realize how charming and lovely she was. She looked at me from across the table. She smiled, but her eyes looked elsewhere. Even her voice was different, full of new sounds.

"You go ahead and eat!"

"I'll wait for you. What's the point of eating alone?"

"But I'm not hungry. I feel like I could fast for months."

"You only feel that way now."

"No. I mean it . . . I've just realized that for so long my life hasn't been much of a life at all. You won't understand."

"I understand everything. Everyone feels that way."

"Do you want me to tell you about my husband?"

"No."

"I agree. There's no need to say anything. But, God, if it goes on like this, I'll die."

"You won't die. You'll be alright. We'll go home in a few days and everything will be exactly the same."

I started eating. It tasted good because I'd just begun to feel hungry. Mi watched me eating attentively, but I knew clearly that she was not seeing anything.

"He's married and has a four-year-old son," Mi said.

"Who? Binh? Yeah. He told me."

"I'm jealous of his wife."

"Don't be jealous. No one in this world is really happy."

Mi smiled and seemed to agree with me. She had often told me about trivial matters and she always seemed to be writhing over them. I usually gave her short, often curt advice, but it seemed to help her recover herself. It had always been like that.

I said, "You should go to bed and try to sleep. Tomorrow morning we have to go to the work site."

"I can't sleep."

"Count to one hundred, then start over."

"I can't. It isn't that simple. But tomorrow morning, I'll be able to go to work. Don't worry."

She looked at the stack of magazines and newspapers on the table. There was a photo of a new president who wasn't even forty years old yet. He was talented and singularly handsome. You could look at him and see a superhuman, the shining star of a big country on the other side of the hemisphere.

Mi gazed at the photo for a long time. "I don't understand

people like that," she said. "What makes them different? They're unreachable. How would it feel to be a wife or lover of a man like that? It would be special, extraordinary. Like that."

"It would probably be the same as with anyone else."

"How could that be? It has to be happiness. True happiness. Such a man would know how to love a woman. Love from the bottom of his heart. True love."

"He wouldn't have the time. I can guarantee it. He has to do his presidential duties."

"Does he know where our country is?"

"Maybe!"

"Well, I'm going to my room now." The sound of her sigh was accompanied by an interjection, "God, oh God."

I ignored it and went back to my own room. Tuan was asleep already. A cup of coffee was sitting on the table for me. Even the coffee smelled like diesel oil.

I was used to getting up early. Everything was still hazy in the August mist and this heralded a very sunny day. I picked up the soap and my toothbrush, planning to go down to the river for a quick swim. I didn't expect to see Binh down by the river but he was already there, sitting on a rock, picking up stones from beneath his feet and tossing them into the water. He seemed pensive. I called to him and made a joke and when he looked up my smile died on my lips. I had thought I would see Mi's brightness reflected in his face. But no. He looked desolate. I had lived with him at Work Site B. He had been cheerful, flirting with the girls, giving them hope and then destroying it, but no one had ever gotten mad at him. He had always been a flirt like that, giving the impression that he would go through life having endless fun. This was the first time I had ever witnessed such sadness in a man. It seemed bottomless.

He leaned over and pulled a pack of cigarettes from the pocket of his trousers. "Have a smoke to wake yourself up," he offered.

After lighting up, I asked, "So?"

The word meant so much, but at the same time it meant

nothing at all. Binh smiled slightly. We went into the water and swam together to the other side and back. There was a slick of oil across the surface of the water and the smell was very bad. After swimming, I felt sticky because of the smell of the oil.

I mumbled as I put on my clothes, "This is awful. The water used to be so clear."

"Yeah. All these factories are going to ruin the rivers."

After he said that, I waited for him to reveal more, but he said nothing at all. He looked even sadder getting out of the water. I wondered if I had ever been so much in love that I would feel that sad. No. Maybe I had never felt love as he was feeling now. The two of us wandered around. There was a coffee house on the other side of the road. We went inside. The coffee we drank smelled of diesel oil and the additional stink of the smoke from the stove.

I said to Binh, "My group will be very busy today."

"So will mine. When you're busy, you feel better."

We shook hands. He walked off in the direction of his guest house. Then, as if on second thought, he turned around and called to me and ran back. He looked as if he had wanted to tell me something for a long time.

"What do you think of it?" He asked. "Am I really bad?"

"Don't be crazy!"

"What would my life be like if I couldn't be with her?"

I took his hand. I hadn't imagined that it could have gotten this serious. I had always thought of affairs like this as just for fun. I could sense his seriousness through his hand, though, and I wanted him to calm down.

He said, "I love her. I should have met her long ago. That would have made more sense."

"This is normal," I told him, "but if it's reached this point, you'd better split up."

"Why should we?"

"Because you love each other. It's as simple as that!"

Binh smiled. He understood me. Real life is such a powerful shock it could even break stones.

He looked over my shoulder and out across the river to where the sun was rising. The bright sunshine had driven the mist into the hollows at the edge of the river. He was looking but he didn't see anything. His expression was like Mi's.

That whole day, my group had to stay on the work site to oversee the construction. The sun had parched everything and we became dazed and stupid from the glare and the dust. Sometimes I looked into Mi's face beneath her hardhat, a face as fresh as a flower, a face that reminded me of things that were soothing and cool. Her beauty had nothing to do with our surroundings. She inhabited her own private world, amidst the hot inland wind, the cement dust, and the acrid stink of the diesel oil.

That evening, after we'd washed up for dinner, only Tuan and I sat at the table. The next day, and then for the whole week that we spent on the work site, Mi simply disappeared each evening. I knew where they were. Half a kilometer to the north of the site, by the river, there was a magnificent forest of young pine trees. The pine needles filtered out all the dust and the air was as pure as when the sky and earth were first formed. I have the bad habit of imagining the lovemaking of my friends, but I thought of Binh with respect. I always did, and I continued to feel that way, even during this love affair.

Every night, next to the tray of food, reading the paper to kill the time, I waited for Mi until very late. Every night, she came back very late, full of the night mist and the cool wind. She was always happy and carefree at first but after conversing for a few minutes would become worried and uneasy, as on that first day.

I could also see the changes in Binh clearly during those days. He lost his cheerfulness and became desolate. One day, he sat with me in the morning by the edge of the river. He squeezed my hand very firmly and gave a long sigh. His whole body seemed to be in pain. I knew for sure, after an affair like this, the woman could forget the man. Women are often like that. As for him, never. I regretted that they had come to know each other.

By Saturday evening of that week, all our work was completely done. A big group of experts arrived at the work site. Lights and garlands of flowers had been strung in the meeting hall and there was dancing. I sat at a table in the back with Tuan and two peasant girls who had just arrived at the site. They were very shy. One of them was always giggling and covering her mouth. Both of them had dark skin, but they wore tons of makeup and looked ridiculous. Their clothes were all imported from Thailand. They wore pungent perfume and their bracelets were garish. Tuan was courting them and I was fidgety while waiting for Mi. From three o'clock until now, Mi had disappeared somewhere with Binh. This last day would be hard on both of them.

In the center of the room, a group of young people began to dance. The music was ear-splitting. With his eyes closed tight, the drummer bent his body and shook his full head of hair. Some of the women wore very wide trousers and a few wore skirts. Maybe they were the interpreters for the big European men who were dancing with them. Except for the Westerners, nobody danced with feeling. They were just trying to stay with the beat, and so they looked as rigid as logs. Furthermore, there was something makeshift about the general atmosphere of this place. It just didn't look like a dance hall. I was beginning to get bored when Mi walked through the front door. She walked slowly, her head held high.

Mi walked through the couples dancing. One young man with blond hair watched her pass by. He was dancing with someone else, but every time they revolved around, he would look again at the most beautiful woman at the dance. It was true. At that moment, Mi was absolutely lovely. The younger women could not even compare with her. Mi sat down next to me and put a hand on the table. It was shaking. Catching me looking down at that hand, she dropped it, and smiled apologetically. The blond-headed man approached our table. He invited Mi to dance. She answered in English that she didn't know how. He looked at her curiously with the blue eyes of the North, as if he were asking himself if she were telling the truth or not. Mi looked distracted. At that moment, Binh came in with two friends. Seeing Mi sitting with me, he walked over to us cheerfully. Mi stood up immediately, gave her hand to the blond man, and the two of them walked out onto the dance floor.

They'd had a fight already. That's what I thought. Any kind of love was like that. Brushing each other off, sulking, and seeing every tiny thing as important—all of these things showed that love was still meaningful. That was the best time to end it. Try to take it one step further and there would be nothing left to continue.

Binh offered me a cigarette. One of the peasant girls gave Binh a sharp glance. The other girl giggled shyly and covered her mouth. Both of them bloomed when Binh sat down next to them. Meanwhile, Binh sadly took a drag of his cigarette.

I asked him, "Hey. Did something happen?"

"The trouble is that neither of us knows how to sort things out."

"Don't do anything. I gave you that advice already. You shouldn't do anything."

"This is not just for fun. It's not something temporary. I don't want it like that."

He seemed determined. At that moment, Mi was gliding through the music with a stranger.

The next day, my group did not go to the work site. I gave Mi the day off and she disappeared immediately. Tuan and I took care of some odds and ends. We left for home in the cool evening to avoid the heat of the day.

Mi got in the car first. Binh stood beneath a tree. He squeezed my hand.

"When will you go to Saigon?" I asked.

"Next Tuesday. I have some urgent business."

He had a strong handshake. All of his feelings were squeezed into and entrusted to it. He looked into the car.

"You forgot your little bag, Mi," he said. "Wait and I'll go get it for you."

Once the car was on the way, I didn't dare look into the ghostly face of that woman. She pressed her lips together until the blood drained out of them. Just behind her ear, a dried pine needle had gotten caught in her permed hair. She had squeezed herself into a corner of the backseat of the car and I sat on the other side. Tuan—a young man who liked to drive a Honda Cub, who was fond of flirting and dancing the frantic Latin steps, a man who easily forgot—had taken a seat in the front by the driver. He had stayed up the whole night courting an interpreter, so now he was sleeping. The driver kept his eyes on the road.

I took Mi's hand to calm her down. Her hand was icy and trembling. Her eyes were completely dry.

The car crossed beyond the work site and went through a town that resembled every other town in this region, then sped onto the highway that cut across the rice fields. The driver had a small cassette recorder. He put a tape in and a maudlin, annoying voice began to sing. I could picture in my mind the sentimental face of the woman singing, the way that she closed her eyes tight, throwing her head back, looking decadent and pathetic. The sun was setting. I tried not to say anything. What could one say at a moment like that?

A few minutes later, Mi suddenly asked, "What time is it?"

"Around six, or a little later."

"I'll soon be home with my son. Oh God, I've forgotten him for a whole week. How awful. I've never behaved like this. I've sinned."

"It doesn't matter. Such things are normal."

"It won't be normal anymore. Pretty soon, I'll take my boy away with me. He asked me to bring my son."

"Where are you going?"

"Anywhere. He said we could go anyplace where we could live for each other. His parents are in Thailand. We'll escape there."

"And from there where will you go?"

"We'll plan that later."

"In my opinion, you should drop the whole idea. Even if

you go to the moon or to Mars, you still can't escape. That's our fate. After a while, you'll be in the same state you're in now. I believe that."

"But I'll be living with Binh."

"It would be the same with anybody."

Mi was quiet for a long while and then I noticed her weeping.

"Then I would die. If things are like this forever and ever, then there's nothing left for me at all. I'll erode a little more every day. I'll become stupid, lethargic, house bound. I'll be mean, wicked. I'll shout at my son, fight with the neighbors, become a penny-pincher. In only ten years, I'll be a forty-year-old crone and no one will recognize me."

"Relax. Ten years is a long, long time. You can achieve a lot in that time."

"He woke me up. He said he felt the same way. He thanked me for letting him know what love is. I love him so much. I've never felt this way before."

"When you got married, you probably said you'd never felt that way before, didn't you?"

"Yes!"

"There. Then you should rejoice that you're alive, right? To be alive in this world is the best you can hope for. On top of that, you are whole, you sleep soundly at night, you're not hungry, and you have no worries."

"You say that because you've lived through the war."

"Probably."

"I always respect those men who carried rifles and ran through the showers of bullets. Oh God, at those moments, what was going through your mind?"

"Not a thing. Because at that moment, there was a place I had to reach. When they have a goal in front of them, people are all the same. They don't think a lot."

"You're beginning to talk like an old man. Binh is not like that at all. He's more confused."

"Really?"

"I hate that you're so confident. How can people be so confident when everything has become so tangled?"

"It's useless to try to wriggle out of it."

After that, we were quiet as the car drove into the night. The woman on the cassette sang nonstop. Why did people continue to drown themselves in things as meaningless as that? A woman's love. Tears. Her lonely world. Heavy sobbing always means a lot of pain.

Mi broke into laughter. "It's horrendous," she said. "How could she sing like that? I want to be like those singers. You eat well. You wear nice clothes. You're carefree."

"You're no worse off than them."

"I'll try to be like that. If you want to go really far away, you have to have a lot of money, right?"

"Yeah. A lot."

"I've got to go."

"You shouldn't go anywhere."

"How can you understand?"

"Why not? If I were you, I would never do anything so foolish."

"Oh God. How much longer before we get home?"

"Another hour."

"I'm going to nap. Talking with you leads nowhere."

The next morning, I went to the office early. The director of our agency told us that our design project had been approved and we'd receive three million. He was planning to award one of those millions to our group. I waited for Tuan and Mi to arrive so they could hear the great news and also so that the three of us could tell the director how our project at the work site had gone. Tuan showed up and he and the director and I waited until ten o'clock. Then the director had to go to a meeting so he made an appointment to see us that afternoon.

He guessed that Mi hadn't arrived yet because she was busy with her children or something. "She works so hard," he said. "A wife like her is really a wife. A mother like her is really a mother. I've never met a woman like that."

I didn't say a word. Tuan left too, saying he'd be back by two o'clock. I sat at a desk and pulled out a stack of newspapers and some letters to read. After a while, I heard Mi's footsteps enter the room and go to a desk in the corner, but I didn't look up. The truth is that I was afraid. A woman's misery was something I could not yet understand. Was it real?

Mi unfolded some papers and began to write. It seemed that she couldn't bear the silence and so she began to talk. It was always the same. She told us about what was going on in the housing project where she lived. The whole place was a rat's nest, she said. Everyone was terrified, because there were so many rats and they were big, old, and very savage. The people themselves were like rats as well. Even in the tiniest spaces, they would crawl in and build their nests. That place resembled the market train: complete bedlam. It seemed like in that housing project all the "flowers of civilization" were concentrated.

"Hey Duc," she said. "Last night, when I got home, I saw something so funny it made me laugh until I cried."

"Tell me."

"There's this toilet and underneath it is a cesspit. People cut a hole in it to get at the shit for fertilizer. And the cesspit is always so full that it overflows from that spot. Then, last night, they forgot to block the hole. The electricity had gone off and somebody's guest went down, groping in the dark. He fell in and almost drowned."

"Go on!"

"He bellowed like a bull. It was a long time before they were finally able to pull him out. To make matters worse, water was scarce and they had to dunk him in the gutter just to get some of it off of him. After that, every house had to give him one bucket of water to wash with. During the night, he ran a high fever and they had to take him to the emergency room."

"Why the fever?"

"He was scared stiff. If that had happened to me, I would have died."

I looked at Mi's face. Her eyes were open wide and no longer showed the pain she'd felt. Here was the face she had always shown us. Severe, completely exhausted, and furious because there was no way she could escape all the troubles of life.

Then she went on to tell another story, about a "Great Duke," a horrible old man who took his whole family with him out of the countryside to crowd into a tiny space of eight square meters. The old man built three stories on that eight square meters. On each floor, the ceilings were so low you could only sit. Finally, when he couldn't build another story, he cut a hole in the ceiling to climb out. That ceiling was shared by many other apartments. He lit a lamp up there and walked back and forth like a ghost all night. One day, the ceiling collapsed and the old man fell onto the top of one couple's wardrobe. People pleaded with and cursed him. He turned his ear this way and that, pretending to be deaf.

The old man used to go out into the street and collect old brooms and tattered baskets, then bring all of that back and shove it in spaces in the housing project. In this corner, he stored a pair of old tires. In that one, he stored a dried tree stump. Over the years, these things had become moldy and smelly havens for mice and cockroaches. But he wouldn't let anyone touch them. He dared even the sub-district committee, even the municipal people's committee to go near them. He announced this dramatically in the courtyard and hundreds of people in the neighborhood were frightened into silence.

The old man lived completely satisfied within those eight dingy square meters, as if he were a great duke living on an estate in his vast castle. He organized the wedding of a daughter and another of a son and he celebrated the longevity of his father. All of this was done extravagantly within those three floors that were more like storage spaces. Guests had to bend over while they ate on those three floors. It was so hot in there that when they finally emerged, they looked as red as boiled shrimp. One day, it was 39 degrees Celsius outside, and inside it was even hotter. The old man sat shirtless, drinking whiskey, eating fish heads, and jiggling his legs while listening to the radio. That radio was always blasting at full volume. He was Mi's nightmare, and the nightmare of every timid soul in the neighborhood. Every day there was a story about the old man, and every day we always had a good laugh.

Mi said, "Yesterday, the Great Duke somehow got hold of some fabric. When he got home, he talked his wife into buying it from him. The two of them haggled over it."

"Then what happened?"

"The old woman insisted on a discount of 500 dong. He grabbed her hair and threw her down from the "third floor." She fell onto the edge of a chair and had to be taken to the hospital where they gave her three stitches near her temple. He left her in the hospital and when he got home, he paced back and forth on the floor just under the roof. He started tinkering with someone's wiring and so he electrocuted himself."

"Did he die?"

"No. Even if heaven struck that man, he wouldn't die."

"That means his story will go on?"

"How could it end? Let me continue."

"Bravo! The old man's story is a tonic. Laughter makes a person healthy."

"Do you remember when I told you once about a professor of philosophy at the university? The guy the children call the Inchworm?"

"You told me a few times already."

"He has three university degrees. One in this country and two in Europe."

"That's too many."

"Yesterday he was caught red-handed puncturing the tire of a locksmith's bicycle. The two families had been feuding over a place to put their trash. He was mad at the other guy, but he didn't say a word. Whenever he's mad at anyone, he never says a word. He waits until dark so he can use a needle to punch holes in the other person's tires. Once he threw his kid's shit into a woman's basket of water spinach and then she stuffed it all back into his mouth.

"Today," she continued, "the locksmith's two sons beat him

with a bamboo carrying pole. Even now, both families are being kept at the police station. The guy's also a kleptomaniac. He's compelled to steal. One day, some children caught him stealing a basket of hen's eggs. And this guy has three degrees. He despises anyone who didn't finish college."

Both of us laughed until our eyes watered.

Mi said, "Maybe he wasn't always so bad. He's eroded. He's eroding himself and dirtying himself. So am I. Sometimes I see myself as a wicked woman."

"No. You can't be like that."

"Still, it's unavoidable. All day, I curse and wish the Great Duke dead. He's the guy that even heaven can't strike. He's from the country. He's been baiting crabs and catching snails since he was little, which gives him supernatural health. He bullies everyone with his giant body and with his voice, which is as loud as a copper bell. Still, I curse him. His apartment is right next to mine. He's like flies and mosquitoes. No one can avoid them. How can people avoid flies and mosquitoes in this country?"

"It's difficult!"

"But we're also flies and mosquitoes bothering other people."

"No!"

"I'll write a letter to Binh and tell him to stop his plan to divorce his wife."

"Right. Neither of you should do anything. You should keep living as you are."

"I can't do anything. Everything's over."

"Mi!"

"No. Let me cry. This morning, when I woke up and was still lying under the mosquito net, I heard someone singing something, a song that was rather familiar but I couldn't remember whom I'd heard it with. I burst into tears. I've been married for eight years and that was the first time I've cried like that. I felt so desolate all morning. When I rode my bike to work, I was crying. I couldn't even see the road through my tears. At the intersection with the train tracks, a whole crowd was waiting for the train to go by. I was still crying, thinking that no one would pay any attention to me. But as it turned out, two guys on a motorbike noticed me. The one on the back looked into my face and grinned. Can you guess what he said?"

"I give up."

"He said, 'Sweetie, what number did you play yesterday that turned out to be such a fiasco? Stop crying. If at first you don't succeed—try, try again.' Finding me silent, he turned serious and thoughtful. Then he said, 'Today, you should play number 74. I've taken such a liking to you that I'm giving you the number. Follow my advice and play 74.'

"The train passed and the two of them edged their way through the crowd and then revved up and disappeared. At that moment, I must have looked like a gambler. But, actually, at that moment, I was thinking of Binh and the fact that I would never live like that again."

"Let's go get some coffee."

"Yes. And let's never talk about this again."

"Right."

"But, God, I've only known him a week and now when I think of him, it all seems like so long ago."

"Think of it like a dream."

"Or like I won the lottery, right?"

"It's all the same."

She was still sniffling, but she seemed to be regaining her composure. Eventually, she'd get used to it.

After that, we went downtown. That day, the weather was still sultry, the kind of weather that made me feel it wasn't easy to get used to anything. The woman walking beside me had frivolously wasted her time. Are such moments necessary to anyone? These days, tears only flow when people play the wrong number. And yet here she was, crying over love, over the trivial things of life, over extravagant wishes.

1991

Tony D

A gloomy looking guy, the kind of hustler you see lurking around the market place, stopped by the home of Old Man Thien. The stranger stood in the doorway. He had the bloated body of someone who had been fattened on starch. It overwhelmed the bland face stuck on his tiny head.

Old Man Thien didn't bother to stand up. "It's about Than, right?" he asked.

"How did you know?"

"Just tell me."

"Than is dead and they haven't found his body."

When Old Man Thien heard this, his gigantic Adam's apple moved like a brick in his throat. Nearly a year had passed since his son, Than, had joined the crowds of people from all over the country streaming into Central Vietnam to dig for gold. This was the third time somebody had come here to inform Old Man Thien of Than's death. The first time, he'd drowned. The second time, he was cut up. This time his body had disappeared. The guy who'd brought the news stood in the doorway licking his lips. He looked hungry. Old Man Thien, who knew too well the evil intent of a man such as this, did not move even a muscle on his face.

"Why'd his body disappear?" he asked.

"The mine collapsed. Couldn't pull him out."

"Three kinds of death!" the old man exclaimed.

"What are you talking about?"

"Three different guys bring me three different deaths. To hell with all of you."

The man looked surprised, then quickly swept his eyes over the room inhabited by Old Man Thien and his son. There was nothing worth taking.

"Scum!" he mumbled, then said. "But I came all the way up here. The train fare cost me a lot. Can't you give me a little food?"

Old Man Thien waved his arm across the dark and narrow space. "Have a look," he said. "Any damn food you can find you can take."

Apparently the stranger was desperate. He stepped over Old Man Thien, extended his arm and grabbed an electric mouse ear fan, its blades dotted with holes.

"May I?" the stranger asked

He put the fan under his arm and walked out. Old Man Thien yelled after him, "Watch out! When my son Than gets back here he'll have your blood to pay for that! Get lost."

Old Man Thien knew very well that although his son was as small as a mouse, he was the sort of guy that even heaven couldn't finish off. He was like a weed burned to the ground seven times that grew back seven times, each time tougher than the last. Once, while committing a burglary, he fell off a third floor balcony and, blessed by his seventy generations of ancestors, landed in a pile of sand. Old Man Thien would bet against anyone who thought he could kill his son.

Still, once he'd kicked the stranger out the door, Old Man Thien felt a bit unsettled. He waited until nightfall, then pulled out the small radio he'd carefully hidden among the dirty bowls under the bed. He began to search for a station. He never let himself hear a complete sentence that anyone said on that radio; his pleasure lay in holding the knob and turning it. Whenever he heard the static of an incoming station, he'd listen for a moment, then continue turning the dial. His neighbors scowled and sulked at the racket. He ignored them. What business was it of theirs? It wasn't as if he had stepped on their ancestors' graves, was it? He couldn't even imagine how a little noise could keep them from sleeping. A bomb could explode next to his ear and he'd still be fast asleep.

For each meal, Old Man Thien ate eight bowls of moldy rice with fermented fishheads and chicken gizzards, all of which he bought cheap at the evening market. Every time the old man ate fermented food, the whole neighborhood held its breath. What did he care? Only strong-smelling foods suited his tastes. He

was a big man, like an ancient discarded tractor. Sometimes
people said he was an apparition from hell who had come back
to haunt the world. So what? His diet made him the fittest person
in the neighborhood. No one wanted to mess with him. The old
man had bragged around the neighborhood that the past three
generations of his family had been utterly virtuous and had even
contributed to the revolution. He was always ready to recount
these contributions to anyone, whether they cared or not. Mostly
his audience was the neighborhood kids who listened with about
as much understanding as a duck listening to thunder. It didn't
matter. When he crossed the courtyard, the whole neighborhood
literally shook like an earthquake because he was powerful as a
bull. He did whatever he pleased and had no respect for the
"intellectuals" and their so-called consciences. When he wanted
something, he did whatever it took to get it. He trampled on
everyone.

   The old man had worked as a janitor until he retired ten
years ago. He once had a house in the country with a garden and
a fishpond, but suddenly he sold everything and moved into the
city. He used the money from the sale to buy gold, then hid the
gold and pretended to be both poor and miserable, forcing his
family to crowd into this stuffy hovel that wasn't even ten meters
square. On one side was the public latrine, which meant that the
place was never lacking for odors. On the other side was a terrace
now occupied by people who had built a bamboo roof over their
heads and partitioned the space into sections so that each family
was surrounded by four thin bamboo walls. It was a colorful
scene. There was a couple from the street theater who would
curse each other like cats and dogs all day and then lie in bed
holding each other and giggling on those nights when a rainstorm
finally lessened the stink in the air. There were the hovels that
contained only men and boys, a gang who would scatter by day
to hustle some money and crawl back at night. When the
electricity went out, their fans were useless, and water was rare,
so they couldn't use it to wash their sweaty bodies. They slept in
nothing but shorts, lying next to each other like fish in a pot.

This terrace where, long ago, the children of the wealthy used to sit and catch the cool breezes, now was filled with the croaking snores of common mortals sleeping peacefully beneath the protection of God's starry sky. At night, they slept like a wretched and miserable herd. By day, they were a band of savage devils, a pack of animals, with the strongest taking the choicest morsels. Their compound was no different than thousands of public housing projects that had sprung up to imprison both human bodies and souls.

Old Man Thien had sold his property in the countryside, wore gold beneath his clothes, and still pretended to be as miserable as scum. Old Man Thien had also crawled into one of those hovels on the terrace, to live among the herd of animals. And among them, he was the creature with the sharpest fangs.

* * *

A few days later, Than suddenly appeared, carrying a knapsack that was bulging at the seams. He strutted into the housing project courtyard and every eye from every lair and hovel converged on the pack that the ruffian was carrying. From underneath the stairs came a flippant voice with an accent that sounded part Northern, part Nghe Tinh Province: "Than!"

"What?" Than turned his head to look at a fat woman with folds in her neck, her face covered with the kind of gaudy makeup one sees on the girls who work the area around the train station. Now she smiled, baring her teeth, on which a bit of green onion had gotten stuck.

"Hey, kid!" she said

"Hey, Big Sis!" he replied.

"What you got in that knapsack that makes you so full of yourself?" she asked.

"Just clothes."

That's no damn clothes. You must have struck it rich if it's that heavy."

Old Man Thien, running outside to greet his son, came to

his rescue. "Shut your mouth about 'struck it rich' or I'll strike you dead," he warned.

"Yeah, strike her dead," said Than, and then, haughtily, he walked up the steps.

The steps, which were built during the French occupation, groaned and creaked, always provoking a sensation of "Quick! It might fall down under me!" But the stairs had been here for many decades and hadn't fallen yet. People said that this was because they had been built during the French time, before laborers had learned how to steal cement. Buildings erected during that time to house five people now housed two hundred.

A group of small boys, who'd been playing cards for money in the courtyard, ran out shouting when they spotted Than. "The Lord's son has returned! Great Lord, treat us to a meal!"

Old Man Thien was called "the Great Lord" because even though he lived like an animal in the dark hovel that he and his son called home, he still put on airs. He even observed birthdays there. Oh Buddha, what parties! All the urchins held their breaths whenever they watched the old man celebrating birthdays. In the past, the old man had worked as a security guard at a fancy office outside the city, and so he knew very well the taste of these kinds of celebrations. He would invite over two good-for-nothing guys who lived down the street and they'd sit slurping beer, eating roasted peanuts, and making up poems like kids farting. One after another. Dozens of poems in an hour. On top of that, the old man commemorated the anniversaries of his ancestors' deaths, as well as Tet. All his relatives would flood into the city from their remote villages for those celebrations.

The old man had great talent. Although his siblings had absolutely no education, every one of them got a job with the government. One of them sold vegetables at the state-run store. Another worked as a security guard. Even after they retired, they still received their salaries. The old man brandished his certificate of "Service for the Revolution" like a weapon to threaten any faint-hearted bosses. He would visit them again and again, ten, twenty times. As much as it took. He'd sit without budging in the homes of these bosses, never bringing any gifts, just his mouth. In that way, two younger brothers, two younger sisters, and dozens of relatives had been planted in government offices, and were receiving ration coupons. When he commemorated his ancestors' deaths, the old man rallied all his relatives together in his hovel, entertaining the lot of them with a single stringy duck. Every year it was the same. The duck was cooked in a watery broth, seasoned, and then the whole clan would squat together and noisily slurp. Cramped in as they were, they figured that being in the city was still better than the boonies. The old man would be in the middle of it all, solemnly pronouncing words of wisdom as he moved through the crowd, weighed down by the gold on his body. There had never been a mandarin or a king who could be happier or more content in retirement than Old Man Thien. The nickname "Great Lord" fit him perfectly; only a king or mandarin could live so grandly in his own kingdom, even though the temperature was over 40 degrees celsius, even with a leaky roof and the stench of dead rats and urine. The old man took care of his own business, and he always ate and slept as he pleased.

* * *

Looking exhausted, Than threw down the knapsack. Then, as if on second thought, he snatched it up and hugged it tightly against his stomach. He looked around the room, and thrust the knapsack into the corner where he and the old man often cooked, using electricity stolen through a wire they stretched to the office next door. Than knew he had to keep an eye on his father. Old Man Thien was bulky but, when he was stealing something, he could be smoother than a cat. All day long, he'd keep a lookout for things that he could pinch. He'd take anything, from women's underpants to a piece of electric cable linking someone's house to the mainline. He'd even stolen a child's potty someone left outside in the courtyard. He'd stuff all his loot into a big sack and when it was full, he'd bring it to the countryside. He had an older brother who still lived in the village because he hadn't been able to haul all ten of his children into the city. Old Man Thien would exchange the things he had stolen for taro and mung beans to bring back to town. The whole neighborhood knew that the old man was a thief, but no one had ever been able to catch him in the act. Than was a disciple of the old man, but he took on bigger challenges. "I wouldn't settle for trash like you do," he'd often shout at his father.

Old Man Thien's wife had died., and he'd had married off his daughter to a guy who lived in the highlands. Now only the old man and Than were left. Than and his buddies roamed far and wide to hustle their living. Sometimes, he'd give his father money, but the two of them never shared a meal. When they cooked, either the old man or Than would eat first. Since they stole their electricity from the company next door anyway, they'd let their pots bubble on the stove day and night. Old Man Thien would stew a batch of fish heads or pork bones he'd bought cheap at the market so that he could enjoy the broth. Even if he didn't have anything to cook, he left the burner on anyway, clucking, "If you're going to steal it, you've got to make it worth the effort. My stealing electricity won't make a dent in anything. I listen to the news about those things. One guy stole billions, and nothing happened to him at all. As for me, I'm only a crippled chicken. All I can do is stay close to the rice mill and pick up scattered grains."

* * *

Old Man Thien was pacing in and out of the room now, sneaking glances at the knapsack. He felt like there were needles pricking his stomach; he'd never seen Than bring home a knapsack as big as this. With great generosity, he shared a loaf of bread with his son. Then, watching Than eat in silence, the old man couldn't stand it a moment longer.

"You hit it big this time, didn't you?"

"Sure."

"So, what have you got bulging in there?"

"My cock," Than spit out the words at his father. He picked a few crumbs of bread off the mat, wiped his face with his hand, then went to the corner and took the lid off the chamber pot. A terrible stench filled the room. After Than finished his business, he crawled into the corner his father had allotted to him, and began to snore like thunder, one of his hands gripping the straps of the knapsack.

Old Man Thien sat on embers while Than was sleeping. He racked his brain trying to guess what was in the knapsack, but he couldn't figure it out. Near dusk, he groped over to the place where his son was sleeping.

"Than," he said. "Wake up. I've got to tell you something."

"What?"

"Look, you've got something big here, right? Well, watch out for Hung. He's been back more than a week already. He escaped."

"Really?" Than sat up, hugging the knapsack. Hung was the son of Old Lady Phan from Nghe Tinh, who was so sly as a trader that she even outsmarted native Hanoians. Hung was twenty-five years old and had already been to jail three times. Each time he served for a year and after each release he became even bolder. Even people like Than had to look up to him. This time, Hung had gotten five years for rape. He hadn't even served for a year when he escaped.

"Are they after him?" Than asked.

"Probably. He's hiding in the attic now. Nobody in the building would dare snitch. He'd slit their throats. So tell me the truth. What have you got in there? Tell me so that both of us can take care of it. On your own, you won't make it."

"O.K., but keep your mouth shut, you hear?"

Old Man Thien spit into his hand and brandished it in front of his face two times, as if he were performing a solemn rite.

Than inched closer to his father. "They're bones."

"You're kidding me."

"I'm not kidding you. These bones are more precious than gold. They're American bones."

Old Man Thien sniffed. He stretched his neck very long, the way he did when something truly moved him. A moment later, he whispered, "Are they real? You might be wrong."

"Dao and I dug them up," Than said. "There was a chain around the neck. Hanging from it was a tag with a name printed on it. The end of the name had peeled off, but the words 'Tony D' were still clear, and you could just read the serial number on it. Dao took the tag to try to find a buyer for the bones. Dao knows what he's doing—these are 100 percent American bones. He even took the measurements."

"If you can sell them, what kind of price can you get?"

"Dao says everybody involved in the chain gets something," said Than. "And there are a lot of people involved. But the diggers get five million and Dao and I will split that fifty-fifty."

"Shit. That is a lot of money."

"Dao is looking for a contact at the port. He's going to wait there and sell the bones to some sailors. They'll take them to America and make a lot of money. If this goes through, I'll give you five hundred thousand, O.K.?"

"It's up to you," said the father. "But if you want to last long in this business, don't try to make too much on this one deal."

"Save the advice, old man," Than retorted. "I'm giving you 500,000 dong pure profit. You don't even have to fucking sweat and you've got 500,000."

"O.K., O.K. Look, get some sleep so you'll feel strong enough to go tomorrow. I'll keep watch."

Old Man Thien squatted next to the thin bamboo door like a dog trying to fit into a kennel; his arms wrapped around his legs. Than felt reassured with his father on guard and began snoring again loudly. After his first emotional fit had subsided, the old man began to experience the strange sensation he often had when he heard that his son had money. Than never lied to his father about how much money he made. Sometimes he even exaggerated—but he never gave his father a thing. On a few occasions he even had a few million, but, after several days of betting on the lottery, it was gone. What comes in easily today goes out easily tomorrow. How could he save his money if he didn't give it to his father to keep for him? Old Man Thien both envied his son and coveted his possessions. Scheme after scheme swirled in his mind. But he was afraid of his son's temper. His mind always churned with this jumbled mix of dark thoughts and sharp fear whenever Than brought home some loot. His mouth would go dry, as if he were sucking on waterfern, and his eyes became dazed, unable to see clearly. That was the state the old man was in now. He began to doze when he felt a hand pat him lightly on the shoulder. He looked up and saw, as clearly as day, the face of an American man that was black as tar, its teeth as white as lime. The American stuck out a bony hand and stroked Old Man Thien's hair. The old man tried to move but couldn't. He felt as if his entire body had been painted with glue and now lay stuck to the floor. He tried to cry out for Than. Seeing the old man in such confusion, the black man roared with laughter, but didn't make a sound. He stood next to the old man. Only his head was intact. The rest of his body was made up of white bones. Even though he was laughing, he seemed filled with misery. In a fit of terror, Old Man Thien kicked hard against the bamboo door and the noise woke him up, and made the black man disappear. Than, who woke at that moment as well, looked groggily at his father.

"Was that Hung?" he asked.

"What Hung? It was a black guy."

"What black guy?"

"Maybe I dreamed it. I saw a black guy laughing at me."

"You dreamed you saw a black guy, Dad?" asked Than. "Shit. I had the same dream. I was terrified. I wanted to call out to you but I couldn't."

Than turned on the light. Today was the first time that this father and son, these two thieves, had ever discovered that there was something mysterious that could dominate human dreams. Something that was stronger even than man's avarice, his stupidity, his thirst for brutality.

"Did he say anything to you?" asked the father.

"No. He just laughed. And something smelled like rotten fish."

"Get that thing out of here. It's terrifying to have it in the house. Give me some incense."

Old Man Thien lit three sticks of incense, stuck them into a can of dry rice and then placed that, along with a cup of water, on the knapsack. All of his life, Old Man Thien had never offered any prayer, but at this moment he felt as if some tremendous force had invaded his body and he prostrated himself over and over in front of the knapsack.

"If your spirit is here with us, then please go to sleep, sir," he said. "Tomorrow, my son will find a way to get you back to your homeland. As it happens, my son has done a good deed for you, sir. He hasn't committed any sin. It's better for you to go back to your parents and wife and children, sir, than to remain in the jungle where no one can find you."

Than quietly listened to his father praying. He'd been to school through the seventh grade: He had trouble believing that the soul of a black soldier named Tony could hold a grudge against him. Anyway, he knew why Tony D had been killed. Evil begets evil. It was just bad karma. The soldier had killed people and so people killed him. He'd ended up all alone in the wilderness and Than, who had found him, deserved to be paid for his efforts. That was it. Besides, Than had heard that over in America people were fair minded about compensation for work.

Once Old Man Thien had finished his prayers, he again urged his son to go to sleep. But the old man didn't dare turn off the light. He sat staring out the window, waiting for dawn. As morning approached, he dozed again. He saw very clearly two bony feet walking around him and exuding a horrible stink that made him nauseated. In terror, he shut his eyes tightly, but he still heard the sound of footsteps walking around him like clanking pieces of metal. Then he fell into a deep sleep until morning.

During the days that Than was gone, Old Man Thien couldn't sleep at all. He dreamed continuously of the black soldier. At times, the soldier had flesh and he looked exactly like a black French soldier who had stayed in Vietnam after the French defeat. That guy had worked as a driver in Thien's village. Thien had still been young at that time and he remembered how once the French soldier had stopped and offered him a cigarette. But that black soldier had been such a good-natured guy. Why was this Tony so inscrutably quiet? He looked exactly like the French capitulationist, but he never said a word. He just stood in the corner of the room, staring out. Every time the old man dreamed, he'd smell the stink of bones and flesh newly unearthed from the grave.

Sometimes, he saw the white skeleton clattering around the room. It climbed onto the bed, up to the windowsill, and then, above that bone mouth, those two empty sockets gazed at him with a horrible stare. Old Man Thien had never been faint-hearted in his life, but over the past few days, his limbs went limp whenever he even considered sleeping. During the day, he locked the door and went out to the flower garden down the road. There, he climbed onto a stone bench that still held traces of night-time sexual liaisons and slept. Old Man Thien slept peacefully here, despite the wind and the glare. Such things had never bothered him. But at dusk, he had to return home. He'd leave the light on all night long and kept fiddling with the knob on his radio. He imitated Old Lady Phan by throwing salt out the window and setting sticks of burning incense in the walkway. And he listened to the noise of the herd of animals sleeping on the terrace.

Next to Old Man Thien lived Xet, who sold dogmeat at the market. Having abandoned his wife in the countryside, Xet had come into the city to open the dogmeat shop and had taken up residence in this hovel on the terrace. For a new wife, he found himself a whore to bring home. She came from the mountains and had a fair complexion and a soft voice. She was mad with happiness because she got to bathe with Camay, wear Thai panties, and use Chinese perfume. Xet pampered his new wife, taking pains to buy her things so that, at night, she would bestow on him the type of happiness an aggressive female could offer a male made extremely virile from dogmeat and liquor. He bought her a "journalist" jacket, bleached blue jeans, expensive shoes. Whenever he saw even a single new style appear among the girls who sold meat at the market, he was thrilled that his wife already had it.

Over the past few nights, the sound of Old Man Thien's footsteps had interrupted Xet and his wife. All that noise had made the tigress incapacitated by the side of the tiger. Xet's wife nestled her head into his armpit, which stank of the sweat-stink a dogmeat eater gets.

"I'm so scared of him," she whimpered in that accent of the mountainous region where, all year round, the wind passes through from Laos.

Xet stroked his wife's head exactly like he'd seen people do in the bedroom scenes he'd watched on TV. He wanted to imitate those movies by saying a few tender words of flattery and caressing his wife, but he wasn't sure how to do it. He tried hard for a moment, then gave it up:

"Fuck that crazy guy. Just ignore him. Turn over here towards me. Damn, you're getting fat as a shaved pig."

The muffled laughter of Xet and his wife sounded like sewer rats looking for food in the night. Somehow that reassured Old Man Thien. He fiddled with the radio knob, sat in the glaring light and waiting impatiently for morning to come.

* * *

A week later, Than, beside himself with joy, returned with a big bundle of money. He flashed a smile that revealed all his teeth. "I hit it big," he said.

The old man went out and bought a big package of pork chitterlings wrapped in banana leaves, a bag of fermented shrimp paste, and three kilos of rice noodles. Together, the two of them finished off the pork and all three kilos of the noodles. But then Old Man Thien realized he didn't see his son's bundle of money anywhere.

"Where'd you stuff it?"

"It's around here," said Than. "Look, I'll be gone a day and when I get back I'll give you 500,000. Don't worry. I'll keep my word."

After Than left, Old Man Thien couldn't sit still. Although it was daytime, he couldn't sleep. He scoured the whole place searching for the money. He dug into even the most secret niches and corners, but, still, he couldn't find it. By the middle of the day, he lay down on the floor exhausted, trying to figure out where else it might be. He only wanted to pull a few grand out of the heap and there was no damn way Than would ever even know. With those thoughts in mind, he dozed again—but bolted up when he saw the skeleton squatting up in the rafters.

"Fuck you!" the old man cursed, spitting out the words. "You're going back to your own country. What the hell more do you want from me?"

The skeleton kept squatting there, moving its head, its loose joints jangling like horsebells. Old Man Thien was shaken to his soul. He gestured wildly to make the skeleton stop, but it became even more energetic. The horrible stink choked him. He fought against the spectre all through his fitful sleep and, when he finally woke up, he felt frail and drained of energy, as if an ill wind had invaded him.

The next day, Old Man Thien had to go back out to the flower garden to sleep. In the afternoon, Than came home, and immediately rushed out to the garden to drag his father home.

"Come back right now!" he said.

Seeing the bloodshot eyes and purple lips of his son's rage, Old Man Thien followed him without protest. Than walked into

the house first. As soon as his father had set foot through the
door, he grabbed him by the neck.

"Where's the money?"

Old Man Thien was stupefied. "Why are you asking me
about the money?"

"I hid the money under this piece of brick. Where'd you put
it?"

Old Man Thien could only shake his head, and step back to
avoid his son's pincer-like hands. He couldn't say a word. Seeing
his father like that, Than became even more suspicious.

"Spit it out!" Than said. "You can't swallow up my sweat
and tears like that. My three million ain't peanuts!"

"I didn't take it!" Old Man Thien finally was able to stammer.

"So if you didn't take it, then who did? Spit it out!"

"I swear to you. I looked for it. I was going to pull out a
couple of bills, but I couldn't find it. I swear to you. If I'm lying,
may a train run over me and crush me."

"You'll never die. If that happens, I'll eat dog shit. Do you
get it? Spit it out! Throw it out or I'll strangle you until your
tongue comes out."

Than jumped upon the old man, grabbing the neck with its
brick-like Adam's apple. Old Man Thien let out a muffled cry
that sounded like an old dog being drowned.

"Spit it out. I wouldn't let you have it all. Spit it out, I have
to pay off my gambling debts."

"I didn't take it! I swear!"

"Your words ain't worth shit. If you didn't take it, then pick
up that knife over there and slash your face with it. If you don't,
then I'm going to wring your neck. Take the knife!"

Old Man Thien was trembling. He picked up the knife, which
was extremely sharp, and looked at his son imploringly. "Don't
make me," he said. "I didn't take your money. Listen, Son, how
could I do that? I'm an old man. It would be a sin for me to do
that."

"Slash your face!"

"No! How can I bear the pain?"

"O.K. If you're not going to slash your face, then chop off a finger. Do it now. I'm not going to believe you until you do it. If you don't do it, I'll strangle you to death. Chop it off!"

The son ran toward the old man. His face glowed with cruelty. Dazed and looking pitiful, Old Man Thien put his finger onto the hard edge of the bed and looked at Than.

"Swear it!" Than screamed. "Cut it off. You insect! Cut it off or I'll pull out your tongue."

The old man raised the knife and swung it down with an awful thud. In a spurt of blood, the index finger of his left hand fell to the floor. Than watched without a flicker of emotion, but when his father's face went pale and his mouth flinched in a spasm of pain, the young man came to his senses. He turned and walked out the door, taking care to step around the blood on the floor. He was burning with the desire to get his revenge against whoever had stolen his three million with so little sweat. The finger lying on the floor had perhaps convinced him that Old Man Thien had told the truth. But who had taken it? How could he find the money to repay his debt? The owner of the gambling den would throw acid on his face. Goddammit. These days, the winner is anybody willing to take a chance. I'll run away he thought. He began walking unsteadily, as if he were drunk, his mind already drifting off to the holy land—Hong Kong.

Seeing Than going down the stairs with such determination, Old Lady Phan wanted to smile at him but didn't dare. His face was so frightening, as if he'd just drunk human blood. She was about to enter her hovel when she heard Old Man Thien moaning.

She had no idea what had happened, but she screamed anyway: "Murder! Someone's been murdered!"

They found Old Man Thien with his head against his chest, sucking on his wounded hand, the blood dyeing his chin red and running down his shirt. This bulky man with such a good appetite but so little desire to think, this brutal bully now, at this moment, became so withered that even a cruel-hearted child would have pitied him. Old Man Thien felt faint. He could see a white skeleton looking at him through the mist, a blurry skeleton, moving slightly and raising its hand toward the top of its head. The old man thought that it was calling to him, so he began to approach it. But no, it turned out that the skeleton was only saluting. This time the skeleton even let out a high-pitched laugh like that of a woman. The old man wanted to return the salute but he couldn't do it. His hands were tied tightly.

Old Man Thien vaguely heard the sounds of voices.

"He's just come to. Go get a cyclo to take him to the clinic. A cyclo will give him the smoothest ride."

Someone said something vulgar. Then there was the high-pitched laugh of a woman. Old Man Thien recognized it as Old Lady Phan's. And the herd of animals with whom he had lived on the terrace all this time had become human beings; huddling beside him. They bandaged his wound, washed his face, and put a new shirt on him. Then he was carried down the stairs toward the emergency clinic.

* * *

Since then, Old Man Thien has never dreamed of the skeleton or the black soldier again. He is at peace, except for the fact that Than disappeared without a trace.

One night, not long after, Xet urged his wife to get in bed earlier than usual. Embracing her plump body with his two dog-killing arms, breathing the stink of alcohol into her face, he said: "You know, Babe, tomorrow, I'm going to buy you a really fancy fur coat."

"Where'd you get the money for something so cool?" she asked. She'd begun to pick up the lingo of the city.

"I found it. But don't go blabbing. I'll cut out your tongue if you do, you hear? Pretty soon, I'm going to get myself a Honda Cub and you'd better tell people it's my money, you hear? If you don't do what I tell you, I'll cut you up. I got myself a big piece of it and if he finds out, they'll put me away. You got it?"

She laughed loudly like someone screaming. Like someone whose throat were being slit. She laughed like that every night. And every night, the terrace is enveloped in heavy sleep after a day during which the tenants had struggled to feed themselves. Now Xet and his wife stay up the latest and make the most noise. The two of them remain animals even when nightfall has made the others human.

Tonight is oppressively hot, and the sky shows signs of a storm approaching. Old Man Thien is experiencing pain in what remains of his finger. He sits on the windowsill looking out, waiting for the rain to soothe his wound. Out there is the city, with its houses piled up against each other. The soldier Tony D isn't bothering him any more. The old man feels content again, like a genuine lord. He only feels dissatisfied at moments like this one, when he is gnawed by a blood-red pain that makes him sick of living.

Suddenly a thought strikes him. It was that black soldier who stole the money! Damn him! No wonder ever since the day he took it he's never shown his face here again. What an asshole!

1991

A Very Late Afternoon

There were thousands of employees in the research institute, but few of them knew each other, or if they did, it was only casually. Near the entrance was a drink shop. The intellectuals, with almost nothing to do, spent their time there downing beers or cups of coffee as dark as night. Tan was one of the people who often spent his priceless eight hours this way.

Tan was sitting there arguing about horoscopes with his friend Quang when Van, a recent graduate of F2, came in and handed him an envelope.

"It's from Hang!" he said, then turned and went out.

Tan opened the letter. On the back of a business card, she had written, "I have something important I want to discuss with you. If you're willing, please come to my house this Monday night. Don't let anyone see this note."

What was so important? He put the letter in his pocket without giving it much thought. When people are over thirty, nothing deserves much attention. And, nowadays, with the future foggy, one had to enjoy whatever pleasures each day brought. The more one could enjoy oneself, the better.

Tan told himself all this in a leisurely manner. But then he remembered Hang. He had only spoken with her a couple of times. Once he heard her deliver a scientific paper. She was a doctoral candidate, no longer young, and there was nothing special about her except that she had very beautiful eyes. Her eyes were of the kind that are usually inherited from one's lineage, perhaps from her grandmothers and her mother, who must have been beautiful women. Also, she didn't dress in the noisy, exhibitionist style of many of the women her age. Rather, she had a strange, almost frightened look about her that only the truly observant would notice. Once, when he had said hello, she had whipped around and her face went pale as she stared at him. Only now did that look strike him as strange. In general, she was quiet, and seemed content with her work, which centered on highly complex scientific problems that a woman would wear herself out pursuing. Looking at her, men would offer her the respect they gave their elder sisters. Nothing else.

Quang, seeing his friend sit so quietly after putting the letter in his pocket, chuckled and winked. "What does she need from you? Is there a meeting?"

Tan shook his head.

Quang said, "It's strange. How can these women live in this country and believe they'll be the next Marie Curie? Marie Curie on a rickety bicycle, living for a whole month on the food that a female black market dealer would eat in a single meal. Their bodies are like dried-out stalks of spinach. Women should be like that woman over there. A delight for the eyes!"

He pointed to a young woman walking by. A drink seller in the institute, she was buxom and fresh and when the wind tickled her behind the ears, she wiggled her neck and giggled. She often blushed and she was so languid that her arms and legs looked ready to go limp at any time. She was soft and inviting, like a foam mattress.

Quang said slowly, "Here's another strange thing. Hang's destiny is the moon and she's both talented and beautiful. But up until now, she's never been in love. And she has no plans to get married or have children, either."

"How do you know?"

"We were in the same class at school. She used to be really pretty!"

Tan, who was not particularly interested in what Quang had to say, was thinking, "Each of us has our own destiny and it's not something I'm going to concern myself with."

That afternoon, Tan caught sight of Hang in the bicycle parking lot. He didn't understand why she turned away just as he was about to walk toward her. The next Monday night, he didn't go to her house. On Tuesday morning, he knocked on her office door. She was wearing a white lab coat and rubber gloves as if she were about to leave for the laboratory. He looked at her pale face and her passionate black eyes, which would have been so out of place in a laboratory, and said, "You asked me to come over, but I was too busy to come. You must have had something to talk with me about. You can talk to me about it here."

A cold look passed over her eyes. "No. I can't talk about it here," she said. "But never mind. I found what I needed. I was going to ask a favor, but it's taken care of already."

Someone called to her from inside the room. She disappeared immediately, but her angry eyes kept haunting him. That afternoon, Tan skipped his tennis game at the institute and went home early. He had recently been divorced and he and his wife had never had children. Their life together hadn't been disastrous, but the two of them had been like two arrows flying in opposite directions. Tan's ex-wife was a singer who performed in the city's youth troupe and it wasn't long before he discovered a labyrinth of relationships. She had the youthful illusion that life is infinite and she never knew when to stop. As for Tan, he had always tried to make her realize life's limits. The two of them were like a couple on the dance floor. Both of them had realized that the lights were going up and they'd better go back to their separate seats.

In this world, which was as annoying as a headache, a family needed a stream of cool water, not the heat of burning conflict. After the divorce, both of them were able to relax. They were both relieved and so they were able to say hello when they ran into each other on the street. Sometimes, when she couldn't find a dancing partner, she'd even come and drag him out with her. She'd already introduced him to three of her new lovers but it seemed that each of those relationships had been inconclusive.

Tan's mother had set her sights on a new young lady for him, a shining beauty. Her face was Hong Kong style, which was so much the fashion nowadays that he often mistook other women for her in the street. She had permed hair, a nose so straight it looked sculpted, a pretty and cheerful mouth, and pricey glasses that covered half her face. The odd thing about those women with Hong Kong-style faces was that they also walked and smiled and talked in exactly the same way. Tan didn't feel much emotion when he went on a date with that woman. She was the result of imported commodities, of sidewalks lit by multi-colored lights, of restaurants, and dance floors. She displayed everything that people desired after long years of deprivation. She was alert, simple, easily moved, and as forgetful as a child. Maybe he needed a person like that.

Seeing him arrive, she always jumped up, smiled, and began to chatter incessantly. At the movies, she would crack sunflower seeds and, without noticing, drop all the husks onto the floor by her feet. Then she would give Tan her hand. Through her hand, she wanted to offer her whole trivial life to this thirty-two-year-old man, much too old for a woman who was only twenty-one.

But on days like this, Tan remembered Hang. He decided, abruptly, to go to her house. He barely knew her, so this was the first time he had ever been there. It turned out that she lived by herself on the second floor of a noisy building, an ancient villa that had once been the warm nest of a middle-class family. After the revolution, the house had been divided into six or seven smaller apartments and now it looked like a merchant train, bent beneath the weight of too many passengers. Opposite was a flea market and under her window was a public water tap. Consequently, the fifteen square meter room sat between two pockets of obscenities, one coming from the market and the other from the inhabitants of her house. Still, when she closed her window, she must have been able to shut out all the noise.

Tan looked around the room. Everything was neat and comfortable, as if it were ready to receive someone. The scent of cheap perfume exuded from the curtain on the door, from the bookshelf, from the tablecloth, and even her hair. For some reason, he felt offended, as if she'd been waiting for him. Would a scientist, even a female one, need such excessive comforts? Near Tan's house lived an artist who worked for the army. He lived alone, far from his wife and children, who stayed in the countryside. The decor in his room resembled that of a cunning hunter out to ensnare the young deer: A statue of Venus. A tree branch stretching out from a corner, giving freshness to the room. An embroidered silk quilt covering the bed. Many wholesome deer had been ensnared there. Tan had some very harsh feelings about that fellow's room. Strangely, he had a similar feeling when he came here.

At first, Hang's eyes brightened with surprise and joy. Or at least Tan thought they did when he stepped inside and bowed slightly to greet her. He hesitated before sitting down on the upholstered chair, his elbows lightly touching its soft fabric. Everything was comfortable, not as wobbly as his things at home. He asked a question and she answered. Then she said something and he asked something else. For the most part, he did not feel at ease. On the wall opposite him hung a painting in the classical style: At nightfall, a forest was turning dark green and the water under a bridge shone violet. Gazing at the picture, Tan somehow felt worried about her and the infinite loneliness of a woman approaching forty. He thought about the women who had been victimized by the war. Their boyfriends were dead. They carried their age with such hardship and, while their beauty grew more faded every day, they were left to watch the next generation grow up and float before their eyes like clusters of colored balloons at a carnival. Nowadays, literature often reflected on this matter, gradually moving even the young people, who had their own achievements but had never held a gun.

"Were you ever on the battlefield?" he asked her.

"Why do you want to know?"

"I thought people your age often went," he said.

"Why would I go?" she asked.

Tan was surprised by her rebuttal. In this country, nobody spoke like that.

Her voice was soothing. "My father and my two older brothers all died on the battlefield at Tay Nguyen," she said. "Isn't that enough already?"

Tan nodded.

She had stayed in school, she told him. She went to university abroad, then studied four years beyond that. Jumping headlong into that cursed program, she became a victim of things that were dark, chaotic, and impractical. Women shouldn't spend their lives around guns, she said, but they shouldn't spend their time immersed in those other things, either. As she said these things, her voice was as soft as a breath.

Tan felt her grow more quiet, and that quiet made him more alert. He said goodbye, asking one more question, thinking he might have already figured out what she needed from him. She needed someone by her side to listen to her innermost feelings because the emptiness of her world made her frightened. He didn't know if he were correct or not, but the thought of this upset him. Although his life wasn't that interesting, how could she have the nerve to turn back toward someone so young?

Still, he repeated his question in order to pull her out of her reflections.

"Is there anything else you need from me?"

"No," she said, "I'm sorry I put you to so much trouble. It was just a technical matter, and I've solved it already."

* * *

Tan searched for ways to avoid her, but it was only a few days before he realized that this was unnecessary. She avoided him. Or, if she couldn't avoid him, she would nod her greeting coldly. Her cool expression sometimes made him angry. Clearly, she was a woman of some experience. When his anger cooled, though, he realized he had been unreasonable. Obviously, something had already pulled her away and she simply didn't notice him anymore.

He continued to take out the curly-haired girl, to listen to the sound of cracking sunflower seeds, to smell the Thai perfume on her cheeks and the scent of French shampoo in her hair, and sometimes he would help her carry her Japanese purse, which was made of soft leather and extremely beautiful. When she flung her bare arm around his shoulders, the Swiss watch on her delicate wrist tickled the back of his neck. Her laughter and her voice were trivial and coarse. Generally speaking, in contrast to their early, happier days, now she often caused him to feel both bored and dejected. He had returned to the state of lethargy he'd experienced following his divorce, and every day became routine.

These days, the institute held many conferences, which, although a waste of time, offered people a welcome distraction. Tan saw Hang at these conferences and during the sessions he often observed her. She looked so sad, as if even the slightest word would make her cry.

One afternoon, an institute van was taking cadres to inspect some experimental scientific projects in another, smaller city. The van was filled with people and Tan took a seat in the back, hoping that he could sleep a bit, having heard that they would arrive at ten o'clock at night and go to the sites immediately. He had barely put his head against the back of the seat and closed his eyes when he felt someone sit down beside him. He glanced over. It was Hang. It seemed that she, too, had only just noticed him and she instantly stood up and looked toward the front of the van to see if any empty seats remained. At that moment, the van began to pull away and Tan grabbed her arm and pulled her down beside him.

He asked, "I haven't seen you in two weeks. Where have you disappeared to?"

She adjusted herself in her seat, then smiled slightly. "Why would I disappear? Where could I disappear to?"

The van left the city. It was mid-afternoon, the end of autumn and rather chilly, a time when a sudden, unreasonable sadness seemed to envelop Hang's soul. It came in a manner that was hard to comprehend, and, though unnecessary, unavoidable. The male scientists would probably call such moments "excessive luxuries." The woman sitting next to Tan put her hands in her lap and turned to gaze out the window. Suddenly looking relaxed, freed of her inhibitions, she was like a young girl before his eyes. Tan put his arm around her shoulders. She wasn't startled and she didn't blush and jerk away, but, a moment later, she gently pushed his arm off.

After a long while, as if out of deep compassion, he said, "Tell me. Why are you so miserable?"

"I'm not miserable at all, but, okay, let me tell you something."

Then she told him her story, which, beneath the rumble of the van, was only loud enough for him to hear.

It turned out that she had had her youth and that she had loved. Just out of high school, with her hair in two long pigtails, she wore black silk pants and high-heeled plastic clogs, the latest fashion for a Northern girl during wartime. One afternoon in the fall, on deserted Co Ngu Street, which ran between two lakes, the chain came off the Unification bicycle she'd borrowed from her mother. She tinkered with it until she was sweating profusely, but she still couldn't put it back.

"Can I help?"

It was a rather unusual voice, unlike the artificial male voices she often heard. It was low and warm, rich in tone, and couldn't have been produced in this poor country. She looked up. He was European, with brown eyes, brown hair, and a beauty that pierced her sixteen-year-old heart.

"I can help you!" he said, immediately bending down beside her. His hands were firm and deft and in only three minutes he had finished fixing the bike.

"Thank you."

"It's nothing."

They spoke and looked at each other. All her trouble faded into the background and there were only the two of them.

"Where do you come from?" she asked. "Why do you speak Vietnamese so well?"

"My name's Louis. I'm French," he answered. "I'm studying Vietnamese here."

"I'm Mai," she gave him the nickname her mother had called her when she was small, then held out her hand to him.

"Mai! Mai!" He repeated the name and smiled. It was such a human smile. She had never seen a man smile so beautifully. It was the kind of smile that made people want to live that beautiful a life. The two lakes seemed to ripple. She and the Frenchman looked at each other strangely, as if they had just discovered in each other something for which they had been searching for a long time.

"You're so beautiful," he said. "Please let me meet you again. Here. Any day this week."

"No!" she suddenly said it loudly. "I can't."

"Why not?"

A man with a white shirt and green pants wearing military shoes peddled by. Then he turned around and rode toward them again. A pair of brutal eyes pierced her face. A shiver ran through her and she felt her skin crawl. People said that in this country talking to a foreigner, regardless of the subject, could get you followed, even arrested. "No! no!" she repeated. "I can't." She shook her head with a force the young man could not understand at all. He was afraid that perhaps he had offended the modesty of this young Asian woman. She got back on her bicycle and began to ride off. When he tried to follow her, she frantically waved him away. The young man watched her go, with a surprised look on his face.

As she was riding through a crowded street, she felt that someone was following her. She rode faster and he rode faster. She rode slower and he slowed down. She turned down a nearly empty road. He followed her. She stopped her bike to buy a baguette from a cart. The man stopped his bike beneath a nearby tree and lit a cigarette. She got back on her bike and he got back on his. Her heart was beating wildly. Even after she got home, she was still trembling as she sat down next to the dinner tray.

When her mother, worried, asked what was wrong, she whispered in reply, "I don't know why, but something scared me."

That night, she dreamed that two eyes pressed like burning coals against her temples, so hot it made her scream.

After that, in the market, or when she stood in line to buy rice, or sat in the library reading a book, someone was always following her. They had different faces, but they all resembled each other with their dark frowns, with their terrible stares that made her tremble. As for the young man, he kept looking for her all over the city. Riding his bike, he ventured into even the smallest and most empty streets, often turning to look at the girls who looked like her. Whenever she went out, she put on a conical hat to cover her hair and conceal her face. Then, at the bookstore one evening, she found herself face to face with him. She couldn't run away.

He stood in front of her, breathing heavily with happiness. "I found you!" he said, and put out an arm to prevent her from running away. "Please, only one minute."

He said something in a trembling voice but she had turned very white. He made a gesture as if to help her. She couldn't hear anything else he said because at that moment a man in a white shirt approached where they were standing, leaned against a bookshelf, and pretended to browse through the titles. The young man gave her his business card.

"Please take this," he said, "and when it's convenient for you, give me a call. I really want to see you."

"Yes, yes!" she said.

"What are you so terrified of?" he asked.

"I'm really afraid. Don't look for me any more. I don't have permission."

"Why not?"

"I don't know. But oh, please," she exclaimed those words and then abruptly turned away. But she couldn't leave because of the look on the young man's face. Putting aside her fear, she smiled to reassure him

On her way home, she had to ride through a small alley. The road was empty. A Soviet military jeep pulled up beside her and screeched to a stop. Several hands reached out and forced her into the car. She screamed. A hand covered her mouth. "It's her!" a rough voice said. "Let's search her to see if she got anything from him." He snatched the business card that the Frenchman had given her, which she hadn't had a chance to look at yet. The car drove slowly through the streets. She saw the people outside. She was terrified because suddenly she had been removed from that stream of normal life.

She screamed, "What have I done? Who are you?" She asked many times, trying to pull herself away, even pinching the arms of the driver. The driver, who seemed the nicest of the men sitting around her, spoke with a Nghe accent, "We're the Red Flag Youth—security. We have a few things we need to ask you."

"But why did you force me into this car?"

No one answered her question. In despair, she scratched and pinched them until they took some parachute cord and tied her hands behind her back. The car drove to the central square, slowing down to let a woman lead her child across the street. The men discussed something among themselves, whispering about the business card. Then they searched her bag, turning every page of the book she'd just bought. They untied the handkerchief that she'd wrapped around some apples, shoved into her bag in the early afternoon, and forgotten to eat. The questions continued.

"How many times have you met with him?"

"Only twice!"

"Why did you pretend that your bike was broken?"

"No. It was really broken!" She cried like a child. "Why? It was really broken."

"Don't lie to us!"

With her tears streaming down and her hands tied behind her back, she had to wipe her face with her knees.

"What was the content of your meetings?"

"There was nothing! We were just chatting."

"Repeat it all."

She was able to repeat every word that she and the young Frenchman had said to each other because she remembered it so clearly. They were normal words but they contained everything that they had felt for each other. She repeated the words but she couldn't describe for them the look in the Frenchman's eyes, or the beating of her own heart. The men showered her with more questions about her family and about her mother and father. They looked at each other when she said that her father and two brothers were at the front.

A week after that, she was ordered to the district prison, which was filled with prostitutes, street vendors, and people who had been living at the train station without any documents. She was called to come there three times, at night, so that her situation would seem more frightening. All three times, she repeated her name, her age, and what she had said in the car among the fierce group of men. Then they gave her a citation—Unlawful relationship with a foreigner—which she had to sign, promising that this relationship would not continue and that, if there were any sign of that boy, she would let them know.

She stepped out the door of the police station and from that moment, she had lost her youth, her trust, and her carefree innocence. After that, she was often jumpy and her arms and legs went limp when anyone suddenly called her name. For months, she didn't dare to venture into the street, because the sight of any military jeep would terrify her. She was afraid of catching sight of any foreigner. At night, she wouldn't sleep alone and whenever her mother worked the third shift, she'd stay awake until her mother came home. But the strangest thing was that, mixed with those horrible fears was a torment, a pain that nothing could surpass, and that was the pain she felt when she thought of the first young man in her life. She knew that he would still be searching for her, on his bicycle, through the streets of the city. Once she barely missed meeting him. He was sitting in a car with a man in front of a store reserved for foreigners. He didn't see her and she cried the innocent tears reserved for a sweetheart.

"With love, we need only that many meetings and that many words. No more than that, don't you think so?"

She asked that question without looking at Tan.

Tan was thoughtful. "Perhaps Louis was a spy, or something like that."

"Not at all. My mother asked an acquaintance who was very high ranking in the security branch. Louis was only a student, completely harmless."

"Why were you still allowed to go study abroad?"

"A year later, we were informed of the deaths of my father and two brothers. My oldest brother was proclaimed a hero. Thanks to that, I was allowed to go abroad. But even while I was abroad, it seemed like they still kept an eye on me. I felt it. I don't know if it was true or not."

"How weird!"

"It wasn't weird at all. In my youth, people thought differently. Now, in our poor country, foreigners have such high status they are thought of as Gods." She smiled bitterly, then added, "From that day on, I became an old woman. For over twenty years, I've only been an old woman. I lost my will to fight. I was constantly afraid."

"It's your own fault. You're too sensitive. That's not good."

"Maybe it's my fault," she agreed

"Are you still afraid now?" he asked.

"At my age, women have been through everything, and can pretty much sleep peacefully. What more could I be afraid of? There's nothing left to fear."

Night had fallen. Tan felt as if she had grown even smaller and he could understand her sorrow. She spoke like this because she had loved so passionately. She had loved that stranger.

Hang leaned her head against Tan's shoulder and said, "I'm hopeless."

He took her hand. It was trembling, youthful and full of desire, not the despair she had expressed. But when he hugged her in the darkness that had descended on the van, she gently pushed him away. "No," she said, "It isn't necessary anymore. The other day, I needed you, because you were the only person around who I didn't feel was a stranger. I left you a message and you didn't come. Now it's over."

Tan continued to go out and continued to be sick of the woman who would soon be his wife. By marrying her, he would be bringing all the colors of the sidewalks, of the dance clubs, and of the posh and elegant restaurants into his family. And through her face, he could have everything, except the emotions he had had with a miserable woman, a scientist, a person who had been stripped of her passion and love for another human being ever since the first day she stepped into adult life. Maybe that group of men had only been carrying out their public duty to prevent an unusual relationship. Perhaps they didn't know that they had destroyed a young person's soul.

These days, Hang seemed to withdraw into herself even more. She very rarely appeared at the institute meetings. She was heading a project for an industrial dehumidifier. Tan went to her office and even to her home, but he still couldn't find her. He felt nervous and worried and was surprised at himself: neither his former wife nor fiancee had caused him as much worry as this.

One cold night, he rode his bicycle all the way across the city to Hang's house. His worries weren't unfounded. She had packed all her luggage, preparing to move to the South to live with her mother and sister-in-law, the wife of her heroic brother. The house looked empty. The painting in the classical style had also been packed and placed on the divan. She was wearing a woolen turtleneck dress that covered her knees and she looked like a young girl. He hugged her, feeling her whole body trembling.

"Why are you leaving?" he asked.

"I'm running away from you."

"Is it so urgent?"

"Very urgent. I must go. I can't stand living here any longer," she answered.

The winter night was long and freezing. The two of them never slept. She was passionate and, yet, as clumsy as a child. The woman's virgin body touched the young man deeply and he loved her.

Outside was the winter night. The train blew its whistle in the station. There were only a few hours left and then they would be separated forever. He knew that after these moments, the two of them would never see each other again.

1990

The Coolie's Tale

The neighborhood of the university professors had long been as quiet as a cemetery. Suddenly there was so much commotion that it seemed like a flying saucer had landed in the schoolyard.

"That wench Canh is coming home."

"She's back already. I heard she just arrived at the airport."

"Now we'll see who's the boss."

Professor Tri said bitterly, "Now is no different from any other time. The toads and frogs always rise to the top. It's scary."

He crossed his legs, his gangly skeletal form looking like a wooden frame beneath his wool jacket. Then he turned his face up to look out the window, his hand reaching up to pluck at some invisible whiskers. He always did this when he began to think that no one else in the world compared with him.

During his time, things were not as awful as they were now. The university had been an ivory tower, high above the masses. Anyone admitted had to fulfill many requirements. Basically, that meant that they, as well as their ancestors, had to have been common laborers who had never eaten a full meal. They had to have lived their whole lives as coolies. It was for this reason that, once they were admitted into the university, they would be able to absorb all the lofty ideas of humanity. The school had been bustling then and people could act haughty, while pretending to be humble in order to assimilate with the multitudes. The staff was free-floating. Teachers who had relatives and friends in the countryside brought them around to enjoy the free government rice while they worked as cooks, security personnel, supply clerks and myriad other jobs that demanded no formal education.

Miss Canh had been the younger sister of the wife of the school's head cook. She was short and had a pockmarked face and because she was so dimwitted she always looked a bit zany. The cook had asked permission to hire her and so she came to the city to become a dishwasher although there were already more than ten. On top of that, she brought along a girl, a niece or something in her family. The two were just alike, making meaningless sounds all day, not quite deaf and not quite dumb, but somewhere in between. But they had their rice ration booklet and their food stamps. They became city dwellers. Miss Canh was allowed a space big enough for a single bed right next to the pigsty in the kitchen. She was in charge of cleaning up the pigsty, and she also washed dishes after the students ate. The advantage of this job was that she could sneak a big piece of rice crust from the bottom of the pot and hide it in her bed so that late at night the two of them could snack on it. At that time, the students never had enough to eat and their food rations only served to coat their stomachs. If it were up to them, there never would have been even a rice crust left over. Miss Canh lived this humble life, well-liked by the professors who found her gentle and diligent. Whenever they came back from somewhere, they would pass her and her niece potatoes, cassava, candy, or maybe some old clothes that she could mend and wear. She accepted it all with the silent gratitude of a person who had kept her nose to the ground her entire life. Things went on like that for a few years.

Then, circumstances changed. The university was bloated with staff and the order to cut back was handed down from above. Anyone above a certain age would be forced to retire. Anyone without a skill had to be transferred somewhere else. Every department was responsible for its own staff. In addition, five slots were reserved for those workers who had made the biggest contributions to the university or who had suffered the most, and these workers would go overseas to become coolies for white people. Miss Canh had made no contribution but she came from the very bottom and so she was chosen first. She sent her niece back to the countryside, then packed up to be on her way. She cried her heart out for the goodwill of the professors and also out of fear: With no education, how could she survive in that strange land? The professors had to endlessly try to cheer her up.

Soon after she'd arrived, that Western country suddenly became reunited. News flared up about the extraordinary power of its currency. Then rumors began to filter back about the great fortune of the guest workers, which was rising with the currency. Because of that, on the day of Miss Canh's return, the teachers closed the door and sat inside, but in fact they were impatient. After five years, the school had changed, but Miss Canh, they reasoned, had probably changed much more. Was she still short? No, she would be tall and plump. The butter and milk were not second-rate overseas. Was she still as dimwitted as before? Not now! In fact, she would be quite eloquent. If not, how could she have survived in a place where people talked as enthusiastically as they worked? After she came back, she would wear skirts and high heels and pay visits to all the professors. Every professor would receive a gift and, because she understood their thinking and their empty stomachs, all of these gifts would be something to eat. Food was the highest priority. All the professors would flatter her as they received their gifts, but, inside, they would burn with jealousy. Damn! They had heard that she was worth eight hundred million now. Even if they sold the whole school and all of its facilities, they wouldn't get half that amount.

Miss Canh bought a piece of land near the gates of the school and built a house so that later on she could do business more easily. The house had to be close to the street so that it would bring in big profits. In no time at all, the concrete house was finished. All the doors were made of wood as hard as iron. There were two stories and a flat roof, exactly like the houses owned by the city's *nouveaux riche*. All around the front she planted flowers. The gate that opened onto the street was made of decorative iron. Also like the *nouveaux riche*, she kept a German shepherd as big as a cow that stood near the gate and growled. On the porch a Pekinese no bigger than someone's hand frolicked and clung to the skirt of its mistress every time she walked in or out. Miss Canh had also sent for the young girl from the countryside she'd once raised. That girl cooked, went to the market and, like her aunt, could anyone consider her stupid? No way. Now she wore backless dresses and looked down on everyone. The aunt and her niece brightened up the gates of the school. It was said that every night the aunt let her niece go to dancing lessons downtown.

Every morning, Miss Canh drank milk and ate bread with butter on it. While she ate, she reflected on the time she'd spent abroad. Because she was poor, she was thrifty, and able to save all the money she'd made. Then one day, an elderly Westerner noticed her and winked. She went with him and experienced the Western smell, which was both fatty and redolent of milk. He gave her money. Great! She told herself that she was poor so she needed to work hard. And because she was hardworking, she was willing to take on this second job as well. She did it for both Westerners and Vietnamese, who were far from home themselves. After she received compensation for agreeing to return to Vietnam, she was even richer. If she hadn't had to pay taxes on it, she would have been even more successful. Diligence brings bounty. Thanks to her hard work, she was able to relax today, drinking milk with her ornamental dog. Usually, after breakfast, she liked to go for a walk in the little road behind the school. She wore a skirt and pulled her hair back into a ponytail with a ribbon around it. Her skirt was the latest fashion, with two front pockets into which she thrust her plump hands as she walked along. The white Pekinese followed her.

"Oh! Oh! Minu! Get on over here," she called out.

She'd learned "Oh! Oh!" in the West. She also tried to imitate the Westerners who called their dogs "Milu," but she was from a region where people couldn't pronounce their "l's."

Whenever he heard her call her dog "Minu," Professor Tri would snicker. "She even gives her dog a Western name," he laughed.

Professor Tri really bore a grudge towards Miss Canh. He came from a line of mandarins that stretched back for three generations. Little Master Tri both went to school and had a private tutor at home. He also had a nanny who fanned him while he slept. Sometimes he greeted his heavily perfumed mother as she stepped down from the family automobile. Eventually, the little master joined the revolution and became a cadre. During the period of reform, he had to sign an oath to break off ties with his family in order to maintain his purity. As a reward for abandoning his parents, he was able to secure for himself a teaching position in a "top secret" school. His parents had arranged for him to marry the daughter of a mandarin and one-time provincial governor, but after a few rectification campaigns he divorced her. Then he married Miss Tham, a district cadre whose face was as big as a winnowing basket. Tham loved to deliver loud speeches to an audience of thousands. At home, every time she opened her mouth, she tried to lecture him on the class struggle. Spending his whole life next to that loudspeaker meant he couldn't think clearly and, on top of that, he had to contend with six wild ducks—his daughters. These days, his wife's love of giving speeches had diminished a bit and she had consented to return to her hometown in order to take care of the altars of her ancestors. While there, she had even managed to grow some vegetables to feed those wild ducks of theirs. As for the oldest of the flock, the mother sent her back to live with her father. Professor Tri put her in a dormitory.

Over the past few years, the number of students in the school had decreased. Now there were more professors than students and, to make matters worse, these professors had spent their whole lives accumulating abstract knowledge and therefore none of them had any skills that would help them earn extra money. His salary, including seniority bonuses and fringe benefits, only amounted to 98,000. He had three college degrees. He had studied until his hair fell out, until nothing was left of him but bones. All his life he had lectured about the future of humanity and now his intellect and energy were reserved for one thing. One lofty thing. That was to sit and calculate how to keep his expenses within the reach of his salary.

He was obliged to send 30,000 back home to his wife. Another 20,000 went toward the studies of his eldest daughter. The rest was for him. He bought meat once a week. Eighty grams. He cut it up into chunks as small as the pieces on his chess set then marinated it in fish sauce until every last molecule was full of salt. He fried it until it was completely dry, then put it in a jar. For every meal, he would take out two pieces. Even those two pieces eaten with rice sufficed to give him the feeling that he was getting his protein. He also had tofu and he made sure to buy the kind that was already fried, so that he wouldn't have to use up any fat. He chopped it and mixed it with fermented shrimp and salt, then cooked it dry. In this way, he was able to have a small piece for every meal. For a special treat, he would boil an egg, cut it in half and use it to flavor his fish sauce. Vegetables were easier to come by because the school had a large yard and if he was willing to put the energy into it, he could have a meal on all the wild plants. Still, he had to spend money on rice, on electricity, and he also needed to save something in case of sneezing or a runny nose. In the past, he had lectured to thousands, feeling full of enthusiasm, adrenaline, passion, and faith. Now, sitting there calculating his small salary gave him a headache.

Miss Canh was not an ingrate. She knew who had helped her out in the past by slipping her potatoes and cassava and now she sometimes returned the kindness. But she had to be fair in returning every kindness, or else the professors would resent each other out of jealousy. She really sympathized with Professor Tri. One day, she brought him an entire bottle of cooking oil. Another day, she brought him half a kilo of pork sausage and a dozen eggs. She only had to take a little pinch out of her marks in order to return every kindness. In the past, had she patronized him this way, he might have hurled curses in her face ("An intellectual like me? Never!") But now, his face, sunken from malnutrition, would brighten. A bottle of cooking oil meant that he could save 30,000, which was no small thing.

He accepted her kindness, but after she left he would snicker, "Damn! The toads and frogs always rise to the top!"

* * *

I used to study with Professor Tri. His knowledge was so impressive that his students could never forget him. One New Year's Eve, I went back to school to visit him. The vast courtyard, which used to be crowded with students, was now as quiet as death. Seeing a little boy playing by himself, I walked over and asked, "Are all the professors out?"

"No, ma'am. They're all asleep."

"But it's four o'clock in the afternoon!"

"Every afternoon, they sleep until almost dark and then they get up to cook their dinner."

I knocked lightly on the door and instantly heard my professor say, "Come in."

The house was pitch dark. I groped for the light switch and when I found it, it gave off a reddish yellow light. The professor crawled out from under a thin blanket wearing a quilted jacket and a wool cap, the whole bit. Everything. As if he were walking outside.

I asked, "Are you sick, Professor?"

He snickered. "No, I'm not sick at all. But without enough to eat in this freezing weather it's best to crawl under the blanket after a meal, to slow one's digestion. It's just a way to conserve energy, that's all. If you walk around a lot, you'll feel hungry very quickly and once you're hungry, you'll really freeze."

His voice sounded lethargic, as if he were "conserving energy." I opened a window to let in more light. From his window, I could see Miss Canh's new house. She was standing inside the fence, wearing a short-sleeved dress. Lord, even in this cold weather, she looked fresh in that dress. One of her hands was caressing the head of her German shepherd and the other was gesticulating here and there. She was chattering with a guy who'd come over on a motorbike and was standing with one leg up on the steps of her house. The guy had a great build and was probably strong enough to strangle a water buffalo. His motorbike seemed no less aggressive and was shining like a great chunk of gold. He and Miss Canh were flirting with each other exactly like the *nouveaux riche* who were popping up everywhere in the city with utter contempt for everyone else.

Once again, Professor Tri said lethargically, "Close the window. Her music is as loud as guns at war. It makes my ears ring."

He sat down in a chair and even in the way his shoulders hunched behind his head I could see that he was "conserving energy."

1989

An Evening Away from the City

The driver raised his hands helplessly and said in that familiar half-joking, half-serious voice, "My dear passengers, this car won't be leaving this afternoon. I'll be looking around this desolate place for spare parts and, when I find them, I'll fix us up right away. We'll all rally back around the car here at nine o'clock tomorrow morning. Until then, go ahead and wander wherever you like."

Tan was the only woman among three colleagues from the same office who were traveling together. The driver's words made her uncomfortable. The three of them began a lively discussion of the situation because they weren't really familiar with the place. Perhaps the only thing to do would be to ask if they could sleep in the village committee building. But what about food? The men, who were in the prime of life, were always hungry. Mostly, though, they were worried about Tan.

"She looks down, doesn't she?" one of them said.

Tan smiled, almost apologetically.

Her friends were continuing to tease her when a plan crossed her mind. More than a year earlier, Vien had written to her and said that she was living in this area, in the housing set aside for hospital staff.

"How far is it from here to the provincial center?" Tan asked.

The driver smiled. "More than three kilometers. In those high heels, don't even think of crossing that field over there."

"I'll just give it a shot," she said, taking off her shoes. She set them down in the trunk of the car and slipped a spare pair of plastic sandals on her feet. The driver looked at the sandals and, nodding his head, winked.

It was still autumn and so the late afternoon seemed lighthearted. The air was clear. Very big clouds, in many different forms, spread out across the sky above the field and they seemed even bigger, limitless, because they weren't cut off by the roofs of the city.

She remembered a certain forest crowded with soldiers. The sound of murmuring, talking, and laughing. All kinds of vehicles rushing forward. All kinds of vehicles, all kinds of engines. It was so much fun being nineteen, with a clear complexion and smooth hair beneath the fingers of the person stroking it. Wherever you went, someone's eyes would follow. Day and night, your vision was cut off by trees, and your space was sometimes limited to a few narrow feet. The two of them would talk about Vien's birthplace in the central region. There were so many white clouds spread above the tea-covered hills. Limitless clouds.

Tan walked more quickly when she thought about the conversations that she and Vien had in the forest. Things had been so easy then. Even their wishes had been lighthearted. In those days, they were both pretty and their youth made them even prettier. The soldiers often teased them and so they tried even harder to take care of their braids and their fingernails. Sometimes they embroidered little flowers on white scarves, which they tied into their hair to make themselves even more charming. Whenever the soldiers stopped to watch them walk by with their two-way radios, the girls would cover their mouths with their hands, and turn their heads away in exactly the same manner, which always made their braids fall over to one side. Then the soldiers would start to walk on their way again, and the two girls would twitter like birds in each other's ears and burst into laughter, which sometimes made the soldiers who had teased them turn their heads to look again. The two girls never wanted to be apart. Whenever one went off on a mission, the other couldn't sleep. At night, a strong wind would blow across the whole valley. There was something immense in the sound of that wind.

There, in that forest, the communications outpost had shaken from the enemy bombs. Sometimes, while they sat together by the side of the stream, sharing the rice porridge from a single ration box, a bomb would whistle by and both of them immediately thought of going off to reconnect the radio wires. Whenever one of them was about to go off on a mission and the other had to stay behind with the radio, they always said goodbye as if they were offering each other their final testaments. Life and death were very close together. Who could know? When they finally parted, they always hugged, which made the soldiers roll their eyes.

But why did it seem that she had put Vien so completely out of her mind these days? Even when she had received Vien's letter complaining of her miserable life with her husband and children, Tan had only skimmed it before going off to the birthday celebration of a local luminary. Afterwards, she hadn't found the time to read it again. Luckily, she had kept the envelope with the address on it and, although she didn't have the envelope with her, she could vaguely remember it. Once she was in the area, the sad sight of the countryside had the effect of reminding her that this was the region where her friend lived. Only now, as she was walking, did Tan begin to ask herself the questions she should have asked when she had first received that tormented letter. What was the problem? Why did Vien complain so much about things that, in the past, she had longed for?

Once, two pretty girls had followed the soldiers to the liberation of the city. Wide-eyed, they had whispered to each other about so many things. How did those city girls get such shiny complexions? How could they bear to sit in these bars with the colored lights without getting a headache? Why did those young couples walk arm-in-arm like that in public? Weren't they afraid of being scolded by their elders? Heavens! Those spring mattresses could make you nauseous. Let's just string up our hammocks. But these windows have no bars on them. How can we string up our hammocks? And the gates of these houses are all locked anyway, and surrounded by walls with barbed wire on top. And yesterday, an old man came up to me, put his hands together and told me, "Greetings, Miss Soldier" and I was so embarrassed. And that "nutritional drink" was really just fruit juice. Here in the South, they have such strange words for things, don't they? And the Lambrettas are so beat up, but they still have Western writing on them. And that man with the sunken stomach and thick lips who sometimes walks past the gate, do you know what his name is? Robert Minh! It's so funny. There's not anything Robert about him!

The male soldiers thought they were naive. Everything shocked them. Then, on the tenth day of liberation, the two ignoramuses started to prepare to go to university. It was time to go. They hadn't seen the North for several years.

The courtyard of the university was filled with white shirts and flowered shirts on their first day. They were twenty-three years old already and just becoming students. But they were still young enough to make people turn to look at them when they crossed the courtyard. Their first year passed. They absorbed knowledge easily because both of them were bright.

In the second year, a slender young man with curly hair and glasses appeared in the dormitory. All of the women knew him. He was in the sixth year of medical school and was about to become a doctor. He was so elegant that the women students said, laughing noisily, that once he put on his doctor's coat, they might go wild. At those moments, Vien would turn to listen to them, wide-eyed and full of panic.

"Why aren't you laughing, Vien?" someone asked.

"Because we're saying bad things about her future doctor!" Someone else responded.

"Who says he's hers? You're kidding!"

"I'm not. They're a perfect match."

The medical student blushed. As for Vien, she jumped down from her bunk with such a thud that people thought she could have broken something, but she immediately recovered her balance and rushed out the door. The other women laughed even louder, but the medical student appeared worried as he looked in the direction she had gone. Tan threw down her notebook, mumbling her anger at their friends, and ran after Vien.

Vien was standing beneath a tree, a place where the two of them often went to gossip and talk about love.

"Oh, Lord," Vien said, "maybe it's our destiny to have a broken heart. Why does it happen so often that way?"

At those moments, they acted like two very old young women, putting their chins on each other's shoulders and heaving long sighs. Beneath this tree, where moonlight couldn't reach, pretty Vien stood with her shoulders shaking lightly from emotion.

"Stop it. Why do you cry so easily?" Tan asked.

Vien answered with sobs, her slender fingers squeezing her friend's hand. Her fingers were icy cold, her slightly oval face covered in tears..

"No, let me cry. Just a little. You don't understand. They embarrassed me. Why would they tease me? He would never even bother to look at a person like me."

Something hot had filled Tan's chest that day. Was it an intuition about happiness? Or about the troubles her friend might meet? At that time, how could she know? Even now, how could she know?

On Saturday nights and Sundays while they were at the university, Tan picked up the rations for both of them, but had to eat by herself. Vien was out somewhere and hadn't come back yet. Her studies were also going nowhere. She would look at the teacher without really seeing him and mumble her answers whenever he called on her. The cheerful and pretty Vien had become pale and her eyes burned as if with fever. And then something unexpected happened. Right after Vien discovered her condition, he was assigned to a hospital in a faraway town whose name couldn't even be pinpointed on the map. If she wanted him to marry her before the news broke out, she would have to drop out of school and go with him. Underneath the tree in the university courtyard, the two "old ladies" had sat lost in thought.

"Oh well," Vien said. "Maybe it's my fate that I can't be far away from him. Look, it's here in my palm. And, surely, he's gotten what he wanted. In the moment of passion, he promises anything, but when I'm faced with disaster, he couldn't care less. Why did I ever fall in love with him?"

The two "old ladies" heaved long sighs, hugging their knees and looking out at the deserted courtyard. And just like all women who have ever complained about this situation, they spoke almost simultaneously:

"Men are like that!"

"Men!"

Another woman moved into the upper bunk when Vien left. One of the other student's younger sister, she was staying temporarily in order to take an exam and was thrilled that she didn't have to sleep with her sister anymore. At night, while lying in the bed listening to this woman loudly grinding her teeth and repeatedly kicking against the bunk, Tan missed Vien terribly. For two nights, she went alone and sat at the base of the familiar tree. But, maybe because she was all alone, the mosquitoes drove her crazy and she had to give up that memory-filled tree. After that, almost every night a group of students would sit there playing chess.

"It's so sad about Vien," one of them said. "And such a shame that she had to give up her studies."

"You can see a fate of misery written in her physiognomy," someone else responded. "That's how it is with girls with such slender bodies, white skin, and thin eyebrows."

"If that's her destiny, then what can be done?"

"Maybe when she has children, things will improve."

"On the day of their wedding, the guy looked so haughty. I hate him."

"He's right to be haughty. A foolish girl has to bear the consequences."

Everybody had one thing to say and all of them were worried. Maybe they were worried about the common destiny of women. Tan wasn't worried about that. Why should she be? She wasn't born into this life in order to bear inequality.

By the end of that year, Tan hadn't received a single letter from Vien. By the next summer, she had many new friends, city people. Why not? She'd suffered a lot. Now she was ready to live well.

See that rather fat girl over there? The daughter of the newly promoted minister? When she goes home to sleep, she even has someone to hang up her mosquito net for her. One evening, she came over to the student dormitory and invited Tan to go with her to see a free movie. Then the two of them walked together to the auditorium and later to a drink shop and the university library.

Then there was the daughter of the university rector, the daughter of a colonel who was a pilot for the air force, the daughter of a physicist. By her third year, Tan was always moving within the circle of the daughters of Mr. This and Mr. That. Some of the university students admired that circle, calling them the "Notables," while others were sarcastic and others still were jealous. Because of that, these young women always seemed aloof and the young men kept their distance. Perhaps they thought that the girls, living only on the reputations of their fathers, deserved to be hated. In the past, Tan had been courted by these young men in the dining hall, in the library, and out on the sports fields. Now they walked by her as if they were walking by a tree. But getting to hang out with these wealthy girls was a feat.

Who was Vien? Tan could barely remember her friend within this maze of complicated relationships, all of which took great effort to cultivate. And owing to this vast web of acquaintances, Tan came to know one particular man, a man past middle age. Then she married him. His house was large, on a tree-shaded street, far from the noise of the bus and train stations, the trolley tracks and marketplaces. He was rather old, old enough to act fatherly toward her: a fashion beautiful and romantic girls have always loved. He was a doctor in a big hospital. He had an ugly face and did housework awkwardly. Still, he didn't appear happy at all that an ugly guy like him had been able to marry such a beautiful wife. Every morning, watching Tan stand in front of the mirror, powdering her face, trying on this dress, tossing aside that one, adjusting the shoulder of a shirt, tilting her neck, he never ventured a compliment. Yet, even the stupidest girl could understand from his gaze what he wanted. Tan would blush. After awhile, she would no longer even dare to put on her makeup in his presence. But even that wasn't important. Women are like raindrops. She had fallen into financial security and that alone meant happiness. So they had to overlook a lot of things in each other. So they didn't have the same interests. But the transformation from being a student sleeping in a dormitory bunk bed to giving out her address as 23 N. Street—Heavens! What an elegant street. Everybody thought so. Now she went to school on a little motorbike. On her way home, wearing her tight jeans and high heels, she drove slowly with the other "Notables," her hair flying behind her. Back home, she changed into something more sheer, satin slippers embroidered with lotus flowers, opened the refrigerator for a snack, then put her head down on a big pillow to listen to music or read a book. On the wall was a blow-up of her and her husband on their wedding day. She was wearing a gold crown and red tunic like Queen Nam Phuong and holding a bouquet of roses in her hand. Oh, look at the bride, so beautiful! And the groom! How ugly he is! That's what the children said to each other while the firecrackers were exploding. But now, lying on the bed, with her head resting on her arm, looking at that photograph still made her heart beat faster. Who could have imagined that she had ever worn a uniform, that her whole body, because of the miserable conditions in the jungle, had once been covered with scabies and tortured by bouts of malaria? Who could have known?

* * *

Now, evening was falling very quickly and the sun was low in the sky by the time she arrived at the center of town, which she had recognized from a distance because of its two watch repair shops and a sundries shop with green and red plastic baskets and basins in front.

"The hospital staff housing?" came a reply to her question. "It's just across this road. Do you see the line where the diapers are hanging over there?"

Tan saw the line on which the yellow-stained diapers hung. A woman, her hair piled high in a bun, was doing something in the yard. Only the two buttons on the neck of her shirt held it closed while the flaps blew open, revealing a white belly. The cuffs of her pants were torn to the knees. Her wooden clogs were very strange. One of them had a high heel and a green strap. The other had no heel and a yellow strap. Consequently, she walked around the yard limping. Tan stood looking across the street. Could this be the Vien she'd known? Vien with the white skin and the long hair? Even during those fierce days on the battlefield, she'd still spent time looking after her fingernails and hair, and if she couldn't go down to the stream one day to bathe she couldn't bear it. Could this be Vien?

A girl with wildly unkempt hair came out of the house, pulling up her shirt and furiously scratching her stomach. She fixed her gaze on her mother, then raised her voice aggressively, "Yesterday, you borrowed two dong from me. Today, you better give back two-fifty."

"Why two-fifty?"

"Money changes its value every day, Ma. You should know."

"Then, yesterday, whose pork sausage did you eat?"

"That was from the money that Dad sent home. If it had been yours, I wouldn't have touched it."

"Okay. This evening, I'll buy some more sausage and if you even go near it, I'll slap your face."

"I wouldn't touch it anyway!"

The woman laughed cheerfully. "What kind of daughter are you? So young and already such a smart-aleck! Come here and let me give you a kiss."

The girl rubbed her tousled head into her mother's stomach. The mother and daughter hugged each other and the mother cooed, "My smart aleck, don't ever leave me like that curly-haired father of yours did."

The girl suddenly looked up, pointed toward Tan and shouted, "That hag over there is spying on us!"

"What? Why do you use such language? I'll slap you for that!" The girl's mother looked up, then exclaimed, "Is that Tan?"

"Vien? Yes, it's Tan!"

"Heavens! That's Tan! Aunt Tan! Say hello to your aunt. Hurry up and come inside. Don't just stand there like that! Come inside and let me help you with your bag. My, you look even younger than before. I've kept hoping and hoping that I'd see you again. I thought you had forgotten all your friends."

Vien's words came out machine-gun fast. Unable to say a word, Tan could only smile. Vien's apartment was a room in a narrow building of a housing project. There was a leafless banyan tree in the front yard and a row of chicken coops next to a well, all of which made the building seem bustling and cozy. Vien pulled her friend inside to sit down on the bed. The smell of children's urine and another strange and unidentifiable odor made the room, stuffed with disordered furniture, seem even more crowded. Tan resisted a feeling of nausea. A baby boy crawled out from behind a corner of a wardrobe, dirty, his chest covered with snot and drool. He raised his two dirty hands in the direction of his mother, who rushed toward her son, picked him up, and held him tightly against her chest. Her eyes were teary.

"You have to be quiet while I'm talking to your Little Aunt Tan. Yes, it must be Little Aunt Tan because she has no children and so we have to think of her as my little sister now. Look here, Little Sister, at your handsome nephew. He just had diarrhea so his face looks a little anemic now. He's a good boy, exactly like his father, except for the fact that he's so greedy when he eats. Quiet down now, son. I nursed you already. Okay, I'll nurse you again."

In the past, Vien had never spoken as quickly as she spoke now and Tan could only look at her friend and laugh. Vien lay down on the bed and opened her shirt. The baby leaned his head against her breast, nursing hungrily, while his mother continued chattering in baby talk, faster than all the mothers Tan had ever known. The baby finished nursing and, while Vien buttoned her shirt, he crawled toward his mother's head and peed onto the straw mat of the bed. Vien sat up quickly. Her long hair, which had come undone, was now wet with urine. Perhaps this was a normal occurrence because she squeezed out her hair and fluffed it. Then she twisted it as if she were washing it, wrapped it into a bun, wiped her hand on a flap of her shirt, and smiled happily.

"Children mess you up, Tan" she said. "But when they grow up, they really love their mother. Every one of them is always going, 'Mommy! Mommy!' all day long. They're more afraid of their father than a tiger, though. These days, he's always going off somewhere on missions for work and so he leaves most of the child raising to me. If he sees a kid's poop, he's completely disgusted. Hey, Mai! Go call your big brother and tell him to come in here and clean the house. It's going to take us a whole day just to catch up, Tan. I've forgotten everything, but I do remember that you married a rich and handsome guy. And after you graduated you stayed in Hanoi and took a job at the Institute of Design. I've been planning one day to bring all three of my kids up to visit you. Little Aunt, do you have enough rice to feed all of us?"

Tan's heart skipped a beat. This messy and dirty mother and children were so different from her bedroom with its white curtain and the light blue plaster on the walls. Heaven forbid, if they were ever to come visit.

"Oh, it's enough now that I've come down here to visit you," she said hurriedly. "It would be too much trouble for you to bring all the kids up on the bus or the train."

"Oh, it's only wishful thinking anyway. We can barely afford to travel from the house to the yard. We always plan this and that but we can never do a thing. It's just like in the past. I was planning to continue my studies with a correspondence course. That never happened, either. Once you've got kids, that's it. Oh! My little rat of a son! You've pooped again. Hey! Where's that black dog gone? This is another diarrhea day. Oh, my poor little son. Maybe you're so miserable because your mother ate shrimp yesterday. Oh, wittle waby, I'm so sorry! Let me wipe you up so Little

Aunt Tan won't laugh at you. Oh, when you've got diarrhea like this, it makes me so upset. Hey! Hey! Black dog! Get in here!"

The black dog came into the house and started to lick up the mess. Suddenly, Vien screamed and, carrying the baby, she ran out onto the stoop.

"Hey! Who's out here teasing my daughter? Is it you, Khanh? I'll slap your face, you brat! Everything was fine. Why did you have to tease her? Come back here, child, and let's see who dares to come in here and pull your hair. Where did she hit you? Poor child! Watch out, Khanh, you hear? I'll even come into your house and slap your bratty face, you hear?"

Vien savagely hugged her baby on the stoop, having almost completely forgotten that her friend was there. With her other arm, she embraced the daughter who had just run home, patting her head and back and crooning her sympathy. The little girl revealed a pencil.

"I stole it from her," she said. "That's why she pulled my hair."

"Go throw it in the fire to teach her a lesson about bullying people. One day, I'll give her a slap. What a brat. Are you hurt? What did she do to you? There's a scratch on your forehead. Run inside and fetch me the bottle of alcohol so I can rub it on the scratch. I don't want you getting tetanus."

"I got it this morning," the girl said. "You put alcohol on it already."

"Is that right? Try to remember."

"It's right."

"Tan," Vien said suddenly. "My older son is on his way over. Here he is, the one I was carrying while we were still at school. Isn't he big? Say hello to your aunt."

The boy mumbled something, rushed into the house, then immediately went back out again, but not before Tan had sized him up and found him completely different from the curly haired doctor she remembered. She could see him open the lid of a pot, give the dog a vicious kick, and mutter a curse. Vien raced over to him and tried to console him.

"Your sister already ate all the rice and I didn't make any more," she said. "Here's five dong so tonight you can go out and get some peanut candy. Now both of you cook some more rice so we can invite Little Aunt Tan to eat."

The boy snatched up the five dong note and stuffed it into his pocket. The girl became jealous and begged her mother for money, too. Vien hurriedly handed out another two dong, then came back in to Tan, smiling happily. That silly smile made Tan cringe. Vien, still hugging her baby, sat down on the chair, opened her shirt again and began to nurse while her two other children quarreled. The boy built a fire and fanned the rice husk fuel until the dust flew into the air.

Vien sighed. "He's away all day, Tan, almost never home. Either he's studying or he's at a meeting. Now he's gone to the South until the end of the year. I don't understand what he's so sick of that he doesn't even care to hold his own baby.."

Vien's voice had become soft but it was still quick. The older boy yelled in from outside. "I told you! He said this house is too dirty and you stink like an owl. He can't stand it."

"Shut up, boy!" Vien snapped. "Who told you to interrupt like that? You brat! Oh Tan, women are so miserable. There have been times when I was really fed up, like the times when I've written you letters. He's had one lover after another, until I'd had it. But in the end I had to think of the children. With them clinging to me, I forget everything. Do you know how cruel he is? Every time I give birth, I'm so in love with the child and so wrapped up in taking care of it that if anyone even touches a hair on its leg I feel like I've been cut apart. And still, he snickers at me and tells me that women having babies are savage, like dogs, like bitches with puppies. I'm so angry I just tell him off—'Get out of here! Just send me money and I'll raise the children. If you don't send money, then don't blame me. I'll take the children and all of us will jump in front of a train!'—That scares him!"

Vien laughed out loud and kept on talking about her children. Tan could only sit and listen. What else could she do? Among those incessant words, there was no way she could cut in.

From out in the yard, the boy shouted to his sister. "Hey, spoiled brat, hurry up! Don't you see your old man's got runny eyes from the fire? The water's about to boil and if you don't hurry up I'm going to kick you!"

The girl, who was washing the rice in the yard, refused to submit. "Are you blind? Can't you see that I've had to pick out the grains that are still in the husk? This old lady has runny eyes, too!"

While the two children were bickering, Vien said, "My oldest boy, when he was only two months old, was so adorable. You can't even imagine, Tan."

She continued to speak without pause about the boy. Finally, the meal was ready. Tan carried a basin out to the well to wash her face. A woman was standing by the well. She drew up a gourdful of water and gave it to Tan.

"So you're a friend of Vien?" she asked. "It's been many years since any of her friends have come over to visit. She's too busy to make friends with anyone. In fact, she did it to herself. The people around here do like her and they're always trying to bring her around but she won't listen. She works at a pharmacy but every month she has to take weeks off because her children get sick. If the kids even lose their appetites, she panics and leaves work. Her husband got sick of it. To tell you the truth, though, he was nothing much to begin with. How do you solve a problem like that? Her parents have been here many times. They've tried to convince her to let them raise the two oldest kids so that she can work harder and maybe even continue her studies, but she won't even listen. She's crazy for her children.

"The thing is," the woman continued, "she's not the only one with children. It's just that she dotes on them so much that they're all spoiled."

Hearing those words, Tan felt sad.

The noisy meal soon came to an end. The children finished their homework and all three of them climbed onto the wide bed. To postpone as long as possible the task of getting into the small bed that Vien had prepared for her, the bed that still stunk of urine, Tan insisted that her friend sit and drink tea with her. Five or six times, Vien climbed through the mosquito net over the bed where her children slept. Then, both screeching and clinching her teeth, she banged her hands together and squashed a mosquito between her palms. If she thought mosquitoes could hear, she would have bombarded them also with curses.

Vien's pain was close to misery. "That mosquito bit my baby," she said. "It drives me crazy. It wasn't my fault. I already checked inside the net for them. I don't know how it managed to get in there. Oh Tan, will you hand me the bottle of perfume on top of the wardrobe? My poor baby, the bite has already swollen."

Vien poured the perfume into her hand, then lay her hand across the baby's bottom. She looked dazed. In fact, the mosquito bite was nothing and Tan felt afraid for her friend. What would happen if Vien kept on like this?

"Don't keep going in and out of the net like that," Tan said. "More mosquitoes will get in that way."

"Oh, right."

"You have to sit down and talk to me a little while," Tan said. "Tomorrow I'll be gone and you'll have all the time in the world for the kids."

"Oh, right. I'm a little overwhelmed. Every day at this time my eyes begin to droop and I can't think of another thing."

The two women sat at the table and Tan had to wait a long time for Vien to quiet down. At night, Vien seemed less uptight, but as soon as she said anything, her next word would be about her children. Both afraid and concerned, Tan held her friend's bony hand, which was covered with scabs, and tried to get her to talk about other things by reminiscing about Vien's beauty, her youth, and her love of life. Vien's eyes began to grow brighter, and her face came alive.

Little by little, Tan could see the Vien she remembered, a charming young woman in a communications operator's uniform, whom all the young men watched as she passed by. The night was tranquil outside the window. The sound of a faraway train whistle made both of them listen. Oh heavens! It was so much like the time they had marched with all the other soldiers to the Vinh station. It was so dark that night and when the planes screamed in the skies the two of them had hugged each other, crying. A captain had made fun of them, knowing that both were new recruits. It had been so easy to cry then.

"Vien, do you remember Hung? The driver who saved his caramel rations and passed them to us?"

"Oh, I remember!" Vien said. "After he was wounded, we always went to visit him."

"His chin was completely fractured and he still tried to tell you that you should become a movie actress. He'd liked your voice ever since that first get-together between our two units and so, when we visited, you used to sing for him. He would shut his eyes tight, his chin covered in bandages. He'd lie there and listen and listen. Oh, we really wished he hadn't died. And do you remember Thuan, the missile engineer? His death was so sad. They couldn't find even enough of his body. We had so many friends who died."

This fact came up so suddenly that it surprised both of them. So many people had died.

And unexpectedly, Tan picked up her friend's hand and, filled with enthusiasm, said hurriedly, "You can't be like this forever, Vien. You can't. Your children are big enough already. You have to go back to school. Right away, this year. Send the two older ones back to your parents to raise. You can take the baby with you and I'll arrange a place for the two of you at the university. Don't worry about it! Getting re-admitted would be simple. My father-in-law's younger sister is on the governing board. She holds a lot of authority and only needs to say a word and it's done. Anyway, you're still a former student of the university. Oh, Vien. I'll talk to her immediately and I'll find you a place to stay. All of the people in my husband's family are high-level. With only a little trouble, it'll be taken care of. You might have to take an exam, but don't worry. I'll help you."

Tears streamed down Vien's cheeks. Tan, still trying to persuade her friend, couldn't understand why she was crying. Finally, Vien spoke through her sobs.

"The truth is that, ever since I came here with him, no one's ever cared about me like you do," she said. "Don't criticize me. Friends from the war are true friends, but ever since I came to this deserted place, I haven't seen any of them. If I'd had you near me, I would have—"

Vien had to stop for a second before she could continue. "Well. Well. Of course, I'll miss my children a lot, but I'll make that sacrifice. If you can take care of it, then I'll go back to school. I want to teach him a lesson. He's so scornful toward me. He always says I'm a bitch that bares her teeth to protect her children. He's always going off with awful women. He's never even picked up one of his children, even though they're so adorable, so sweet, so—"

"Listen! You have to go back to school," Tan hurriedly interrupted.

"Well, I know I still have the ability. I'm determined to do it."

Both of them were crying and now they smiled through their tears, thinking of their miserable life. Memories, plans, and new hopes washed over them, transforming them. Now they looked at each other and saw their former selves, pure and rather silly, but so fine. And the bed, stinking of children's urine, could no longer disgust Tan. Someday she'd have a child of her own; she couldn't be clean and carefree forever. When, near dawn, they finally went to bed, she fell asleep easily.

When Tan had to leave to meet the car, Vien came with her two older children, carrying the baby in her arms. Both she and Tan were full of hope and promises.

"I'll take care of it soon," Tan said, "and I'll write to you immediately. Remember, once you get my letter, you'll have to get ready to go right away."

"Goodbye, Tan! Children, say goodbye to Aunt Tan." Vien held up the baby, saying, "Hey! That's Aunt Tan. She's going to help us go back to school. She's your mother's good friend. She won't ever forget us. You're going to come to school with me. Tan! Goodbye Tan! I'll wait for your letter from now on."

Oh, that was an exhausting trip, full of so many impressions. She had to get Vien out of that life. She had to take care of it immediately. Oh, here was Hanoi already. She'd only been gone a week, but it felt like years. It was Sunday, so her husband was probably at home.

"There! I guessed right, didn't I? You're home," she said when she got there. "I'm starving. But I have to bathe first. And these clothes have to be boiled before I'd dare to wear them again. Yuck! The conditions at that workshop we went to were so awful. The well water was muddy and they still used it for cooking. Look at this, my skin is covered with spots. I give up. I cannot leave Hanoi. Do you remember the time I told you about my friend Vien who was in the army with me? I have to tell you."

Throughout the meal, the man listened quietly while his wife told him about Vien. His way of life was entirely different from his family's and even rather opposite to that of his wife. He recognized her pure selfishness, her fondness for making friends with important people, and her contempt for the life she had led during the war. All of this had made him lose some of the respect he'd had for her when he first met her. He had to take care of almost all the housework because she liked to go out and have fun. He listened attentively while Tan described Vien's children and depicted her terribly depressing life in that remote corner of the country. He also thought of Tan's tiny hometown, which he had once gone to see. It had been a long time since Tan went back home for a visit. Seeing Tan speak so honestly and enthusiastically, with tears even welling up in her eyes, hearing her telling him that she would take care of everything so that Vien could go back to school, he kept quiet.

That month went by. Many times, she planned to go over to her father-in-law's sister's house, but she hesitated and never did it. Once, she did go over there, but she completely forgot to mention Vien. Tet came and went, leading into a magnificent spring with lots of new kinds of skintight sleeveless sweaters.

One day, she said to her husband, "I met the cutest girl. Her father is an ambassador from Latin America. She keeps inviting me to visit the residence. One day, I'll have to invite her over here. It's so great to get to know her."

In the mornings, as she got ready for work, she stood in front of her cosmetic case, trying to decide which shade would match the day's weather. The Institute of Design was full of fun-loving people, what with meetings and evening birthday parties for this person or that. They always had icing-covered layer cakes. With candles, just like in the movies.

Summer passed. In the autumn, the physicist's daughter, that member of the "Notables," was going to get married.

"Do you know who she's going to marry?" Tan asked her husband. "The son of a famous professor. The guy usually lives abroad and he's coming back to marry her. After the wedding, they'll leave for Northern Europe, where he'll be working for several years. He's going to ask permission for her to go with him. Will you look at these *ao dai*? Which one should I wear to the wedding? Only elegant people will be there."

When Tan tried on one of the *ao dai* to check the color, her husband asked impatiently, "What about that other business?"

"What business?"

"Have you done anything to help Vien?"

"Uh, uh. I'm going to take care of it."

"Have you written to her yet?"

"Not yet, but you should know that she wouldn't even have time to read it. She has so many children. It's terrible."

The man softened his tone. "What's terrible about it? Women are like that. There's no one like you. You're less scared of tigers than you are of having children. You might not know it but, in my opinion, you're very unusual."

Tan's eyes followed her husband as he walked out the door and she shivered with fear and anger. Who am I, really? she thought. But, never mind. There was no time. Those things were trivial. She was still a good friend. If not, why would she have gone to visit her and made those promises? The problem was that she had so little time.

More than a year had passed since Tan's visit. On those nights when her children lay sleeping, Vien went to the front door and looked out at the street that led toward Hanoi. Sometimes she recalled her friend's youthfulness, her pink fingers, her fragrant nightgown, and she smiled warmly to herself. Tan had been able to keep her beauty for so long. And as for herself, she was going back to school. She would catch up with her friends. She only needed Tan to help her. As soon as she received Tan's letter, she would get ready to go.

Tan never wrote.

A group of scientists were preparing to go on a mission to several European countries. They needed someone to act as a receptionist. Someone sophisticated. Tan knew she'd have to speak to all the "Notables," because their parents were people of authority.

In the disappointment he felt after reminding Tan about the letter, her husband, that intelligent and ugly man, thought that shallowness could be a kind of crime. Trouble was, this was difficult for people to see.

1982

A Small Tragedy

On assignment from the biggest newspaper office in town, I went to District V to investigate the murder of a man committed by his son. He'd killed his father very deliberately, according to his own confession. After killing him, he dragged the body into the back garden and slit open his belly to pull out his liver. I did not dare ask him any questions, so I only observed him through the bars of his temporary cell, planning to do a small survey on the increasing crime rate in this region after the war. Upon my arrival there I'd received a letter from Uncle Tuyen. In it he told me that at the end of the month, my cousin Cay—his oldest daughter—would come up from Ho Chi Minh City with her fiancee to visit the family. Taking advantage of the investment law, the young man, Quang, had returned from abroad to try out a shrimp breeding program in the town of K as a joint venture between the town and the French Company S. He didn't meet Cay at the office. In fact, he met her at a gathering at which some overseas Vietnamese who had returned to work under the investment law met with about twenty intellectuals representing the City. After the conference, people sang and recited poetry. Quang happened to be an amateur musician and singer. He sang so beautifully that Cay couldn't take her eyes off him. Under the circumstances, they discarded all barriers, got to know each other, fell in love, and decided to get married. The children of my father's oldest brother, Uncle Ca, and Cay's brothers and sisters had already moved to Ho Chi Minh City. All of them were young and had made their way in the world. Some of those cousins of mine had married foreigners and so the love that blossomed between Cay and Quang, who carried a French passport, was nothing unusual. Uncle Tuyen and his wife were reassured because so many of their own children and nephews and nieces had witnessed Quang's introduction to the clan down in Ho Chi Minh City. Now Cay was about to formally present Quang to his future in-laws in the North. After that, Quang would return to France on company business and also to bring his mother back here to take charge of the wedding.

I felt bad about my unfinished business in District V. I kept thinking about the man who murdered his father: Outwardly, he looked so normal, even boring. But he had a very pale complexion. Twice on the streets I had witnessed murders. The killers were never big or fierce. Rather, they were pale, cold, delicate and determined. Those people could kill without feeling or remorse or pity. The man in District V was like that. He seemed content, detached and extremely cold. His wife had taken off with their child because he had murdered his own father—how could he have any pity on them? People were beginning to try to find out if he was insane. As for him, he seemed indifferent, sitting there behind the metal bars.

But I had to set my work aside and go back. I got a ride with a group of reporters from Hanoi, as they also had to go to my provincial town. This way, I could save a little money and afford to buy a pretty good present for Cay on the occasion of her engagement. Among Uncle Tuyen's children, I treasured Cay, who was good-natured and beautiful beyond compare. She was born in 1957 and ever since then she had lived in a family that received the rationing vouchers reserved for very high-ranking officials. She went to Europe at the age of seventeen to enter university and pursue the odd profession of cremation. As stubborn as she was, no one could have swayed her. So she studied abroad for six years.

By convincing those specialists who traveled to Europe on business to take things to his beloved daughter, Uncle Tuyen was able to take such good care of her that the young men of France were greatly impressed. In the summer, in her dorm room half a world away, Cay could fill a vase with fresh lotuses from home that had been refrigerated on the plane. Following the specialists' most recent business trips, she could enjoy fresh blood oysters. She ate fresh green water spinach and fish sauce, and she could even wash her hair with citronella leaves or other kinds of herbs. She enjoyed all those things as if they were as plentiful as the very air that we breathe. At that time I was also living in a dorm, in Vietnam. I got the lower bunk and developed allergies because of all the dust that came down from the wooden slats on the bed above: my friend on the upper bunk never bothered to dust her bed before going to sleep. During those years, the boys ate their meals in a common kitchen and never used bowls. The rice was tossed into a basin and then the food went in, too. With their heads almost touching, they leaned over the basin, each with a spoon. Those stairways in the dorm were covered with trash and urine. The future intellectuals spent their days at the university gate drinking tea on credit. Their hair was long and unkempt, their complexion pale from malnutrition. There were days when there was no rice at all, and then everyone got one "fist"—a handful of boiled flour that was as hard as a rock and a piece of water spinach as long as your arm. I told Cay these stories about my student days, but she seemed indifferent and sometimes smiled. I asked her if she was aware of such things. Of course, she answered and laughed quietly. I did not know what she was laughing about but I knew she was not indifferent. Perhaps she was thinking: Everything's the same. We have to put up with misfortune as it comes. It's destiny. No one would will such things.

Cay joined the Communist Party while she was in Europe. Then she worked as Youth League leader for several years. Things came to her as naturally as air. She fell in love with a young man from Poland but refused to follow him back to his country. They were deeply in love, but she wanted to return to her homeland more than anything else. If your family has all the modern conveniences, living in a poor country is so much better than living abroad. You don't have to exert an ounce of effort, and for Cay there was never a lack of anything back home. Materially, that is. As for her spiritual life, Cay had a strong personality and never wanted to assimilate herself into a strange new life. Why should she? she asked me. If he loved her, then he should follow her to Vietnam!

After returning to Vietnam, she had to make a choice between the six best and most prominent institutes and finally she decided to join a research institute. Her knowledge of cremation was tossed aside. Where could they find enough electricity to burn corpses in Vietnam? she asked, smiling! Then she went to work in the research institute and was able to keep herself fragrant and so clean her feet never picked up a speck of dust. She lived with her parents in one of the villas set aside for high-ranking municipal government officials who'd been sent from Hanoi to work here in the second-largest city in the North.

These villas belonging to cadres like Uncle Tuyen always posed a riddle to people. Once, upon returning to the capital, I went to visit a friend. She was the daughter of a cook who worked for a high-ranking cadre. She lived with her father in a room in a cordoned-off area of villas. On the edge of the place, a soldier in green stepped out of a green guard hut. He sported a stony face and suspicious look: What do you want? He scrutinized my personal documents. Then he left me standing there and, with his rifle on his shoulder, he went to ring the bell on the iron gate. A soldier in yellow approached, also fixing me with a steely glare. The two of them exchanged a couple of words. The soldier in yellow disappeared into the villa. A moment later, a man in civilian clothes came up to me. He stared into my face the way a lab worker examines a bacterium under his microscope. When the cook's daughter appeared, I had already broken into a cold sweat. After this experience I didn't want to see her any more. What would a cook's daughter be doing in a place like that?

All those bothersome safety measures forced the young people living in those villas to alienate themselves from everyday society and this drove me to nourish an extreme hostility towards Uncle Tuyen's children. In the provincial towns, things were pretty much as they were in the capital, even more troublesome in many ways, and this made me sick. Cay had very few friends and she loathed every minute she had to live in the villa with her parents. Very often she would flee to my room in the communal housing project, squeezing into my single bed. On rainy nights, we would huddle on the bed in the cold because the rain kept leaking in. It wasn't that she was really fond of a meager life like mine, but only that because of her life of abundance, she often suffered from depression. She told me: The satisfaction of every need isn't necessarily delightful! Perhaps a little hardship makes life more interesting! I became her friend after that.

During all the time that Uncle Tuyen held office, I never once set foot inside his well-guarded villa. Impenetrable as it was though, one artful fellow did manage to enter. At that time, color photos were still very rare. This guy was an engineer working in an office near Cay's research institute. He asked her permission to come and take a few photos of her family as a gift. Uncle Tuyen's wife came from a merchant's family and in her maiden days had worked as a salesclerk in a grocery store out at the edge of the city. Needless to say, she was crazy about having her picture taken. She told Cay to invite the engineer to come by. The "aristocrat" and her "aristocratic" children were thrilled over the color photos. Uncle Tuyen also had his picture taken. He was dressed in a suit and stood pompously by his Volga. He let his Pekinese squat on top of the car, so in the picture my uncle looked like a bigwig in some foreign country. Only Cay was indifferent. But by a strange twist of fate, when the engineer became a frequent visitor and had dinner a few times with my uncle and his wife, Cay accepted his proposal of marriage. The guy was very handsome, intelligent and cheerful. He was tall without being gawky and he had slender fingers. Cay, of course, knew that a man with beautiful and soft hands would be useless and could even bring unhappiness to his wife, but she nevertheless put on the bridal clothes. They lived together for almost a year. There were nights when she would suddenly appear at my place and sit there listlessly. She seldom spoke ill of her husband, but she looked deeply dejected. I supposed that this was because of the spoiled nature of girls and women upon whom fate has always doted. Then one day she whispered into my ear, as if she were about to blurt out a terrible secret:

"Do you want me to tell you something?" she asked.

"Of course," I said.

"I've never been lucky."

"Who knows what's lucky and what's not?"

"But it's true," Cay asserted. "I've never known happiness."

"Happiness is something very rare, don't you think?"

"Maybe that's true, but I've been going around in circles without getting anywhere. A person like me going around in circles, don't you find it strange?"

Having become the son-in-law of a high-ranking municipal official, Cay's husband was now entitled to choose any destination abroad to go and conduct useless research. He flew to Europe safely, even though he was deeply miserable because before his departure Cay had asked for a divorce. No one could prevent her from her wish. I reproached her many times.

At long last she calmly said, "Look, who came out the winner in this marriage? He did, right? He was the big winner. He wouldn't have had a chance in hell to go to Europe if he hadn't married me. He got too much out of our marriage."

I have never met anyone who abhorred a man as much as Cay abhorred her ex-husband. Whenever she talked about him, she had trouble breathing and seemed to be deeply frightened.

And then she abandoned her family and went by herself to live in the South. Before going away, she came to visit me in the newspaper's living quarters and we went to eat noodles with crab. She was in the prime of life. She was tall and dignified. I was very proud of her because her beauty wasn't the kind you often saw. In the streets you could only see faces embellished to follow exactly one model, but hers stood out from the very first glance. Her eyes, her eyebrows, her lips, were all prominent and well-defined within her brown complexion. Hers was a rare beauty in the North. Northerners prefer women of small stature with a fair and soft complexion, so very few of them ever paid her any attention. But on the street, her beauty actually sparkled, while she remained totally aloof from her surroundings. She liked eating good food and wearing beautiful clothes, enjoying the happy moments as they came. Apart from that, she didn't really care much about anything. I often teasingly called her a countess. She laughed: It's destiny; everything has its price. Perhaps she was paying a price for something she wasn't aware of.

* * *

I was sitting in the car going toward my town, the provincial capital. Ours is a big province, almost as big as a small country, and it would take the whole day to cover the distance there from the remote district of V. The reporters from the capital were investigating a story in town. They kept mum about it. They had come to District V to meet with a couple of folks from the inspector's office and then they hurriedly left for town. They were three young men. The nature of their business made them seem serious, but they still managed to have a lot of fun on the way. They told funny stories about the press, laughing together while I sat thinking about my cousin Cay and Uncle Tuyen's letter announcing Cay's upcoming engagement reception.

Uncle Tuyen had retired three years ago. His villa no longer had security guards or any more irksome formalities. Now he had his meals with his wife and children, watered flowers in the garden, or swung in a hammock tied between two tall shady trees. He had lorded it over his subjects for so many years, enjoying the highest salary and all the best privileges and perks in town. Inside his house, from the paperweight on his desk to the paintings hung in the living room, from the bookshelf to the doormat, absolutely everything had been furnished by the State and when he retired they became his own. He had enjoyed everything as if it were the very air that he breathed, so it was inevitable that in his retirement he would feel deeply his impotence in the humdrum of everyday life. The life led by ordinary citizens was like some dirty scraggly stranger worming his way into Uncle Tuyen's house. And he could do nothing about it. In the marketplace he was naive. He got mad over the declining purchasing power of the currency, the rudeness of the salesclerks, the fact that "everything had gotten completely screwed up," and so forth. He was like so many of his powerful contemporaries in that he never tried to find out why things had reached this wretched state. Of course, he would vehemently deny that he was one of the people responsible for "screwing things up!" He got mad because nowadays they would put down in his rationing booklet even a kilo of ground pork or the half kilo of butter he wanted for his breakfast. The grocery store that served the high-ranking municipal officials, and that was a big secret tantalizing the university students who only got vouchers for one-tenth of a kilo of sugar a month, was gradually depriving him and his family of the power to enjoy everything on earth.

The reporters in the car didn't know that I was a niece of Mr. Tuyen. Perhaps they never expected that his niece could be such an impoverished-looking reporter—a reporter who only had a rickety bicycle to toss onto the roof of the car when getting a free ride, a reporter who took out a notepad when working, having neither tape recorder nor camera.

From the passenger's seat, the young man with a buck tooth turned around and asked me, "You're a reporter in town. Have you ever interviewed Mr. Tuyen?"

"No!"

"What a pity! I can't understand why you haven't spoken to a man with such a big reputation."

The man sitting next to me laughed:

"He would never have agreed to meet with you. In his day, he only wanted to meet with . . . how should I say it? . . . with those who would take a picture of him from the chest up. Because he buttoned all the way up. And the people were only allowed to see him from the chest up, buttoned to the chin. I wondered sometimes if he ever used the bathroom and what he wore in bed."

They all laughed. I couldn't. No matter what, Uncle Tuyen was a relation of mine.

Dusk was gathering. The car crossed a river that was still

shallow because the water hadn't risen for the season yet. Corn, sweet potatoes, and pumpkins grew on both sides of the river and there were children chasing each other, filling the air with their laughter. The iron bridge which was restored after the war was painted a quaint green, contrasting with the sky and water. A long time ago, this bridge was truly majestic, but it was bombed during the war.

The young man with the buck tooth turned around again. "At the start of the war, it was fierce here," he said.

"Really?"

"At that time I was an artillery soldier on the other side of the river, so I know. The F105 planes bombed every day, until there was no fresh air left to breathe. Even so, one day we saw people coming out in droves, thousands. When asked, the company commander, who later sacrificed his life in another battle, grumbled: It's an order from the chief of the municipal political committee. These young people are ordered to fill the bomb craters. What? In broad daylight? Of course! The commander blew a fuse. What a stupid order. On a sunny day like this, it'll be a slaughter. True to his prediction, at 8 a.m. the AD6s had already winged in the distance, showing the way. Then the F105s dove down, wave after wave. Our anti-aircraft artillery kept firing. We shot down an AD6."

"And all the people?"

"The vanguard youths? I've never seen so many people die like that. They were empty-handed, puny, running like ants on the naked riverbank where all the trees had already been mowed down already by bombs. I tried to dig into one depression to pull out three young girls but they died in such a tight embrace I couldn't even untangle them. I started sobbing. Later, the old cook somehow pulled them out. They were all city folks. I've never seen so many people die like that. It was nearly dawn before we finished carrying all those bodies away. And the American planes attacked a second time, in the middle of the night . . . Those were fragment bombs."

"What happened to Mr. Tuyen?"

"What?"

"Was he punished for sending those young people out to fill bomb craters in broad daylight?"

"No. Nothing happened to him. There was only this report in the newspapers: At the G Bridge we shot down an AD6. The soldiers and people put on a magnificently heroic struggle."

Everyone in the car was silent. Even the driver slowed the car down. Almost twenty years had passed since then. I looked over my shoulder, almost certain that I would see the eyes of the dead, still so full of accusation and reproach.

After a few moments of silence, the man with the buck tooth said, as if wailing, "Countless people died and it could have been avoided. It could've been done at night. Why order thousands of people to come out in broad daylight on the open ground?"

"Don't forget that in '76, there was another scandalous event here."

"I know what happened!"

The driver turned to see. He was in the South at that time, so he didn't know.

The man with the buck tooth took his time. "It was Mr. Tuyen again," he explained. "He was supervising a big project that required manual labor. He threw thousands of young people into the irrigation project. The geology of the Q area wasn't stable. It was near a limestone mountain and there were pockets of water hidden under the ground. The geologists warned him but he wouldn't listen. The drums beat; the flags waved; everyone was full of zeal. The banners and slogans were all bright red. But there was no machinery and when the ground caved in, there was nothing with which to dig out all the people who were buried."

"How many people died?"

"They didn't report the number. Do you happen to know?"

"No, I don't."

"Actually, I knew about that. It was like a small earthquake. A hundred and eighty-six people died. All of them were young."

The man with the buck tooth sighed. "After the cave-in, there was a serious decline in enthusiasm. The whole project went down the drain. Who knows how many millions of dong were lost? The eye-popping figures were always kept secret."

"In our country things are truly funny: everything is kept secret. In order to protect someone's reputation, everything becomes vague, no one knows what to make of anything."

"Before he retired, he was involved in one more debacle. Or maybe a few more."

"Tell us."

"There's that incident the press have been probing recently. It happened during the flood season. He ordered all three counties to dig fish ponds. The young people had to set all their other work aside to go dig those ponds. Then it started raining. The water began to rise and soon covered all the ponds. That was the end of the fish and people were exhausted. I heard that some people even died of starvation."

"It was a foregone conclusion!"

"Do you know about that? You lived here then, didn't you?"

"No. I don't know about it," I said.

"Then you're truly an innocuous reporter. You only write what they tell you to write?"

"Yes!"

I said yes to avoid the subject. There were so many stories like this about Uncle Tuyen. The reporters in our town knew them all but never mentioned them. We were always advised to protect the reputation of our comrade leaders in town. Sometimes it hurt me because it was my Uncle Tuyen who had indirectly murdered countless people and made life miserable for so many others. He gave up his office with spotless hands and feet and a clear conscience because he had fulfilled his duties. Since he retired, he often called me and asked me to come over. I was angry at him, so I didn't go see him during the first year of his retirement. But Cay sent me letters from Ho Chi Minh City asking me to visit him. She said that he had no friends. At home, he was even lonelier because all his life he had been a tyrant to his family. He paid attention to what jobs they got, what food they ate and charted their destiny, but he was distant with his emotions. At home, he created the same feeling that people got when they looked at his portrait hung on the living room wall: reserved, strict, and indifferent. But now he was weak. That's what Cay told me in one of her letters.

I didn't think he was weak. Because of my job, I often went to his political sermons at the top agencies in town. He would go here and there to spell out a new resolution. Then, a few months later, he would go again to condemn the old and extol the new. It went on like that for years. I always found him relaxed and aloof in front of the masses. Sometimes I had a feeling that he held his audiences in contempt but was trying to hide it. He never had to pull out his handkerchief to wipe away tears when talking about the people from the podium. He was self-controlled and found it difficult to shed a tear. I liked him for this trait.

The reporters from Hanoi were still discussing my Uncle Tuyen. They were no longer holding anything back, and it's appropriate to say that they all had sharp tongues. Even the driver joined in. He expressed a thought that I often had.

"It's just like that," he said. "There are always millions of people in the hands of just one. However much they might want to change it, they still can't."

The man sitting next to me snickered. "The whole world's that way, in the hands of a few people, or even in the hands of just one. Whenever he feels like it, he'll blow it up, and then we're all finished."

They all laughed loudly, having fun. The man with the buck tooth turned his head again: "Do you think Mr. Tuyen enjoyed doing all that?" he asked.

"Perhaps he did. He's smart enough to know what should and shouldn't be done."

"I think so, too!" The driver said, tilting his head. And they were all silent, as if something was going on in their minds that couldn't be joked about.

Following Cay's wish, I went to see Uncle Tuyen. As it turned out, it was rather interesting to talk to him, so I went more often and became his confidante. He praised my articles. As for me, I wanted to find out what was behind my uncle's reserved appearance. I thought that he had nothing to lose now, nothing to hide. Perhaps I could even ask him a couple of questions. And so in every visit, I asked him about the things he had done that people were still speaking so bitterly about. But I wasn't able to extract any explanation from him. For the most part, he listened rather attentively and then smiled benignly.

He often asked me: "Is that so? Did they really say that? What do you think?"

"Why did you do it?"

"But I wasn't alone in this, you know."

"Right. But you could at least have kept other people from doing it."

"I couldn't have done anything. One day you'll understand. Now, let's drop the subject, shall we?"

He and I often sat on the marble steps leading into the garden. Our conversations were always like that. He wanted to conclude the chats on a conciliatory note, which was never my idea. Very often he appeased my fiery head with a cool smile behind his graying mustache.

"Why do you dig things up to make life more complicated?"

"But one day people will have to know all this."

"I know. But when that time comes, I won't be around any more. They can't drag me up from my grave, can they?"

I sighed. It was too true. He had fulfilled his mission. In every respect, his work was complete.

Night was beginning to fall when we arrived in town. The reporters all went into an inn to have a cheap dinner. They insisted that I join them for a little party.

The man with the buck tooth looked at me: "Imagine an 'elitist' reporter riding a rickety bike, living in a six-square-meter room, having no boyfriend, looking so serious all the time, acting as if this world were full of important issues. Do you realize this makes you a truly outdated product?"

They all broke into laughter and I couldn't help laughing too.

The man with the buck tooth kept teasing me: "We ourselves are the losers. We reporters are the fools who keep prying into frivolous things. And what about Mr. Tuyen? He enjoys all the gifts from heaven and his children enjoy the leftovers. Only the leftovers, but that's still a life of luxury to us."

The driver calmly advised, "Stop it. That's nothing to joke about."

I said good-bye to the reporters from the capital and walked the bike along a few narrow streets. All of a sudden, I no longer felt excited. I thought about Cay and had to admit that the man with the buck tooth was right: "The children are enjoying the leftovers." Even now she was still very lucky, having gotten hold of a guy with a French passport and flown here with him from Saigon. I could never live that way. Any man would be repelled to enter my six-square-meter room with its single bed and bookcase. He would see all the things that had been eaten away by termites and a face pale from loneliness and privation. I could never afford to live the way I'd like. As for Cay, she had been enjoying everything in life without having to sweat for any of it.

I entered my room, flung the bag onto the bed and sat listlessly, not bothering to even wash my face. Sometimes, one suddenly thinks of one's lot and is filled with self-pity. Perhaps there are many people like that. Those for whom life is fragile and unprotected.

The operator on the night shift appeared. I looked at him: one more soul whose life wasn't worth a thing. He was a gangling guy who often coughed and kept a lot of pieces of newspaper in his pockets to wipe his nose with. He suffered from chronic nose problems. No girl dared accept his proposal of marriage.

"Hello," I said. "What's new?"

"You've just come back?"

"I just got back this minute!"

"Someone gave you a call late this afternoon. Someone from the town center. Do you know anyone there?"

"Only a casual acquaintance."

"She reminded you to come by. It was a woman named Cay."

From my jacket I fished a few cigarettes I had pilfered at a meeting in District V and gave them to him. He was overjoyed. Perhaps the phone call wasn't important, but these cigarettes were.

"Oh, wow!" he said. "Thank you. Thank you."

I decided to take a quick bath. But when I got to the public tap, no water came out—not even a drop. A few moments later, all the lights went out. The newspaper's living quarters were suddenly like a busted beehive. Girls and women dragged their chairs out their front doors and chattered away noisily. Dogs barked, cats screeched, children shouted . . . And still, no one could see anyone else's face. I don't think a scene from hell could be any worse than that. I was sick of it all, so I hung up my mosquito net and prepared to go to sleep. As for Cay, to hell with it. That was a world that didn't belong to me. That was a world that was full of light.

The next morning, I was still in bed when I heard someone knock and call out my name in a voice that was rather unfamiliar. I jumped out of bed and threw a quick look at my hair in the mirror. The sun streamed through the window. I looked at my face and all the troubles seemed far away. I flung the door open: Cay.

"Hello, little sister!"

Cousin Cay. My heart filled with excitement in the face of her magnificent beauty. She was so much more beautiful than before. She had shed her indifference and aloofness. Her passionate eyes locked me in a loving embrace.

"I waited so long for you last night," she said. "I got here in the morning."

"When I got home, I was too exhausted."

"Something was wrong. Something happened, right? I can tell you weren't too tired to come to see me."

I could only smile. Cay was too smart. She was always able to read my mind.

LE MINH KHUE   193

"Can you straighten things up? We have a guest."

"Who?"

"Quang."

"Oh God! Why did you bring him here? You'll kill me."

"Never mind. I know it'll be okay."

Together we folded the mosquito net and fluffed the pillow. Cay took the broom and gave the floor a quick sweep. During the week that I was away, a thick film of dust had accumulated on everything. Cay urged me:

"Go wash your face!"

I opened the suitcase, pulled out my least tattered shirt and sprinted to the public bath. How lucky. The water was running. The lights had come on. The sun's rays filled the yard and back alley. I took a bath and went into a neighbor's to comb my hair. In the mirror I actually looked presentable. When I got back to my room, Quang was already seated inside. His expensive Honda Cub was parked in the front yard. My heart missed a beat when I found Quang sitting on the decrepit chair I'd been using to write my latest sensational stories. The chair was both rickety and rotten from termites. Cay was sitting at the foot of my bed. She waved me in. Quang jumped to his feet.

"Good morning," he said. "I'm Quang. Cay's told me so much about you. You look just like I expected."

I looked him in the eye. I had never met any man as attractive as he was. I turned to look at Cay and found her smiling sweetly. They were equally attractive, as if they were born for each other. And I instantly believed what the physiognomists said: that a husband and wife always have some similar features. Quang looked like Cay in some respects. Their marriage would last. I thought so.

He looked uncritically at all the things in my room, the shabby room of an unmarried person. It seemed as if he used to live in a room like this, even though judging by his discreetly simple suit I could tell that he was wealthy. Those who are wealthy and take their wealth for granted never show off through their manners or their dress. His natural nobility was not something that could be created by a university degree. I felt reassured when he sat on my old chair in that room I now no longer felt so ashamed of.

"How's your life going, Thao?"

"You can look and see. This is how I live."

"In France, we have more conveniences, but we don't have things like that, because we have so little time."

He was pointing to the landscape painting on my wall. "Above the Eternal Tranquillity." Every morning I looked at the serenity in that painting and couldn't help shedding a tear before the loftiness and sacredness of that place where all of us will eventually dwell.

"I bet you often look at it in the mornings."

"Yes."

"Then you cry, right?"

I nodded. We all laughed. What was strange was that I had a sisterly feeling for Quang. He didn't seem like someone from another land. There was something about him that reminded me of my dead brother. That feeling came softly, and it was deep. I wanted him to stroke my head or hug me as he would hug his little sister. I hadn't felt so close to anyone for a long time.

After that he pushed the scooter into my room and we all went out for breakfast. He walked between Cay and me. Even though I met with and talked to countless men every day, I had never met a real man before. In this land, the worry about food, the struggle over trivial things, and the mediocrity and insignificance of pleasure had deprived men of their dignity. They became identical with women and so, wherever you went, you only encountered one kind of person and you got so bored you lost the habit of distinguishing between men and women. I hadn't experienced the feeling of walking beside a man for so long.

"Why don't you get married?" he asked. "Living like this is so sad."

Cay looked at me out of the corner of her eye.

I answered Quang truthfully. "There's no one who loves me."

"Because you've never met the right man. Right?"

Cay giggled. Quang was thoughtful: "Sometimes that's just a feeling. You must get rid of any hostile feelings. Don't nurture any hostility that isn't necessary. Everything will be fine once you have a lifelong companion."

"It's easier said than done. You have Cay, so you can say that and force everyone to listen. How can I be like you?"

He laughed easily and swung an arm over Cay's shoulder. We walked down a slope to enter the neighborhood where there were restaurants. He grabbed my hand and pulled me out of the way of a car approaching from the opposite direction. I was thrilled. The previous afternoon, when I was in the car coming back from District V, I had pictured Quang quite differently when the man with the buck tooth mentioned those children who enjoyed the leftovers from big guys like Uncle Tuyen. I had imagined Quang as a man with a thin mustache, loosely holding a guitar, singing with a hoarse voice, eyes closed out of arrogance. He would snap his fingers for a cyclo without even bothering to look at the driver, or act cool in public in order to charm the ladies. I don't know why, but I had pictured Quang like a hip singer-songwriter I often saw on TV.

"What dish are we going to treat Quang to?" Cay asked me.

"What do you like the best?"

"When I was small, I lived in the South; and since we went to France, whenever I eat at home, my mother only cooks southern dishes—sour shrimp with boiled pork, raw vegetables and herbs, crisp fried noodles, ground shrimp barbecued on sugarcane, and soft-shell crab with sesame rice paper, which we eat while drinking shots of wine."

"Lord, you make my mouth water!"

"I've seldom had a chance to try Northern dishes. So treat me to something really delicious, okay?"

"Cay, let's go to fat Mrs. Tu's for *bun thang*," I suggested.

"Perfect. I haven't eaten that for so long."

Mrs. Tu had a little place at the end of a long alley lined with banyan trees. Even though the shop looked shabby, the noodle dish was beautiful. Mrs. Tu saw Cay and ran outside to greet her. "Hello, Miss!" she said. "I heard you left for the South long ago."

"Yes. I just came back. This is my friend Quang who's back from France. He wants to try your noodle dish. I'd be honored."

"Please come in and sit at this table where it's cool. Kien! Bring me three china bowls."

Quang seemed very touched. He leaned back comfortably against the foot of the banyan tree. I could see Cay's smile in the corners of her eyes.

"The owner's so excited, Quang," she said. "She's got a customer from abroad."

Quang smiled rather sadly: "Well, I'm a French national but I'm considered a foreigner in France. And here in Vietnam, even though I have residency, people still think of me as a foreigner. How can I be happy?"

"Then it's better for you to return to the place where you were born."

"Unfortunately I don't know where I was born. Of course, I want to come back here. I don't want to live like an exile in France, like an exile in Vietnam, like an exile in the community. I even feel like an exile in my own family sometimes."

It seemed Quang and Cay had talked about this subject many times. Quang spoke softly, somewhat nostalgically. I didn't quite know what it was all about, so I kept silent, listening to them whisper.

Quang turned to me. "I forgot to tell you, Thao," he said. "My parents were also Northerners, but they both passed away. My adoptive mother brought me to Saigon and we didn't leave for France until 1970."

"I know all that from a letter I got from Cay recently."

Cay stood up and walked over to where Mrs. Tu was parboiling the noodles. Quang followed her with his eyes.

"It's a sad story, isn't it?"

"Yes, it is," I told him. "But you're lucky to be living in France."

"Not very lucky. There's something that keeps urging me to come back here. I'm telling you the truth. I'm not trying to be dramatic or anything."

"I understand."

"I'm afraid it isn't that easy to understand. I don't know why I can't be content in France. I have a job and I'm earning money, but I'm not at peace with myself. It's just a feeling but, you know, sometimes even a trivial thing can make you lose your appetite and your sleep."

"Yes. Sometimes that's true."

"After the wedding, we'll live in Saigon."

"What about your adoptive mother?"

"I'll bring her with me. She can't bear to live far away from me. What do you think?"

"I think it's better if you don't come back here to live. This land is full of sadness; how can you put up with it? Once you're married, I don't think it'll matter greatly if you have to live in France."

"Maybe that's true. This is a photo of my birth mother that my adoptive mother was able to hold onto for me."

He opened a small wallet and handed me a small photo. It was still in good shape even though one could tell right away that it was taken long ago. I fixed my eyes on the woman in the photo. It was a noble face, beautiful beyond expression. Inexplicably, I felt moved, maybe because of that lofty portrait. On the back of the picture these words were still legible: "My darling Ti, keep this photo so that you will know your mother. Love Mother Han as you love me. The village of Sam, 1953."

"Why were you called Ti?"

"That was my nickname when I was a kid, because I was born in the year of Ti. In Saigon, my adoptive mother didn't change my name until I was ready to go to school, but at home she continued to call me Ti."

Mrs. Tu carried over a tray containing three bowls of snow-white noodles. Cay followed her, holding a plate of lime slices and chilis.

Mrs. Tu said sweetly, "I have a foreign customer and so I prepared the dish myself. It's been a long time since I've done this myself. Usually, I just give orders in the kitchen."

"Please don't call me a foreign customer. I'm a hundred percent Vietnamese."

"But you're a French citizen. You're no longer a Vietnamese. A person like you deserves to carry a French passport. Vietnamese look very dirty. From a life of hardship, you know. You and the young ladies should squeeze some lime juice into your bowls now. Wow, a Frenchman."

I saw that Quang was saddened to hear Mrs. Tu speak so enthusiastically. Cay saw it too. She cut in. "Tell me the secret recipe for this famous dish of yours."

Mrs. Tu pulled up a chair, sat down, and watched us eat. She smiled brightly. "It's delicious, isn't it? When I do it myself, no one complains. You have to pick a certain kind of castrated rooster, ones that weigh at least three kilos. After it's boiled, you have to take it out and use a toothpick to puncture the pocket of water under each wing so that the bird will dry out quickly. That way the meat won't break into small pieces when you chop it up."

"What about the broth?"

"It has to be the water the bird was boiled in. Then you put in shrimp, pig bones—it's got to be the knees—chicken bones, mushrooms, fish sauce, MSG, onions deep-fried in chicken fat. It's really an art to do it right, you know. As for the ingredients that go in the bowl, you have to pay attention to both color and scent. Everything has to be both tasty and pleasing to the eye. Thinly cut boiled eggs, shredded sausage, pickled sugar beets, finely ground shrimp, chunks and thin slices of boneless chicken placed right next to each other. Then you also have to put pepper and chili into the fish sauce. Can you recognize all the different ingredients by their smells?"

"This is first-rate. No one in Saigon can make a dish as delicious as yours."

"There are many people who can make this dish, but you

have to understand that the spices from other regions don't always go with this kind of noodle soup. They have to come from the North. The flavor that comes from the rice paddy beetles and the herbs of this region are especially delicious. You can't get them anywhere else."

Mrs. Tu sat at our table until we finished eating. She smiled contentedly when Quang finished the last spoonful of broth.

"You really know how to enjoy this dish, not wasting a drop," she told him. "Leaving even one spoonful would mean not doing justice to the person who made it. Isn't that right?"

She walked with us to the street, insisting that we should all come again. We walked to the embankment by the large river that goes through town. All of a sudden, Cay turned to Quang and asked, "Why don't you try to find the village of Sam?"

"I have to go back to France and ask my mother for more detailed information. She's never told me where the village is. She says no one lives there anymore. Everybody's dead by now. And so there's nobody who would know who we are. She seems terrified whenever I mention it."

We stood on the embankment. A breeze blew from the other side. From where we stood we had a good view of the whole town. There was a port; there were factories and strips of marketplaces that had begun to prosper over the past year.

Quang squinted. "The North is so beautiful," he said. "I've never seen nature in more splendor than this."

"You're biased!"

"No. I'm telling the truth. Other countries have too much steel and concrete, too many cars, and too much pollution. Our land still possesses something pristine and pure."

"And our stomachs are in a pristine state, too!"

Quang gave me a light knock on the head. All three of us held hands and ran down the slope to the sandy edge of the river. Except for Quang's worry over his birthplace and that intangible thing that kept drawing him back to this land of Vietnam, except for a certain sorrow that dwelled in my soul, we were filled with joy. We were still young, and still had so much to do. Things seemed to be opening up in front of us, looking brighter and more pleasant, not so brutal or dark as before.

"Have you met Uncle Tuyen yet?" I asked Quang.

"Not yet."

"Why?"

Cousin Cay leaned her head on Quang's shoulder and said, "He went to Hanoi to fetch his oldest brother, my uncle Ca. When we got home yesterday morning, he'd just left. Maybe we'll see him this afternoon."

"And you can see I'm getting very nervous, Cay!"

"Relax. He'll like you at once, you'll see."

"I can't tell how it will be talking to a great statesman."

"No. He used to be a statesman. Now he's only an old man living in retirement, having to start a new life."

We said goodbye to each other after making a plan to meet in the evening. I returned to my empty room and sat listlessly, a prey to sadness and desire. If you're going to love, it should be a big love like Cay's. That's not easy to find, is it?

* * *

I rode my bike to the big villa just before the city lights came on. In the courtyard I found the small car that my uncle was still entitled to use whenever he had to make a long personal trip. The first person I ran into was no other than Cay.

She whispered into my ear, "The old man seemed pensive when he met his future son-in-law."

"Is that so?"

"I don't know if he's pleased or if something's bothering him."

"I'm pretty sure he's pleased. Who wouldn't want to have Quang as a son-in-law? What more could you need?"

The whole clan was there. I came in to pay my respects to Uncle Ca. He was 80 years old and had a snow-white mustache and goatee. Long ago he held the position of mandarin or some high office and even now he still retained the aristocratic air of a fire-breather. Uncle Tuyen waved me over. He looked nervous, not as indifferent as he used to be when I came to see him. He asked me about my business in District V. I told him the story of the guy who killed his father. He was paying attention to me but following Quang with his eyes.

The living room downstairs was decorated with tapestries from various nations that Uncle Tuyen had visited. A big Persian tapestry depicting an old legend was hung in the middle of the room and it created a festive atmosphere. The tables were arranged end to end and covered with a white tablecloth. Uncle Tuyen's wife had ordered all the food for the occasion to be delivered by the hotel across the street. Two uniformed waitresses had come to serve the guests. My aunt wore a long white *ao dai* embroidered with blue flowers. She still had the showy habits of a big lady in a small town, which really didn't suit a sixty-year-old woman. Because of that, she seemed out of place among her children and nephews and nieces in their laid-back, less ostentatious outfits. She came up to me and smiled: It's been so long since you've been here. What do you think of all this? There's plenty of room at home, so instead of going to a restaurant I ordered the food and had it delivered here, where it's cozier. I told her: Everything's perfect! She wanted to say more, but I turned away. I don't like women with "three generations of pure revolutionary credentials" who, once married to revolutionary leaders, become even more snobbish than anybody else. She seemed to respect me because she saw I couldn't care less about what she had. I had never stayed for a meal here, nor had I ever tried to curry any favor because of the mountain of wealth that seemed to fall from heaven into their house. I found it strange that Cay seemed not to have inherited any characteristics from her mother. It was as if she were of a different blood.

People began to stream into the banquet room. They were all relatives living in town. The old people sat grouped together. The younger ones hurried in and out. Uncle Ca occupied a seat at the middle of the table. Quang came in from the yard, made his way to Uncle Ca, put his hands together and made a low bow. Then he turned to Uncle Tuyen and made the same low bow, following the ancient ways. Everyone broke into laughter. Uncle Ca seemed to appreciate Quang's gesture.

"Why are you laughing?" he asked. "Vietnamese should observe manners like this. For so many years our people were too busy with the revolution to remember these traditions. It takes those who live overseas to cherish them. Treasure it, son."

"Yes. We Vietnamese living abroad have to try to maintain all the traditions that belong to our culture, because if we don't, we'll lose them. We're not like Europeans, who feel free to conquer, to re-establish their own civilization wherever they go."

I sat near them so that I could overhear their conversation clearly. Uncle Ca listened attentively. He sat leaning forward. He always ignored his age, wanting to partake of everything in life. Uncle Tuyen sat across the table, facing his future son-in-law. He was the type who seldom revealed his emotions, but tonight he was deeply agitated. From the moment Quang entered the room, his hands were trembling. I noticed it because he was smoking a pipe and trying to prevent it from shaking. While carefully observing Quang talking with Uncle Ca, I saw his face betrayed a certain deliberation and even some panic that couldn't be concealed. I thought it was because he loved Cay and wanted to learn more about her fiancee before he could feel assured.

The feast was splendid. I'd hardly ever eaten such dishes before and so I didn't really know what they were. The room was filled with anticipation. Maybe it was because everyone could sense Cay's happiness. Her beauty shone brightly and her dark eyes sparkled like pools of water. She looked to the right and to the left, and raised her glass to toast one person after another. Quang squinted and cupped his chin in his hand, looking at Cay. This wasn't a particularly striking posture, so I didn't know why it mesmerized Uncle Ca. When he looked at Quang, his hand, grasping a fork with a piece of sausage on it, trembled ever so slightly. Then he sat back and spent the rest of the meal deep in thought. Whenever Quang spoke to him, he only responded with vague nods. He didn't look at Quang anymore. Instead, he fixed his eyes on a tapestry from India, which depicted two beloved girls of Krishna herding cows. I was worried.

When the meal was over, Uncle Ca and Uncle Tuyen went upstairs to rest. The older guests left one by one. As he said goodbye, Quang put his hands together to bow to them, which touched them and made them smile. The young people stayed for a while longer. Quang picked up the guitar and sat down, surrounded by Cay, me and the others. He was slightly drunk and I could tell he was more relaxed.

He adjusted the strings and, turning to me, said, "While living abroad, I imagined people in the North to be very poor, concentrating so hard on making a living that they never thought about anything else. But now I see that's not true. I can really talk with you, with Cay, with all these people. And this isn't poverty. A living standard like this is hard to find even in France."

I laughed. "Uncle Tuyen was not just anybody," I said. "He was a V.I.P. A life like this is rare."

Quang wrapped an arm around Cay's shoulder. "When I first met you, I could never have guessed that you were an aristocrat."

"A lady wouldn't have meant anything to you," she told him. "If I were just that plain girl you met that day, you wouldn't have even cared, would you?"

After that Quang started to sing. Then he told us about his first days in a foreign land, days of hardship, loneliness, and indignity. He had to struggle to find a place among strangers. And it had to be a dignified, decent position, so that no one could look down upon him. Life was so much harder than it was back home.

While listening to him, I silently leafed through the pocket-sized photo album that he carried with him. There were a few photos of pretty young girls standing smiling by his side, and the rest were pictures of his adoptive mother. She was a white-haired woman wearing an *ao dai*. I could see that, even in an elegant setting, she was still a good-natured woman of humble origins. In the photos taken with Quang, she often wore a black dress with flowers embroidered on its front. There were also pictures of the yard in front of their small house. A tea table stood in front of the door, which was covered by a magnificent blue curtain. Even though they were wealthy, they seemed to lead a peaceful and simple life. It was a very beautiful house.

Uncle Tuyen appeared at the window that opened onto the inside hallway. I was the only one who saw him because Quang was singing and the others were concentrating on his voice. Uncle Tuyen waved to me. I stood up and left the room.

"My wife said that Quang has a picture of his birth mother with him. Is that true?" he asked.

"Yes, Uncle."

"Go get it for me."

I returned to the living room. The picture of Quang's birth mother was placed on the first page of the album. I got hold of it and carried it to Uncle Tuyen. He said he wanted to bring it upstairs to take a good look at it. I didn't quite understand, but I felt there was something to worry about.

About half an hour later, Uncle Tuyen came to the window and waved me over again:

"Come upstairs with me. I have something to tell you."

I followed him. He was short of breath and his body seemed to shrink considerably on the steep stairs inside the house.

"What's wrong, Uncle?" I asked.

He made a gesture with his hand as if to tell me: Quiet. And he pointed a finger to the living room where the young people were laughing noisily. When he got to his bedroom, sweat had already broken out profusely on his forehead. I hurriedly took out a handkerchief to wipe away the sweat streaming down his face. His forehead was icy. He sat at the foot of the bed, looking like a pariah who had just lost his last few cents to a pickpocket. Looking at him, I almost started to cry.

"What's the matter, Uncle? You're scaring me."

He didn't look at me. Instead, his eyes fixed on the empty wall in front of him. He said, "You're a virtuous girl. I've always had a lot of affection for you, so I have to let you know. You have to stop them at once. Don't let them go any further. It's enough. Don't let them sleep together."

I panicked. He pointed downstairs. Laughter echoed all the way up. I understood. "They" were Quang and Cay.

"He's Ti. I abandoned him. God sent him back here to punish me. He's been sleeping with his sister for months already in Saigon. That's how young people live nowadays. They sleep together before they get married. The way they look at each other tells me that they've slept together already. God sent him back to punish me."

I sobbed out loud. "You're wrong, my poor Uncle!"

"How can I be mistaken? He's the boy named Ti who was born in the village of Sam. His aunt Han took him with her. I know everything. I couldn't do anything at the time. It wasn't my fault. When I first saw him here, I had a premonition. My heart's been throbbing with pain ever since, and I didn't know why."

He rocked back and forth, talking as if he were in a delirium, as if an excruciating pain were piercing his body. Unable to stop myself, I ran to get Uncle Ca. It turned out that Uncle Ca wasn't sleeping either. He made a motion with his hand: he knew everything already. He followed me to Uncle Tuyen's bedroom. Uncle Tuyen was hugging a pillow tightly. I gave him some water and rubbed some medicated oil onto his hands and feet. I was about to call his wife, but he pulled my arm in panic. "Don't say a word. Don't say a word to anybody. Nobody!"

I nodded.

Uncle Ca said resignedly:

"It's fate, so let it be. What can you do? Send Ti away, and that'll be the end of it. During the meal, it startled me to see the way he sat. He looked just like you looked back when you were still a student in Hanoi, as alike as two drops of water. It's fate. We're still rather lucky."

Laughter from downstairs drifted up again. I was horrified.

* * *

In fact, nothing was really so terrible in a country that had seen nothing but uprootedness, war, and sorrow. I used to think that in old times, people just made up the story of "The Stone Woman Waiting for her Husband's Return." I thought they were wrong to believe that human struggle was futile within the grip of fate and wrong to lament over the heart-breaking predicaments of the world. But who could have guessed that such a misfortune could happen to Uncle Tuyen's family? However, each era reaps its own tragedies.

My paternal grandfather was from the village of Sam. When he resigned from his mandarin's position at the royal court in Hue, he brought my grandmother, a true girl of Hue, up here to start a new life. When I was growing up, I never heard anyone call it the village of Sam. It was always called March Forward Cooperative - the village of March Forward. The beautiful original name of Sam had sunk straight down, totally lost in the tidal waves of the revolution. Nowadays, that name only lurked in the memories of the old people.

Uncle Tuyen passed the national post-high school exam and got a job with the railroad department. My paternal grandmother married him off to a young lady of the most noble bloodline in town. She was so beautiful that, once she came to live with the family in the countryside, she seldom dared go out. Because of her beauty, none of the tenant farmers could eat or sleep.

My paternal grandfather had passed away long before and two years after Uncle Tuyen's marriage, my paternal grandmother also died. The inheritance from an honest mandarin wasn't much—a little land for farming, a tea plantation which they had to hire laborers to harvest, and a compound of tile-roofed houses—but in comparison to the poverty of the countryside at that time, it seemed so big, so comfortable that people were jealous. Uncle Tuyen inherited the property because Uncle Ca had followed his daughter to live in Hanoi. My parents also remained in the village. Every day my father went to teach in a town nearby. My mother opened a small tea shop to earn money to send my older brother to school. After her mother-in-law died, Uncle Tuyen's wife stopped wearing her *ao dai* and bracelets, rolled her hair into a bun, and carried a basket out to the tea plantation. The women were jealous when they saw her: Why is that bitch so beautiful? Why is her skin so fair? She's probably never even had leeches on her feet!

The women's gossip cut into her graceful body. She kept silent and went on with her work in the fields. At that time, it was forbidden to hire anyone to work for you. The tea plantation stretched as far as the eye could see, and she was pregnant with Ti.

By early 1953, Uncle Tuyen, who had joined the government in the provincial town, could already sense the smell of death pervading the political atmosphere in the countryside. He wrote a letter telling his wife to wait and not to worry because he would return when peace was established. His wife cried bitterly, because although she was pregnant she had to do all the work. Luckily, my parents were still living nearby.

But no one could do anything once the guerrillas began appearing every night around my grandfather's house, and began to cock their triggers and point their guns at the people inside the house. And as for Uncle Tuyen, he disappeared into the boiling sea that was politics in those days.

At the end of that year, Tuyen's wife gave birth to Quang, whom she called Ti. When he was only three months old, his mother came down with severe tuberculosis. At that time she was kicked out of the house and forced to live in the rice storage shed at the back of the garden.* Fits of coughing exhausted her health. My parents had been separated and therefore weren't able to come and help their wretched sister-in-law. One night my mother did sneak into the garden to bring Tuyen's wife a few handfuls of rice. A hand reached up out of the grass, grabbed her foot, and yanked her backwards, causing her to tumble into

---

* During the Land Reform campaigns of the 1950s, the property of so-called wealthy landowners was confiscated and redistributed.

a pile of logs left after the garden was cleared. The rice flew in all directions and disappeared into the grass. My mother was caught and imprisoned in a dark cell for two weeks, accused of making contacts to conceal the property of a landowner. In her desperation, caused by hunger and her child wailing all night for milk, Tuyen's wife suddenly remembered her cousin Han, a distant relative who was living alone and earning a living as a merchant in the town. She sent a message to Han. Han had to exhaust all her tears in begging in order to get permission to visit her cousin. Tuyen's wife gave Ti to cousin Han: You must go! Find a way out of here and save his life!

Tuyen's wife had managed to hide a necklace of pure gold that her parents had given her as dowry when she went to live with her husband's family. Han took the necklace and began to weep:

"Oh, cousin! How can I do it?"

"You must go! Wait until very late, then take the baby on the shortcut to the river, then go to the station near the town market. From there, take the baby to Hanoi. Maybe there isn't any trouble there. Then go wherever you can. You have to raise my child for me."

"Oh, cousin! I'm so scared."

"You have to help me. If I weren't so sick I would have escaped already. Here's the photo of me taken a few days before my wedding. Keep it for him so that he'll know who his mother was. Tell him his father died already. Don't ever let him come back to Sam village. You have to keep him from coming back. If he ever comes back here, I'm afraid disaster will strike him. Promise me."

"Yes, I promise!"

"The farther you take him from here the better. Don't tell him the way back to Sam village, do you understand? After I die my spirit will watch over you and your son. From this moment on, you call him your son."

The moment of leave-taking took place on a rainy night when the cold pierced to the bone. Hunger kept the child from even crying. Han took a handful of raw rice and chewed it to a pulp to feed the baby. Tuyen's wife lay on a pile of banana leaves, raised her hand to feel the baby's face and arms and legs, then waved Han away: "Go! Go!"

Han left her cousin some rice she'd brought with her, then disappeared with Ti into the dark night. Outside, it was cold and rainy and the guerrillas had abandoned their posts in order to take refuge inside my grandparents' house. The light from the hurricane lamp shone brightly in the living room and the fits of shouting and laughter enabled baby Ti to go quietly away. Han carried Ti to Hanoi, then down to Haiphong. She found a way to board a certain ship headed to Saigon, and thus disappeared from the North.

When they had a chance to meet, Tuyen's wife told my mother: "I sent Ti away, I can die now." She coughed up blood for a few more days and then she died, curled up like a shrimp on her pile of dry banana leaves. My parents were allowed to wrap her in a straw mat and bury her in Con cemetery. Uncle Tuyen had never returned, although Uncle Ca had told him that Han had taken the three-month-old baby and that his wife had despised his cowardice and had died a raging death among strangers. He still didn't return to visit the grave of his wife, although he could have done so secretly. He had dove very carefully, very deeply, and when he resurfaced, he already occupied a very high position. He married a woman from a very pure background, completely safe, who came from a lowly peasant family and became a saleswoman after the land reform campaigns. For many years, he was a high-level cadre, standing at the top of the local government, which answered directly to Hanoi. His feet took him all over the world and his hand signed treaties in many regions. Between these pleasant trips and his great accomplishments were cases of evil, like the brazen deployment of thousands of young people underneath the American bombs. Throughout all those years, he never lifted a finger to save one single life.

Five months after my mother gave birth to me she died of

complications. There was no medicine and no rice. The family couldn't do anything without being watched or forbidden by the guerrillas. My nine-year-old brother Toan snuck into the fields to steal sweet potatoes and to scrounge for grains of leftover rice to feed me. My father was lying seriously ill in the house. He heard me crying but couldn't do anything to help. At that time, my village was full of Southern recruits for the army. They were poor peasants in soldiers' uniforms and they hated the children of landowners as much as the landowners themselves. As soon as they spotted any of them they would jump on them and beat them. The landowners' children were so terrified they didn't dare to go outside during the day. The soldiers came to my house in the morning when my brother Toan had gone out to look for vegetables. They surrounded my bedridden father: Down with this son of a landowner! My father was so terrified by the sound of these Zone Five accents that as sick as he was he leaped from the bed and ran out into the yard. Two men used poles to beat him on the head. He jumped into the pond where we had once raised lotuses. The two men were so out of their minds with hatred that they jumped after him and used rocks to beat his head in. They only went away when he was dead. My father died with his head in the water, his brains and blood spreading across the surface of the duckweed-covered pond.

Toan came home and found our father dead and me wailing and limp from hunger. He was only nine years old! The sound of our crying was enough to move one kind soul, the old tenant farmer who used to do housework for my grandfather, who helped bury my father, then brought us home. Every day the old man was able to give me one meal of rice. I was barely alive as a wheezing kitten, but I managed to survive. After some time, the atmosphere of hatred dissipated and my aunt returned from the town to carry us home with her to raise. Toan went into secondary school when I was still very small. He reached the seventh grade, then studied pedagogy for three years and became a teacher. He grew into a very big and tall young man, but was constantly depressed. It was only now, remembering the face of my brother, that I understood why, when I first met Quang, he reminded me of Toan.

During a rectification meeting for teachers in a district near the town, one man wearing white glasses stood at the podium and said sweetly: "Among us there are probably many people who were falsely accused during the land reform campaign. Comrades, please speak up and be frank."

Toan approached the podium and said with passion, "My grandparents contributed rice to feed the soldiers. My father participated in the overthrow of the government in 1945. He was on the district resistance committee. My grandfather's family contributed two revolutionary martyrs. Why was my father beaten to death and why has the revolution never done anything about it?"

The gentleman in the white glasses gently shook my brother's hand, and promised to speak to his superiors.

Toan returned to teaching and two weeks later received a summons to the office of the principal. "You are guilty of being in an immoral relationship with a woman. The educational system needs people of good conduct." The principal thrust an expulsion notice into his face, which bore the signature of the head of school district. Naturally, Uncle Tuyen, as the head of the town, had to know about this order but for a long time his relatives had not dared to contact him. He refused to recognize any of them. Now Toan understood. He was in love with a teacher, Kim, who taught in the same school. She was married. At that time this was a serious crime, but he knew that he was being expelled for something more horrendous and that it meant the end for him: He was ordered to return to his birthplace, to return to the village of March Forward, full of awful memories and peasants who still hated the children of the landowners. They were afraid that the parcels of land that had been distributed to them would be demanded back or that there would be trouble of some kind. He came to our aunt's house to visit me. He held me in his arms and cried. I insisted that I return to the village with him.

"I'm not returning anywhere," he told me. "You have to stay

here. You have to study so that you will become an educated person."

I was still so small, how could I understand his state of mind? My brother went off in the direction of the train station, then he leaped under the train bound for Hanoi. My aunt wouldn't let me go near, but I heard people describe the head, the arms, the legs of my brother, all reduced to a pulp, mixed together on the train tracks. My whole body went stiff. The feeling of fear overpowered the feeling of love. I was still too small to understand the meaning of misfortune.

During those years, my Uncle Tuyen lived in a guarded villa. When Cay grew up, she went off to study in Europe. Uncle Tuyen allowed her brother Vi to go study chemistry and then, when Vi returned to the country, arranged a job for him at the municipal planning committee. The third child, Huong, studied physics and then worked in the municipal nuclear science institute. As for the youngest son, Hoang studied automation and his father planted a job for him on the price control committee. The professions of the children fit into all the sectors of society, and would never be affected by politics. He was far sighted in all respects, except for in one way he never anticipated: Two of his children, through the ups and downs of life, met and fell in love with each other, and were about to be married.

* * *

The next morning Uncle Ca insisted on returning to Hanoi. Uncle Tuyen made Cay drive him back in the car. She was a very good driver. Quang stayed behind. Quang and Cay were surprised to see the sunken face of her father. He motioned to Cay to come closer: "I feel rather tired. Let Quang stay so I can discuss matters with him. You take Uncle Ca and then come back tomorrow."

Quang and Cay held each other as they walked down the stairs. I peeked out the window: They were kissing under the big *muom* tree in the garden. Their kisses were not at all discreet. I thought of the stack of hotel room bills that Cay had in her purse. They had rented a room in an expensive hotel for two weeks. I prayed to the heavens that she wouldn't have a baby. In cases like this, a child would probably be missing its arms or its legs. Or perhaps its eyes or nose would not be as normal as the eyes and nose of a child whose parents came from different families.

Uncle Ca was packing his things and mumbling to himself while shaking his head. "How miserable. How shameful. Enough. I'm ready to die." He turned to me. "What's the point of living longer?"

When Cay had gone, Uncle Tuyen said, "Tell Quang to come in here."

Quang was standing with Hoang next to the fence. When he heard me call, he ran up. In the daylight, I was startled: he looked so much like Uncle Tuyen, especially his eyebrows, chin, and lips. Even his large, noble ears had that particular quality that only belonged to people of that lineage. He stroked my head. "The old man is calling me, huh?" he asked. I nodded. He hurried upstairs.

I didn't dare to witness the moment when the father and son acknowledged each other. I went downstairs to the kitchen to help Uncle Tuyen's wife make spring rolls. Today, only the family would be eating. She was upset because of Uncle Ca's sudden departure.

I said, "Old people are as unpredictable as children. Why worry about it?"

Although my aunt was a crafty woman, she had no idea that twenty-something years before her husband had abandoned a wife and child in a cauldron of boiling oil, abandoned them in a most cruel and brutal way in order to protect himself, like a beast.

She rolled some spring rolls, lifting her hand to brush a lock of hair from her forehead. A pot of soup with ribs in it began to boil so she lifted the lid off then set it right down on the floor. Although she had become a lady, this careless manner of doing things was still in her because she had grown up in the countryside. Somehow she'd managed to acquire a soft and sweet voice, soft as cork, sweet as syrup, and it always sent shivers down my spine. When her husband still held office, she couldn't care less who I was. From humble origins herself, once she became a lady she despised with all her heart the rank and file. She used to follow her husband on all his official visits to wealthy countries. But wherever she went, in her greed she cleared her hotel rooms of everything from the matchbooks to the bars of soap. She couldn't suppress her greed for trivial things, which was a mark of people who shared her origins. She was nasty to everyone from her chauffeur to the saleslady in the state grocery store. She was like a servant girl who goes into a wealthy house and doesn't remember she's a servant girl anymore. Whenever I looked at her, I was suddenly filled with hatred and thought about her with condemnation. She gave birth to Cay, but after this event I always had a feeling that Cay was actually the daughter of my aunt—the woman who gave birth to Quang. And so they came from the same mother and, unfortunately, the cruel hand of fate brought them together again after a painful separation.

An hour later I tiptoed upstairs. Uncle Tuyen was lying there as if unconscious. I sprinted down to the garden. Quang was sitting on the stone bench near the fence smoking a cigarette. I went to sit down next to him. He silently took my hand.

I've never seen a man's face as sad as that. For so long I'd only seen despair in the faces of those who had lost their bets in the lottery, in those who had been unable to grab one more meter of public housing, in those who were tormented by low wages or lack of food or trivial gossip . . . I had never seen a face like this, a melancholy so infinite that nothing in the world could lessen it. Perhaps behind every happiness or every sorrow lies the imprint of a particular culture. Wherever people come from, they express happiness and sadness in keeping with that culture.

I spoke, and yet I wanted to burst into tears. "So no one's suspicious, wait until tomorrow to leave!"

"No, I'm leaving this afternoon. Tell everyone, tell Cay, that

I had to go suddenly in order to arrange for my mother to come over here, as requested by the old man. You'll also have to invent something because I'm not going to come back here again. I'm going to abandon the shrimp farming in the South. Cay will think that she met a womanizer. It's better that way."

The atmosphere at lunch was like that of a funeral. Uncle Tuyen was sad. Quang was sad. Who could be happy? Cay's siblings and their girlfriends and boyfriends were all puzzled. Only Tuyen's wife didn't notice a thing. Superficial souls like her prove to be very useful at a moment like that one. She thought that the spring rolls were too salty and that explained why people didn't eat with relish. When Quang said that he had some urgent business and had to catch the Reunification Express at two o'clock, everyone expressed astonishment. He said, "I'll be back in exactly one week!"

From that moment until the end of the meal no one said a word, except for Uncle Tuyen's wife who kept on chattering. She was the happiest person in the room because she never imagined that anyone could have any trouble. If she hadn't kept on chattering, I think everyone else would have started crying.

I was in Uncle Tuyen's room when the father and son said goodbye to each other. Quang hugged the stranger who had become his father and sobbed, "Father! Father, please forgive me!"

"No, it wasn't your fault. Go ahead and go. After awhile I'll talk to your sister. Please forgive me."

Both of them began to cry.

The Reunification Express crossed the city and went into the station. Quang stepped into the sleeping car. He looked at me and Cay's siblings through the train window. His face was pale. I sensed that life had gone out of that face already.

The next evening Cay returned home. She wouldn't listen to any explanations. She was even angry with me.

"What do you know? You've never loved anyone so how could you understand? No, don't try to stop me. Why did he leave? We were so deeply in love."

She caught the Reunification Express that night. Uncle Tuyen got sick. The spacious villa looked emptier and even more spacious. I stayed with him a few days and finally I had to go back to work. The newspaper requested that I finish the investigation of the crime in District V. At this moment articles of this nature were badly needed by newspapers. It was only necessary for the hawker to yell: "A son kills his father and slits open the belly" and the papers would sell like fresh shrimp. We'd get paid, we'd get a bonus, and life would be extremely beautiful in the most literal way. I was so sick of it but I had to do it.

Before returning to the district, I received a telegram from Cay: "Looked everywhere but can't find Quang. Come help me!" But how could I go? Not to find him was very lucky.

They had taken the man who killed his father to the municipal police headquarters. I no longer had to travel. He sat at a table on one side of the iron bars. I sat on the other side with my reporter's notebook open in front of me. What I wanted to know was why he had killed his father in such a brutal way. I asked him softly, in a friendly way, not in the style of an interrogation, only for the purpose of serving to educate young people. He glared at me. He seemed full of hatred, no longer aloof. I took this as a hopeful sign that he might say something, although he still looked pale, gaunt, cold, and ruthless. I waited patiently for a long time. I even smiled at him.

Finally, as if he'd been pushed by something inside himself, he leaped forward like a beast, baring his teeth and beating his fists against his chest.

"What do you want to know?" He growled. "Why do you want to know? Such an evil person had to be killed. Evil his whole life. Who could bear it? Whatever you want to do with me, go ahead and do it. Slice my flesh then throw it to the dogs to eat. As for him, he was evil, without a conscience, I couldn't live with him."

He kept growling horribly, as if he was out of his mind. Someone had to grab him and drag him back to his cell. I sighed. Another awful story? If you wanted to know, you'd have to search from the very beginning, but the story of Uncle Tuyen's family had left me exhausted.

I returned to my small room. I really needed to go back to that simple place which I now considered my oasis, where there was no one to bother me, and no tragedies. I would have the freedom to enjoy a good sleep, to think by myself, and to gaze at my painting "Above the Eternal Tranquillity."

I opened the door and went inside. A telegram had been pushed under the door and was lying in front of me. I opened it and read:

"Vu Duc Quang killed himself in the hotel M, fifth floor, room number—. The victim asked the hotel staff to inform you. Please come and assist us in our inquiries."

Perhaps the story had to end that way. But I couldn't bear to think that my cousin's handsome face would fade away like that, slowly decomposing in the black earth.

1990

The River

When I was really exhausted, I often told myself: Well, I should go back home for a rest. But I'd never been able to do it. All it took was buying a train ticket, spending a day on the train, taking the public van, and then I'd be home. But ever since the last visit I made after the war ended, I hadn't gone home again. It wasn't true to say that I was too busy. Maybe it was inertia that kept holding me back. The prospect of movement makes people hesitant. There are times when I couldn't concentrate enough to figure out what I had left in this world.

At the end of October, the rice harvest season in my village, Kim, the daughter of my aunt, wrote me a letter. "Cousin," the letter said, "Mother has passed away. When she was sick, I thought you were too busy. Because you wouldn't have made it in time anyway, I didn't let you know. I took care of the funeral and everything myself. The Hundredth Day Ceremony is coming up. I wanted to let the relatives in Hanoi and Saigon know about it so that, if they could arrange it, they could come here to light incense for mother."

Throughout the afternoon, I sat in my office, more listless than I'd been in years. Now, I sat by myself, my heart filled with the loneliness that children feel when the evening comes. I thought of my aunt, the woman who had been like a mother to me ever since I was a tiny child. Now, she had fulfilled her duties in this life of hardship. Now she could be at peace in the next world, with no more bothersome ties, no more miserable torments.

The next day, I asked for a few days off, then went straight from my office to the train station. From the train I looked out over a city scarred by too much construction and jammed with throngs of people. As the evening approached, the train entered a region of limestone mountains dotted with caves. A white mist flowed like milk from the caves, rising above the mountains and descending toward the water that covered the fields. It was still more than fifty kilometers from here to my village, but I could already smell my childhood, and see again the life that was as natural as that of the grass and trees. A sense of sadness spread through my heart.

My father and mother died when I was still very young. A short time after my father's death, my mother died of misery and sorrow. I still remember very clearly how, as a very small child, I stood watching the people carrying my mother's casket. Only when my aunt arrived, having traveled 200 kilometers to get me, did I burst into tears, finally vaguely understanding the extent of my situation. In a wide-brimmed straw hat and a tiny army jacket, I carried the black sack that held my belongings. With my other hand, I held on to my aunt and we walked along the shady village road that led to the bus station. She was my father's younger sister, a teacher at that time, and she had come to take me to live with her. We spent a day riding in the public van and after that, it was still such a long walk from the bus station home that sometimes I had to sit down by the side of the road to rest my aching feet.

At one point, I rolled up my pants to cross a shallow spot in a river and while we were walking over the vast expanse of the dry riverbed, she finally said, "We're almost home, child."

My aunt had just gotten married. The two-room house was located in the center of a very small tea plantation, right on the edge of the eroding riverbank. My aunt's husband was also a teacher and I still remember clearly that during those days he rode an old-model French-style bicycle that was unwashed and unadorned, but had a bell so loud you could hear it several kilometers away. In the summer, whenever he had free time, he ran down to the river for a swim. As he ran back from the pier, he stomped his feet against the dirt and sang a French song. And each time my aunt heard it, she would burst out laughing. Little by little, I also learned the song, because he sang loudly, with zest, his eyes blinking, and his mouth becoming livelier with each of the many repetitions of the refrain.

During those first few days, my mind was not accustomed to my mother's absence. When my aunt and uncle were at school, I often went to the top of the slope leading down to the river and wandered around.

When I was old enough, my aunt took me to her school. We usually left very early in the morning. All the villagers would ask my aunt with friendly respect, "Are you on your way to school, teacher?"

Then they would rub my head or shake my hand and ask, "Teacher, where did you find this handsome young man?"

My aunt would also joke with them. "One of my relatives has just sent him through the mail," she'd say.

My aunt's school was in a pagoda located precariously on a promontory jutting into the river. The land was eroding on this side of the river and so my aunt explained that sooner or later this promontory would also erode. Because of that, they were building a new school for the pupils in the village. I still remember that this school was very noisy, full of small children like me. The third and fourth grade were located in the rooms on the other side of the sloping brick yard. Some of the fourth grade girls were adults already. There was one girl with lacquered teeth and hair rolled inside a scarf coiled around her head. Every time she crossed the brick yard, we children would look out the window, whisper, and follow her with our eyes. My friends said that she was married already, and that every time she returned home her mother-in-law would curse at her. They even said that, once, her mother-in-law was so angry that she took the girl's hair and tied it to a pillar in the house to keep her from going to school. That girl loved me, and sometimes she would call me out into the schoolyard to thrust into my hand a piece of peanut candy that she had made the night before. After school she would go to the town market to deliver the candy to an eatery, which was her way of earning a little money for herself.

I studied in my aunt's class. She usually stood with her back to us, her plump hands meticulously tracing the alphabet across the blackboard. In those days my aunt was very young, with her hair brushed high above her head and her cheeks round and rosy. When she saw villagers approaching from far away, she would be the first to say hello. Even long after they had passed, a smile lingered on her fresh lips, which showed that she continued to feel the emotion of her greetings.

She led me through the hamlet which specialized in the production of tofu. The steam rose from the cauldrons of simmering soybean milk and drifted above the courtyard of every house. Wooden tubs of tofu-filled water sat in rows in the courtyard and down the paths. The place exuded the sour smell of the soaking tofu and you could even smell it from far away. The villagers usually spent half the day making tofu and half the day working in the fields. These people cherished the teachers who taught their children. They often gave me a hot glass of soybean milk mixed with a lot of sugar to drink, and I would simultaneously sip and blow on it while my aunt discussed business with them. Sometimes they invited her to chew betel nut with them and her cheeks became even redder as it intoxicated her. I watched and drank the milk until my stomach nearly burst. Even now, I can still remember the taste of the soybean milk, so hot and so sweet.

Sugar was abundant here because another hamlet in the same village made sugar from sugarcane. During the season, the sugarcane press squeaked and groaned from morning until late at night. The melancholy oxen pulled the shaft of the press around and the juice poured out into a cauldron sitting above a flame. That cauldron simmered day and night. The sugarcane season was a season we children really loved, because we could eat sugarcane and sugarcane candy to our hearts' content. The children often pulled me along to participate in their pranks. We'd crawl into the sugarcane fields and find the biggest plants. Then we munched the tastiest sections, most of our joy coming from the fact that no one even knew we were out there.

I was doted on like that until Kim was born. Then the household became chaotic and I was nearly forgotten. I stood in a corner of the kitchen watching the women running in and out.

My uncle was singing that French song of his while he went back and forth to the river fetching water to fill the big earthen container next to the areca tree.

The baby grew quickly. In no time at all I saw her walking. I really loved her because she was so pretty and smart as well. The two of us often played together in the tea garden. I ran all over the garden picking wildflowers that grew along the fence. I used straw to tie them into bunches. Kim held the flowers with her all day long and when she slept she placed them next to her pillow. As soon as she knew how to run, I took her down to the river to play.

It was a strange river. That August, the water flooded both banks, rising all the way up to the slope where I used to play. The water was muddy and covered by yellow foam. People went out in woven basket boats to collect fallen branches floating down from upstream which they would use for firewood all year long. They said that one year the water had risen so high it even swept away houses. Every time the river rose higher, I clung to my aunt with fear. At those times, the river became vast. But when the water ebbed, it revealed a sandy bank covered with rotten, dried out fruit. During the dry season, it was beautiful, so clear that you could look down and see every grain of sand at the bottom. People who worked in the district center or went across to the provincial market would only have to roll up the cuffs of their pants to walk across it.

I led Kim down a footpath that cut across a cornfield. The stalks were fat and the yellow pollen settled on the banks of the river. Beyond that lay the pumpkin patch, the vines spreading all around. Anybody could break off and take as many tips as they wanted because the more times the tips were broken, the more easily they'd branch.

At that time, Kim wasn't walking steadily yet. The two of us often played with sand near the edge of the water but no one was concerned because the river was very shallow. At dusk, my aunt would walk out to the slope above the river and call us home. One day two very big geese appeared on that bank and attacked Kim while she was playing at the edge of the water. At that moment, I was in the pumpkin patch. Kim ran toward me. I was terrified of the geese because they were so large, but for some reason I raced toward her, screaming and picking up handfuls of stones to throw. One of the geese was about to bite into the tiny patch of hair at the top of Kim's head when a stone hit it in the neck. It quacked loudly, pulled its head in, and ran away. The other goose ran after it. Kim flung herself into my arms. Her face was pale. She wasn't crying but her lips shook and she seemed to want to say something. For several days, she wouldn't dare to go back down to the river.

With her eyes open wide, she kept repeating, "The geese. The geese might bite me."

My aunt gave birth to a lot of children. Kim was barely two years old and another one was born already. Every day, holding Kim by the hand, I had to carry baskets of the baby's diapers down to the river. Kim would play in the sand by herself while I washed the diapers. When we were ready to go home, I also had to bring back a small tub of water. Kim picked two young pumpkin leaves, spread them over the tub so that the water wouldn't spill, and then followed me home, walking and chattering all the way. Sometimes Kim would sing the song that my aunt often sang to tease the two of us: "Carry the gold and hurl it into the Ngo River!" But she still sang like a baby and it made me laugh.

My aunt gave birth to a series of boys. My schooldays were full of hardship because the family got poorer and poorer. When I finished high school, I entered the army. I left when Kim was in fourth grade. She came to see me off at the meeting point for new recruits and she was crying bitterly. I will remember forever that thin young girl wearing her mother's flowered shirt, which was patched on its shoulders and altered down to her size.

That was the year that the American enemy began to attack the North and my hamlet was the first to be bombed. After one year in the North, I was permitted to go fight in the South. Before setting off, I went back to visit my family. The American enemy had bombarded day and night. As the crow flies, the distance from my house to the provincial power station was five kilometers. Nearby, there were also several recently completed industrial buildings, a multi-storied high school with a red-tile roof, and more. Because of all those buildings, the Americans concentrated their attack there.

The pleasant village that made sugar and tofu had long since changed. Those unnecessary industries gradually disappeared as the farmers concentrated all their attention on growing rice. In addition, many young people had gone away, so when one passed through the village, it seemed much quieter and more deserted than before. At night, the airplanes droned by, dropping their flares. My aunt and uncle carefully shaded the oil lamp while they graded their papers and every time an airplane flew by they would have to extinguish it. The flame, fed by crude oil, produced clouds of smoke and the two of them had terrible difficulties even deciphering the words through that kind of light. It was usually around midnight before they'd finished grading the papers. Kim and my aunt would go into the kitchen and sit in the dark, silently splitting wood into sticks which they would take to sell at a shop that made incense in the provincial town. After they'd finished their lessons, Kim's two younger brothers would go with baskets and traps to catch fish in the watery rice fields behind the village. The smallest children would have to take care of the pigs and chickens.

As the family grew, the salaries of my aunt and uncle were no longer sufficient. Teaching in the schools during the war grew harder and harder every day. I had been home on leave for several days already and still hadn't gotten a chance to sit down and talk with my aunt and uncle. They always seemed so busy. As soon as they'd finished teaching, they had to work on the construction of trenches and underground shelters and they also had to go to classes. Often, by the time they got home, it was already late at night. The children had cooked and eaten together, so my aunt and uncle would eat the leftovers, hardly noticing what they were putting in their mouths. Whatever was left was already cold and there was never enough to fill their stomachs. Some nights they had to go to sleep without having eaten anything at all.

My aunt's back grew hunched from bearing so many children and working so hard. My uncle had long since stopped singing that French song of his. The bicycle was also broken and they had to go everywhere by foot. But I never heard them complain. They were easy-going, conscientious in their work, and selfless in the way that I'd seen in people of that generation. Perhaps they had done the most beneficial work, without ever asking themselves what they had done. They went about their business, forgot themselves. I still wonder if, were I in their position, I would have the strength to do the same.

The villagers in the area loved my aunt and uncle very much. The war had made everyone poorer, but their hearts were still as truthful, honest, and affectionate as before. When they saw me returning home from the army for a visit, one person brought me some sweet potatoes, and someone else brought a bottle of homemade sugar syrup.

When my aunt walked with me through the village, everyone would greet her saying, "Oh teacher, you're going for a walk! When will your boy come to offer us the betel nut for his wedding?"

My aunt still exchanged a few words with them, although she didn't have as much time to stand and chat as before. After we had walked some distance away, I still saw the smile lingering on her face that had grown so thin. Her face showed the imprint of so many hardships caused by working so much and bearing so many children.

I fought throughout the war and almost never had the chance to write home. After the liberation of Saigon, my unit and I stayed in the city, up to our ears in work. After many years, I received a letter from home. My aunt and uncle still lived in the same village, still worked as hard as before. Life was hard because of the large family and each child needed to be fed and clothed. They loved their parents very much and so they tried to excel at school. The family had had to build the house three times on the same foundation because it was destroyed by American bombs. After each raid, all their possessions were lost, but they always managed to replace them. Generally, the family, and the other villagers as well, had managed to overcome the difficulties of the war against the Americans, contributing to a common victory.

Then my unit received orders to return to the North. I was thrilled, because it had been so many years since I'd had the chance to visit my family. I bought a blue bicycle frame for my uncle, a pair of satin pants for my aunt, and a shirt and pair of pants for each of my cousins. Those things alone filled my knapsack to capacity. I had to carry the bicycle frame in my hand and as for the aluminum tubs I was carrying, I had to tie them to the outside of my knapsack.

The whole family stood frozen when they saw me. Some began to cry. Others laughed. The youngest children just looked at me shyly. The house looked ramshackle. It was rebuilt after the most recent bomb raid in 1972 and was smaller than the one I had left when I went off to war. How many things had happened during all those bombings? There were frightening stories.

When my aunt was about to have her youngest child, my uncle had to take his students to prepare trenches for an artillery battle. He was gone for a week. My aunt lay in the underground shelter, all the small boys beside her, while the B-52s dropped their bombs. The mother and her children heard their house explode in flames and the bamboo walls pop and crackle. In the hamlet, so many houses were burning that everyone had to take care of themselves and no one could come and help the teacher. The two oldest boys comforted the younger ones. They were so afraid because a bomb had never fallen so close before. Just at that moment, the worst thing happened. My aunt's contractions began and she lay there twisting and turning on the wooden plank inside the shelter. The children were terrified, huddling around their mother's body, crying hysterically.

Thang was the third oldest child, an eighth grader, and was the first to calm down. He gave out assignments to the other children, and calmed them down with his voice, which had only just broken. The family had been expecting the birth of the child, and so the supplies had been set in the shelter many days before. Thang ran into the house and pulled a saucepan out of the burning structure. Just as the fire grew stronger, he ran to the well to get some water and then boiled it at the entrance to the shelter. All around him, the villagers were urging one another to abandon the area, which was still being targeted by the B-52 bombs. The atmosphere was chaotic because the planes could return at any time to bomb the place again and the family didn't know how to escape. Thang tried to calm both his mother and his siblings. Without him, I don't know how my aunt could have survived. On that fierce night when the B-52s were dropping their bombs, the eighth grader became a midwife. My aunt was in so much pain, but she had to clench her teeth and tell her children what to do. Even when the umbilical cord was being cut and she was on the point of passing out, she still had to give detailed instructions.

Thang kept encouraging his mother, "Don't worry! Don't worry!"

Hearing his voice, my aunt knew that he was holding back his tears. Until now, my aunt still didn't understand how she and her children were able to live through that terrifying night.

Thang had entered the army and now he was stationed in the South, which was liberated one year after he joined up. After the night he acted as his mother's midwife, he had, by himself, overseen the rebuilding of the family's house and taken care of his siblings while his father was away. One evening, he went out to take a fish trap into the fields. He was gone for a long time and it was after one o'clock in the morning when he came home, with two big fish in his hands. In the weak lamplight, his face looked very pale. He had stepped on a piece of glass sticking out of the ground and his foot had swollen up.

He tried to calm my aunt, "I already went to the village infirmary. They washed and bandaged the cut and gave me a shot for tetanus, so don't worry about me."

But his pain pierced his mother. She sobbed while he tried to smile and console her. The next day, when he offered her some fish he had braised, she couldn't even swallow it.

When her story reached that point, I hugged that child who had been born in that fierce year of 1972. The little boy was pretty and looked exactly like his older sister Kim, only more plump than she'd been at his age.

"On that day, Kim had to go prepare trenches for the artillery unit. Everybody had to go do this or do that . . ."

I loved my aunt and my cousins so much it hurt me. I imagined Thang's swollen, glass-pierced foot and tried to remember what he was like as a baby. But I couldn't remember him as clearly as I remembered Kim. Maybe it was because there were so many boys and the character of one got mixed up with that of the other. It was never like that with Kim.

* * *

A few years ago, my aunt and uncle began to speak of old age, and in reality they were old before their time. They still worked selflessly while all around them people were developing a different outlook and rushing toward a new lifestyle. So many generations of students had been influenced by the good nature and conscientious attitudes of my aunt and uncle. My aunt was as small as a child, her face thin and withered, and her tired eyes seldom lit up as they had when I was small. Whenever I received a letter from her, I still trembled, remembering her warm hands as she led me across the dry riverbed. I thought of the soybean milk mixed with sugar syrup that my aunt often made for me when I was only a little boy, when my hands were stained from the purple ink of my homework

* * *

When I returned to my village, I searched for the same shortcut across the river I'd always taken before. In the river's natural state, it flowed from a source far upstream. People could not control it with embankments, lining its sides with dirt so that they could expand the land available for their concrete houses. More here than anywhere else, the river flowed as it always had. Vast fields of mulberry trees and corn still lined its banks, interspersed with patches of red pumpkins, an edible vegetable which people used for making sweet puddings, soup, or for eating in place of rice. It wasn't very tasty, but it could be used to prevent encephalitis or to cure headaches. Ever since I was a boy, I have always liked to eat ripe red pumpkin cooked with black beans flavored with lots of sugar syrup. It was a dish that my aunt often cooked on sultry summer afternoons.

Asking for directions from the villagers, I went to visit my aunt's grave, which was near the area where the river had shifted, leaving a heavily silted expanse of land covered with reeds. The wind was so strong that all the reeds bent toward the ground. Hills covered with mulberry trees surrounded the cemetery and stretched along the riverbank all the way upstream to a forest which still bore the traces of the great Le Dynasty. The king was originally a villager himself, who had rallied the chivalrous and patriotic people to rise up and obliterate the cruel armies from the North. He returned to this forest to build his encampment. When I was small, my aunt often took me to that place. She would lean against the base of a tree reading a book, while I wandered in the forest. I remember being thrilled to discover those huge moss-covered boulders, the relics of the pillars of the king's palace. How many boulders were there? And how many pillars? The palace disintegrated over time after the king moved his capital to Thang Long. But those indestructible boulders remained as testaments to the Golden Age of the Le Dynasty.

This land has produced so many kings, but Le Loi left the most lasting relics over time. One day, my aunt said to me, "In your life you will go many places, but whenever you feel sad, come back here."

I bowed my head and turned my body from the wind. Striking a match, I lit a stick of incense and placed it on my aunt's grave.

Just as my aunt had said, my heart felt calm after returning to this place. I wanted to lie face down on the ground to enjoy the fresh and healthy taste of the soil, the smell of the earth, so far from the city, so far from the noise, not mixed with the smell of gasoline or nightclubs or the exotic dishes in urban cafes. I turned around and walked away.

"Dear brother, why are you only coming back now?"

Kim, the little girl with whom I had spent my childhood, suddenly burst into tears as she reached to help me with my bag. Looking at her, I was startled to see the image of the mother in the small young woman. Kim looked exactly as my aunt had looked around the time of the war. Kim was now a village teacher. She had given birth to four children very quickly and now her back was bent a little, her hair rather stringy, and her clothes untidy. She cried for some time, wiped her nose, and told me about her children and her husband, who had once worked as a motor mechanic on a state farm but turned into an opium addict.

"I already gave him the boot!" she told me.

"Where did you boot him to?" I asked.

"Into a rehab program. He drove me nuts."

At dinner that night next to the oil lamp, she handed me a morsel of tofu cooked in soybean sauce. The sauce was homemade and Kim had learned to make it from her mother. I ate the dish with gusto. It had been so long since I had eaten it.

The village was not as quiet as it had once been. I could hear the buzz of motorscooters. From a house somewhere came the noise of an electric generator. I also heard some guy loudly singing the words of an English song.

But listen . . .

Mixed in with the urban noises that had invaded the countryside, I heard a creaking.

"What is that?"

"You don't recognize it? They're making sugar syrup. People don't like the machines yet. They still use the oxen pulling the shaft. The syrup is still very delicious."

Then I remembered. The stream of syrup ran through the pipe and down into the cauldron to be boiled. Oh, the froth of the syrup that was made into sugar candy . . .

1986

LE MINH KHUE is currently an editor at the Vietnam Writers' Association Publishing House in Hanoi. A veteran of the American/Vietnam War, she served as a member of the Youth Volunteers Brigade (Sappers) and as a war correspondent for *Tien Phong (Vanguard)* and *Giai Phong (Liberation)*. One of the leading writers of Vietnam, her works in Vietnamese include *Summer's Peak, The Distant Stars, Conclusion, An Evening Away from the City, A Girl in a Green Gown, A Small Tragedy*, and *Collected Works*. She was the co-editor, with Wayne Karlin and Truong Vu, of *The Other Side of Heaven: Postwar Fiction by Vietnamese and American Writers*, published by Curbstone in 1995.

THE TRANSLATORS:

BAC HOAI TRAN is an instructor of Vietnamese at the University of California, Berkeley. He was educated in Ho Chi Minh City and Dalat University. An Associate Editor of *The Tenderloin Times*, he has written the textbook *Anh Ngu Bao Chi: Introductory Vietnamese/ Intermediate Vietnamese*, and served as a consultant on the documentary film *Which Way Is East*. He was one of the translators for *The Other Side of Heaven: Postwar Fiction by Vietnamese and American Writers*.

DANA SACHS is a journalist specializing in topics relating to Vietnam. Her work has appeared in *The Far Eastern Economic Review, Mother Jones, Sierra*, and *The San Francisco Examiner*. In collaboration with her sister, Lynne Sachs, she made the award-winning documentary film about contemporary Vietnam, *Which Way Is East*. She was one of the translators for *The Other Side of Heaven: Postwar Fiction by Vietnamese and American Writers*.

THE EDITOR:

WAYNE KARLIN served in the Marine Corps in Vietnam. He is the author of four novels: *Crossover, Lost Armies, The Extras,* and *Us,* and a novel/memoir: *Rumors and Stones.* In 1973, he contributed to and coedited, with Basil T. Paquet and Larry Rottman, the first Vietnam veterans' anthology, *Free Fire Zone: Short Stories by Vietnam Veterans.* In 1995 he co-edited, with Le Minh Khue and Truong Vu, and contributed to *The Other Side of Heaven: Postwar Fiction by Vietnamese and American Writers.* He has received a fellowship from the National Endowment for the Arts and three individual artist awards in fiction from the State of Maryland.

ABOUT THE SERIES:

VOICES FROM VIETNAM, a series of contemporary fiction from Vietnam, is an ongoing project of Curbstone Press. Over the next decade, Curbstone will publish some of the best contemporary writers of Vietnam, including (as of press time) Ho Anh Thai, Ma Van Khang, Nguyen Minh Chau, Nguyen Khai, Nguyen Khac Truong, Nguyen Manh Tuon, Nguyen Thi Minh Ngoc and Vu Bao. The series will also publish *To the West of the Eastern Sea: Folk Tales of Vietnam,* compiled by Nguyen Nguyet Cam, Dana Sachs and the artist Bui Hoai Mai.

CURBSTONE PRESS

is a 501(c)(3) non-profit publishing house dedicated to literature that reflects a commitment to social change. Curbstone presents writers who give voice to the unheard in a language that goes beyond denunciation to celebrate, honor and teach. Curbstone builds bridges between its writers and the public – from inner-city to rural areas, colleges to community centers, children to adults. Curbstone seeks out the highest aesthetic expression of the dedication to human rights and intercultural understanding: poetry, testimonials, novels,and stories.

This mission requires more than just producing books. It requires ensuring that as many people as possible know about these books and read them. To achieve this, a large portion of Curbstone's schedule is dedicated to arranging tours and programs for its authors, working with public school and university teachers to enrich curricula, reaching out to underserved audiences by donating books and conducting readings and community programs, and promoting discussion in the media. It is only through these combined efforts that literature can truly make a difference.

Curbstone Press, like all non-profit presses, depends on the support of individuals, foundations, and government agencies to bring you, the reader, works of literary merit and social significance which might not find a place in profit-driven publishing channels. Our sincere thanks to the many individuals who support this endeavor and to the following organizations, foundations and government agencies: ADCO Foundation, Witter Bynner Foundation, Connecticut Commission on the Arts, Connecticut Arts Endowment Fund, Greater Hartford Arts Council, Junior League of Hartford, Lawson Valentine Foundation, Lila Wallace-Reader's Digest Fund, Andrew W. Mellon Foundation, National Endowment for the Arts, Puffin Foundation, Samuel Rubin Foundation and United Way-Windham Region.

If you'd like to support Curbstone's efforts to present the diverse voices and views that make our culture richer, tax-deductible donations can be made by check or credit card to Curbstone Press, 321 Jackson St., Willimantic, CT 06226. Telephone: (860) 423-5110.